'You don't k̶̶̶̶̶ ̶̶̶̶̶ ̶̶̶̶̶ ̶̶̶̶̶ ̶̶̶̶̶
I've wanted ̶̶̶̶̶ ̶̶̶̶̶ ̶̶̶̶̶
like withou̶̶̶̶̶ ̶̶̶̶̶ ̶̶̶̶̶
between us.̶̶̶̶̶ ̶̶̶̶̶

Rebecca shud̶̶̶̶̶ ̶̶̶̶̶ ̶̶̶̶̶
dug into his shoulders.

'Do you know what it's been like for me? Do you have any idea?' Mike asked. 'Do you know how close I came to turning onto some back road and stopping the bike so I could do this?'

The thrill of his words, the spell of his virile body, held Rebecca speechless. Her lips parted. All she could do was hang on.

'But you're not that type of woman are you?' His voice dropped to a throaty whisper. 'You wouldn't want to park in some farmer's field and make love on a motorcycle, would you?'

Wouldn't I? she wondered.

Dear Reader,

Welcome to the wonderful, exciting world of Silhouette Sensation®, the home of the best romantic suspense novels around.

Sara Orwig returns to the line to give us our sexy **HEARTBREAKERS** title, *Galahad in Blue Jeans*: Matt Whitewolf coped brilliantly when he found a little girl wandering alone down a quiet road, and then discovered she'd had her very pregnant mum with her as well!

And we've got three more names you'll recognise as firm reader favourites. Suzanne Brockmann continues her latest **TALL, DARK & DANGEROUS** trilogy (*The Admiral's Bride*) and Marie Ferrarella finishes this set of stories about **CHILDFINDERS, INC.** (*Hero in the Nick of Time*). Maggie Shayne's *Out-of-This-World Marriage* could almost have been called 'The Girl Who Fell To Earth' and is very special—take a look.

Magaret Watson and Ingrid Weaver complete the selection with *The Fugitive Bride* and *True Blue*, both the kind of thrilling, pulse-pounding reading that makes Sensation™ so much fun.

Enjoy!

The Editors

True Blue
INGRID WEAVER

SILHOUETTE™
SENSATION

*First published in Great Britain 2000
Silhouette Books, Eton House, 18-24 Paradise Road,
Richmond, Surrey TW9 1SR*

© Ingrid Caris 1994

ISBN 0 373 07570 7

18-0007

*Printed and bound in Spain
by Litografia Rosés S.A., Barcelona*

INGRID WEAVER

admits to being a compulsive reader who loves a book that can make her cry. A former teacher, now a full-time homemaker and mother, she considers herself lucky to have an understanding husband and three amazing children who have encouraged her to pursue her dream of writing. When she isn't trying to squeeze in time on her word processor, her favourite activities include watching old *Star Trek* reruns, and waking up early to canoe after camera-shy loons.

To Joe

Chapter 1

The man stood tall and lean, his sandy hair blowing in the breeze that carried wisps of smoke from the wrecked car and the clanging of alarm bells from the bank on the corner. On the sidewalk at his feet, a second man cowered. He had just been told that he faced a .44 Magnum, a weapon that could blow his head clean off but he couldn't remember whether the man fired six shots, or only five.

"You gotta ask yourself, do I feel lucky? Well, do you, punk?"

Rebecca Stanford clapped her hands in glee and rewound the scene. This was her favorite part, and she always sneered the words right along with Clint Eastwood. Of course, she made sure to lock her doors and pull down the shades before she indulged in a Dirty Harry movie. She even drove to a different neighborhood to rent the videotapes, so there would be no chance of another teacher or worse, one of the parents, witnessing what she modestly considered to be her one vice.

As far as the good members of the Silverthorn PTA were concerned, their third-graders couldn't be in better hands than those of the gentle, soft-spoken, and utterly respected Mrs. Stanford.

Even though there was no longer any "Mr." to go with the "Mrs.," most of the PTA were of the opinion that anyone was better off without a husband who would run away with a nineteen-year-old stripper. After Rebecca had worked past the pain, and the shame, of Ted's desertion she had come to share that opinion herself. As far as she knew, her ex-husband was much happier with his tasseled bimbo than he ever had been with the respectable, bespectacled schoolteacher.

"Why are you thinking about Ted when you've got Clint on hold on the VCR?" she asked herself.

Good question. Perhaps she was getting nostalgic, now that school was over and the summer stretched emptily in front of her. For Rebecca, September, not January, marked the beginning of a new year. Her days revolved around the school calendar just as her life revolved around her students. With no children of her own—Ted hadn't bothered to father one before he had decided to run off with one—until September there would be no bright-eyed faces to greet her in the morning, no gasps of wonder at a bird's nest she discovered, no squeals of delight as she sang the songs she had learned at camp one summer...

Good Lord, she was becoming maudlin. There would be another set of students in the fall. And they would be bringing their spitballs and stomach flu and pet worms along with their smiles.

Tucking a stray wisp of brown hair back into the bun at her nape, she pointed the remote control at the television and started the scene over again. She liked Clint. He was simple. In his movies everything was either right or wrong, good guy or bad guy.

And she wasn't his only fan. As the sixth gunshot rang out once more, a gray ball of fur skidded to a halt in front of the screen and barked enthusiastically.

Rebecca smiled and patted the cushion beside her. "Come over here, Princess."

The dog turned her head, tongue lolling stupidly.

Rebecca tried again. "Come, dog."

Pointed ears tilted forward. Then the animal yapped once more and bounded to the sofa, settling herself comfortably with her chin on Rebecca's knee.

Absently Rebecca stroked the dog's coat, then twitched her nose at the handful of hair that clung to her fingers. The animal was in need of a thorough grooming. She had given it a brushing last Sunday when it had arrived on her front porch. Though that had taken care of the dried mud and dead twigs that had adorned the shaggy animal, within a day the dog had discovered the compost pile and the petunias. What Princess really needed was another bath.

"Well, girl? Do you want a shampoo?"

The ears flattened and a low growl vibrated through the dog's throat.

Rebecca sighed. The dog had a strong aversion to soap and water. How had her owner managed? Was that why she had been abandoned?

There had been no collar or tags around the sturdy neck. Nor had there been any notices in the paper about a lost dog. Although she had called the local pound daily, there had been no inquiries about a dog fitting Princess's description, so Rebecca had come to the conclusion that the animal had been cast aside by some callous person who probably didn't want to be burdened with an animal during his summer vacation.

Yes, Rebecca decided, Princess was probably better off without her owner. Anyone careless enough to lose a lovely animal like this was probably too busy vacationing in Las Vegas with a nineteen-year-old stripper and had probably left a perfectly nice, unsuspecting, mild-mannered wife at home with her nose pressed to the window, wondering why she was alone....

"No. You are not going to think about Ted," she told herself firmly. The dog appeared to agree. With a happy snuffle it nudged Rebecca's hand onto its muzzle.

What an enjoyable companion Princess was turning out to be. Of course "Princess" probably wasn't the dog's name, but it seemed to fit. Even as Rebecca had given in to the prompting of her conscience and placed an ad in the newspaper, she was already regretting it. What if the dog's owner actually called?

Her hand hesitated on the silky fur behind a pointed ear. She had never done a dishonest thing in her life. As a teacher she strove to set a good example, to preserve her values and her reputation above all else. If some part of her had yearned to keep the dog for herself, that part had been overruled by her strong sense of right and wrong. Putting the ad in the paper had been the right thing to do. If the dog's owner responded, she would have to give Princess up.

The dog bestowed a sloppy lick on her motionless fingers then inched its way onto her lap. Moments later it was snoring contentedly, its light gray paws twitching with doggy dreams.

Rebecca smiled. No one had inquired about Princess yet. Maybe she would be able to keep her after all.

Mike Hogan tugged off his tie and tossed it onto the passenger seat beside the diamond-studded dog collar. Steering the black Mercedes with one hand, he peered through the dusk to check the house numbers. How the hell had Bootsie gotten this far? The last time he had seen her, the shaggy gray fur ball had been dodging traffic in front of Monsieur Aldo's Canine Grooming Parlor. The dumb mutt must have had a guardian angel on its tail to have made it all the way across Chicago without getting hit by a truck or eaten by a pit bull.

Still, Mike couldn't really blame the mutt for running away. Dogs were supposed to chase cats and roll in mud puddles, not sit in pink velvet chairs and have bows tied in their fur. He just wished Bootsie had made her bid for freedom when she had been in someone else's care.

A sudden shaft of anger caused him to tighten his hand on

the wheel as he recalled that last scene with Witlock. It had taken place on the patio, beside the pool. Witlock's flaccid skin had been dripping with the same oil that he probably used to slather his hair, and he hadn't bothered to open his eyes. He had balanced a reflective collar beneath his chins and barely moved his lips as he spoke.

"So, Mr. Hogan. I have been told that you misplaced my Bootsie. This is very unfortunate." The thick lips had pursed briefly. "Yes, very unfortunate. I trusted you, Mr. Hogan. Do you know what happens to people who betray my trust?"

Mike did know. His present position as chauffeur had become available when the last chauffeur had been snagged by a fisherman at the foot of the yacht club pier. Witlock wasn't subtle enough to be content with putting horse heads into someone's bed.

"Do you remember what it felt like when that fullback snapped your knee, Mr. Hogan? You carry the scar and the limp even now, don't you? Your hopes for a football career ended that day," the oily man went on. "We wouldn't want your hopes for a career in my organization to end so, ah, painfully, now, would we?"

With a conscious effort Mike relaxed his grip before he cracked the steering wheel. Witlock was pushing him, trying to see how much he would take. But Mike was in this for a payoff that was a lot bigger than a chauffeur's salary. As long as he kept his goal in mind he could put up with the threats and the ever-present risk of violence. After all, he had endured far worse.

He glanced at the diamond collar and set his jaw. Once he found the damn dog he would be that much closer to being fully accepted by Witlock, and that much closer to what he really wanted.

But first he had to find the dog.

He drove right past the house the first time. It was set back from the street, almost hidden behind the huge tree in the center of the lawn. With a muttered curse he slammed on the brakes, then threw the car into reverse. This had to be the place. The ad had described Bootsie perfectly.

Gracefully trailing branches of a weeping willow brushed the roof of the black sedan as it pulled to a stop in the driveway. Headlights reflected from the distinctive back end of a Volkswagen beetle beside the house for only an instant before Mike hit the switch and pocketed the keys. Reflexively he reached for the cigarette pack that he no longer carried, then cursed and popped a fresh toothpick between his lips. The ad in the paper had given only a phone number, but by using Witlock's connections it had been easy enough to get the name and address that went with it. Now it was time to pay a call on one R. Stanford.

As he walked silently toward the front steps he caught the whiff of freshly cut grass. Moonlight gleamed from squeaky clean windows, crickets chirped in the beds of petunias. In a shadowed corner of the porch a wooden swing hung motionless, evoking a quick image of lazy evenings and laughter. Pausing outside the front door, Mike noticed that the shades were drawn on the windows, but light seeped past the edges, along with the muted noises from some cops-and-robbers TV show.

His mouth quirked. So Stanford liked crime shows, did he? Fine. If Bootsie was here, the dog was probably feeling right at home.

Drawing himself up to his full height, he closed his hand into a fist and thumped the door.

Rebecca jerked. Princess stretched, smacked her lips and snored on.

Mike knocked again.

Uneasily Rebecca swiveled to look at the door. Who could that be? she wondered. Her friends were all fellow teachers and had already left town for the summer, so it was unlikely one of them would drop in unannounced. The house was far enough away from the street to discourage salesmen and canvassers. No one had ever disturbed her before during one of her Dirty Harry binges. Guiltily she glanced at the TV screen, then pressed the pause button on the remote.

In the sudden silence Princess opened her jaws wide, curling her long tongue out and then up in a totally uninhibited yawn. She cocked an ear toward the door.

Rebecca eased the animal from her lap. Brushing the dog hair from her skirt, she padded barefoot toward the door and peeked through the peephole.

There was a man on her porch. A big man. The top of his head was almost level with the doorframe. His face was hidden in shadow, but there was no disguising the breadth of the shoulders beneath the pale shirt. "My goodness," she breathed.

Princess's nails clicked across the floor behind her, and a wet nose pressed past her calf to sniff the door.

"Well, what do you think?" she whispered to the dog.

Princess growled, a low, menacing sound that was no less threatening for her diminutive size.

Mike thought he heard a familiar noise from inside. Hope flaring, he knocked a third time. "Hello? Is anyone home?"

Princess barked and wagged her tail. Eyeing the dog for a moment, Rebecca switched on the porch light and opened the door as far as the chain would allow.

Mike had only a glimpse of pointed ears, a shaggy gray coat and light gray paws before the dog ducked out of sight behind the woman. But that glimpse had been enough. "Bootsie!" he called eagerly. "Hey, Bootsie!"

Too many reactions hit Rebecca at once. The man on her porch was not only big, he was handsome. Gorgeous. Tousled black hair and sparkling blue eyes, lean cheeks with shadowed lines framing his mouth, square chin, strong sharp jaw... The impact of his appearance would be enough to knock any normal woman just a bit breathless. But it was what he said that made her heart thump in her throat.

"Bootsie?" she managed.

"Yeah," the big, gorgeous man replied. "The dog. That's her name."

No. Please, no. "Are you saying you recognize my dog?"

"*Your* dog? Didn't you put an ad in the paper about a small, shaggy, dark gray dog with light-colored paws?"

She was holding on to the door with both hands so she used a twitch of her nose to push up her glasses. "That ad only listed my phone number. How did you get here?"

"Did you put that ad in?"

"How did you get here?" she repeated.

Mike braced his hands on either side of the doorframe. It would be easy to force the door, but he hoped he wouldn't have to. From what he could see through the meager crack that the chain allowed, the woman looked as if a strong breeze would knock her over. The top of her head barely reached his chin and the knot of chestnut hair at her nape seemed too heavy for her slender neck. Behind wire-framed glasses, caramel-warm eyes were at odds with her pinched lips. His gaze dropped slowly. Not much to see, considering the buttoned-up blouse and the skirt that reached her calves. Yet beneath the primly flowered hem, her ankles were slim and her feet unexpectedly bare.

Delicate but feisty, he decided. Perhaps Bootsie had chosen her new home well. "I have connections," he answered finally. "Is Mr. Stanford here?"

The caramel-warm eyes blinked rapidly. "No, Mr. Stanford isn't here. Why?"

"The phone number is under the listing of R. Stanford."

She hesitated. "That's me."

So the petunias and the porch swing belonged to her? "I'm sorry to bother you. I guess I should have called first, but I'm very anxious to get Bootsie back home."

"Oh. Of course."

"Do you think you could get her for me? I don't want to take up any more of your time."

She glanced over her shoulder, then squinted nervously past him to the street. "Okay. Just wait here a minute."

Before he could reply, she had closed the door in his face. Mike frowned. He was sure that dog had been Bootsie. Maybe she expected him to pay her a reward.

Rebecca spun around and pressed her back against the door. He wasn't perfect. Those lean cheeks and deep lines on each side of his mouth bore the shadow of a beard that probably had to be shaved twice a day. His forehead was high, with a hairline receding endearingly at the corners. The long, narrow nose was crooked, as if it had been broken at some time during his youth. Still, he was definitely the most gorgeous man she had ever seen. Her gaze flicked to the frozen image on her television. He even beat Clint.

Crossing the floor, she shut off the VCR and slipped the tape into a bookshelf. "Princess?" she called. "Come here, Princess."

The dog must have gone into the bedroom. Despite all of Rebecca's efforts to break the habit, Princess had staked out the center of the bed as her own. Snatching a pair of sandals from the floor as she walked, Rebecca continued to call the animal. "Princess?"

She leaned against the doorframe, balancing on each foot in turn as she fastened her sandals. There was no sign of the dog on the bed. She bent over. No sign of the dog under the bed, either.

Maybe it was the name. "Bootsie?" she tried, even though she couldn't imagine anyone naming their dog Bootsie. Ted might call his bimbo Bootsie, but a dog?

There was a loud knocking from the front of the house. Evidently the gorgeous not-perfect man was short on patience. Hurrying back, she slid the chain from its slot and opened the door.

His fist was poised to knock again. It was an unnerving sight. Good thing it was only the door that was his target.

"Sorry to keep you waiting like this," she began.

He gazed past her. "Where's the dog?"

"Princess seems to be hiding. Would you like to wait inside, Mr....?"

He uncurled his fingers and extended his hand toward her. "Hogan. Mike Hogan."

"I'm Rebecca Stanford," she answered, automatically putting her hand in his.

His palm was warm and dry, his clasp firm without being aggressive. Nevertheless, Rebecca felt a sudden shock at the contact with his flesh. Stepping back quickly, she led him into the living room.

He limped. It came as a surprise, since at first glance he had appeared to be so completely, ideally masculine. Beneath the fine wool of his black pants there was no obvious deformity of his legs. Quite the contrary. With each step he took, the fabric tightened over beautifully molded thighs. He wore regular leather shoes, so the problem didn't appear to be with his feet. It must be his knee, she decided, glancing at the way he didn't bend his left leg as easily as his right.

"Miss Stanford?"

Good heavens, had she been staring? "Please, sit down, Mr. Hogan. And it's Mrs., not Miss." Hurriedly she brushed the dog hair off the sofa. "I'll just be a few minutes."

He remained where he was. "I'd like to get Bootsie home tonight. It's very important to me."

"Oh. Of course. I know she's around here somewhere."

"Thanks." He balanced a wooden toothpick on his lower lip. He had a way of rolling it from one side of his mouth to the other with his tongue, giving him the appearance of a boy who was trying to look like a gangster.

With chagrin Rebecca realized she had been staring again.

He cleared his throat. "I'd be willing to compensate you for your time and trouble. Bootsie can be, uh, uncooperative."

"She's been pleasant company, Mr. Hogan."

"Yeah? You must have found out she likes beer."

"What?"

"Beer. You been giving her any?"

"No, of course not. I never buy it."

"Then it must have been the cops-and-robbers movie you were watching."

She whipped her gaze to the VCR. It was off. The tape was out of sight. "What makes you think—"

"I heard the gunshots outside the door." He rolled the toothpick to the other side of his mouth. "Bootsie never minds that kind of thing."

At that moment a low growl sounded from behind her. Whirling around to face the window, Rebecca saw a bulge at the bottom of the curtains. "I've been calling her Princess."

"That suits her. She always did behave as if she were royalty."

Two shaggy paws appeared at the hem of the curtain. "Are you sure this is your dog, Mr. Hogan?"

"I'm sure."

"You only saw her for a few seconds."

"I recognize the growl."

A black nose pushed its way between the paws. Odd, Rebecca thought. At the first glimpse of Mike Hogan the dog had run away. If this was his Bootsie, shouldn't the animal be happy to see him? "Are you fond of your dog, Mr. Hogan?"

"Can't stand the mutt. About your compensation, would fifty bucks be enough?"

Slowly she turned toward him, disbelief on her face. "Excuse me?"

Mike frowned. Wasn't fifty enough? "Do you want a hundred?"

"You said that you don't like your dog."

"Bootsie doesn't like me, either." A sharp yapping seemed to confirm his words. "But she isn't my dog."

"But you just said—"

"She belongs to my boss."

"Then why are you…"

"I lost the stupid mutt. It's my job to get her back. Would two hundred be all right?"

The curtains billowed forward. Nails scrabbling on the hardwood floor, head low and hackles raised, the mutt in question crept closer until it reached Rebecca's feet. Giving the woman's ankles a sloppy tongue kiss, Bootsie glared at Mike.

Putting the ad in the paper had been the right thing to do, Rebecca told herself. But how could she hand this defenseless animal over to someone who had just said that he didn't like the dog? How did she know that it belonged to his boss? "How did you lose, uh, Bootsie?"

He opened his left hand, letting the thin leash he held uncoil. The empty collar clunked against the floor. "It happened in front of Monsieur Aldo's."

Light glinted from tiny stones that were set into the collar. Of course they couldn't possibly be diamonds, but they were pretty. "Is Monsieur Aldo your boss?"

"No. It's a beauty parlor. For dogs."

Hugging the floor with her stomach, Bootsie inched closer to the collar, nose quivering as she sniffed.

"She didn't want to go inside," he continued. "The next thing I knew she had wriggled out of her collar and run off through the traffic. Bootsie hates baths."

Princess hated baths, too. Rebecca sighed. Her skirt pooled around her as she knelt down to stroke Princess's fur. "Now that you can see her, are you sure this is the animal you lost?"

"Positive." The toothpick tilted upward as his jaw clenched.

"Oh." Well, she had done the right thing. In a matter of minutes the little gray fur ball that she had grown fond of would walk out of her house and her life, along with the gorgeous man.

Still holding the leash, he reached into the back pocket of his pants and drew out a black billfold. "So is two hundred okay?"

From her position on the floor with the dog, she had to tilt her head back sharply to look at him. "What?"

"Two hundred dollars. I thought you agreed, but if you want more…"

"I don't want your money," she said fiercely. Princess growled. "I just want to do what's right."

Mike tucked the billfold back into his pocket slowly, taking the opportunity to study Rebecca Stanford more thoroughly. This delicate, feisty woman was actually serious about wanting to do what was right. It had been a long time since he had met anyone like her. A female who wasn't interested in money? And who lived in a cozy, well-tended house? And where the hell was the husband? "Sorry, no offense meant."

"Are you sure you want to take her?" she asked tentatively. "Maybe if your boss knew that she had a good home he might be willing to sell her."

He shook his head. "You don't know my boss. He doesn't part with anything that he figures belongs to him."

Her hand moved tenderly along the back of Bootsie's head. "Well, I guess that's it then."

She actually seemed to like the stupid mutt, he thought incredulously. Stepping closer, he coiled the leash and unbuckled the collar. "Would you help me fasten this on her? She usually gives me trouble with this, but it seems as if she's really taken to you."

"Okay." She sniffed delicately. "Might as well get this over with."

"Great." He squatted in front of her, looping one end of the leash around his wrist.

She hesitated.

"Mrs. Stanford?"

With a sigh she lifted her hand from the dog's fur.

It happened quickly. If he had been watching the dog instead of the woman, he might have reacted in time. As it was, he hadn't had a chance. One minute the dog had been crouching on the floor, the next it had launched itself through the air.

At the sudden movement, Rebecca jerked and wavered off balance, knocking into Mike's shoulder, moving the collar that he held out of range of the snapping jaws.

To give Bootsie credit, she had probably been aiming at the hated diamond-studded collar. But with the mindless accuracy of a SCUD missile, the animal's strong white teeth locked around Mike's wrist.

Chapter 2

"Just hold still and I'll be done in a minute."

Mike clenched his jaw and held his arm stiffly over the sink. He perched on the toilet seat lid, his sleeve rolled past his elbow. Blood spattered his shirt and the pristine white tiles of the tiny bathroom. He hated blood. The sight of it always made him queasy, a fact that he had successfully hidden since the age of seven when Tommy Kowalski had told all the kids in the neighborhood how Mike had thrown up over a skinned elbow. That was the last time. Mike hadn't thrown up over the bloody nose he had given Tommy.

Tough. That's what the streets of his childhood had been like. That's what you had to be to make it in the world. Especially when you were an all-star quarterback whose college scholarship was destroyed along with your knee, along with all the other dreams of the future—

"Damn," he muttered.

"I'm sorry. Did I hurt you?" Rebecca's fingers rested lightly against his knuckles.

"No. I'm fine."

Why was he thinking about those old dreams now? Maybe it was this house, with its lovingly tended yard and lazily inviting porch swing. Maybe it was this woman, with her warm eyes and gentle hands.

He focused on the place where she touched him. Pale and slender, with neatly rounded nails bare of polish, her fingers looked especially delicate against the stiffened tendons and curving veins on the back of his hand. It had been a long time since he had felt a touch as gentle as Rebecca's. Maybe he never had. He couldn't remember much about his mother, but he did remember that there had been no gentleness in the series of foster homes he had been bounced around to. As for the women who had drifted through his life since then...well, they knew what he was and what they wanted, and it had nothing to do with gentleness.

"You really should go to the hospital and get a shot or something." Shutting off the water, Rebecca patted Mike's wrist gently with a clean towel. The skin was broken in a jagged slash that welled red droplets as quickly as she could blot them away. Holding the towel more firmly to the wound, she reached around him to retrieve the iodine.

"You don't need to fuss," he said. "This isn't the first time Bootsie's drawn blood."

"If you'd like I could drive you to the hospital."

"We've both had our shots. Me and the mutt."

The dog was sitting in the doorway, her tongue lolling, her muzzle puckered in what looked suspiciously like a canine grin.

"I'm sure she didn't mean to hurt you—"

"Ha!"

"But I'd better disinfect it, and this is going to sting a little."

Mike turned his head, making sure he kept his gaze averted from the blood-soaked towel. Rebecca was regarding him hesitantly, the glass rod from the iodine bottle poised just over his arm. The drab bun at the back of her neck was in shambles.

Rich chestnut hair spilled over her shoulders and curled almost to the small breasts that pressed saucily against the prim white blouse. Drops of water had turned the cotton practically transparent in places, and he had a peekaboo view of some lacy underwear.

"Do you mind?"

He smiled, enjoying the view. "No, I don't mind."

"Okay." She touched the iodine to his wrist. And again. And again. "There. That should do it."

Yeah, that did it, all right. It took his mind off what was underneath the prim white blouse. He had no business thinking about a respectable woman like this anyway, no matter how pleasant her touch felt. In a few minutes he would be walking out of her life with the dog that would allow him to get on with his.

"Mr. Hogan? Mike?"

He looked up. Her glasses had slipped down her nose again. Without the barrier of the lenses, her eyes were luminous, filled with concern. "Thanks." He smiled. "I'll be fine now."

That smile should be registered as a lethal weapon, Rebecca decided. His blue eyes crinkled at the corners. The lines on either side of his mouth deepened to slashes. One of his front teeth was chipped a little, just enough to strengthen that naughty-boy appeal.

She blinked, then pushed her glasses firmly onto the bridge of her nose. "Let me wrap your wrist before you go," she said as she leaned back in order to swing the medicine cabinet door open once more. She had to unroll the gauze one-handed since she didn't want to relinquish her light grip on his arm.

"This is really nice of you." He propped his elbow on the edge of the sink as she wound the bandage. "Are you a doctor or something?"

She snipped the end and tucked it in a fold of gauze. "No, I teach third grade."

"A schoolteacher," he mused. "You have a nice place here. I like the flowers in the front."

"Do you? So does Princess."

"Yeah, she would. My boss doesn't let her dig up his gardens."

"What kind of work do you do, Mike?"

He was silent for a moment. "I'm a chauffeur."

Something in his tone made her look back to his face. The smile was gone from his eyes. He looked older, harder. She didn't know what to say, so she ended up blurting, "I like to drive."

"Yeah, well, it's not so bad."

"I've never met anyone who can afford a chauffeur."

"No, I don't imagine you've ever met anyone like my boss."

This wasn't a good topic. Although she was curious about why a man who appeared to be in his middle thirties, fairly intelligent and in good health, despite the limp, would be working as a chauffeur, she let the subject drop. "Maybe you could bring Princess over for a visit sometime."

"I might not get a chance."

She grimaced inwardly. It must have sounded like a clumsy proposition. "I only thought that since school ended last week I haven't had much company..." Worse and worse! "I'm going to miss her," she finished lamely.

The hard look gradually melted from his eyes. "I'll see what I can do."

She put the rest of the gauze roll back into its box and closed the medicine cabinet. Then she rinsed out the towel and wiped the sink. "Are you going to need some help getting Princess back to your boss? If your arm is too sore I could give you a ride."

"You're a decent woman, Rebecca."

She paused, surprised. "I'm only trying to do the right thing."

"If you like that mutt, why didn't you keep her? How come you put that ad in the paper?"

She glanced at the doorway. Princess was lying on her

stomach, her muzzle cradled between her front paws. "She isn't mine. I didn't really want to advertise in the lost-and-found column, but keeping her would have been dishonest."

"And you're always honest?"

"I try to be." She hesitated for a moment, twisting the wet towel in her hands. "Would you mind answering a question for me?"

"Sure."

"Is Princess happy with your boss?"

His forehead creased. "Happy?"

"I mean, she did run away."

He shrugged. "My boss gives her everything she needs. A place to stay, plenty to eat. Even a chauffeured limo to the beauty parlor."

Briefly she wiped at the sink again, then leaned over to toss the towel into the hamper. "I just wanted to be sure."

"Like I said, you're a decent woman." The lines eased from his brow. "Don't worry about Bootsie. She ran away because she didn't want to see Monsieur Aldo, that's all. But I couldn't really blame her. He always puts these stupid bows in her fur."

Rebecca laughed, picturing the way Princess had looked that first night. "I'd say she prefers twigs and mud."

"Yeah. Females look better just a little mussed up." He smiled again.

The lethal effects of that smile went all the way down to her toes.

He flexed his arm and inspected the bandage. "Thanks again for taking care of me."

Rebecca didn't know where to look. Not at the beautifully toned bicep that was flexing against the rolled-up shirtsleeve. Not at the sad brown eyes that tilted toward her from the shaggy face in the doorway. And not at the flushed, disheveled, bright-eyed woman reflected in the mirror of the medicine chest. "I'll get the leash," she offered, stepping over the dog and escaping down the hall.

* * *

It was half an hour to midnight when Mike finally pulled the Mercedes into the five-car garage. Beneath the overhead lights, the rest of the cars all gleamed with the same somber black finish. From the back seat, nails scrabbled against the door as Bootsie whined.

"You'll get your beer in a minute," he said, and immediately the dog settled down.

Even though Rebecca had helped him fasten the collar on the stubborn mutt, he had needed to resort to beer bribery to get Bootsie into the car. If it weren't so important to him to please Witlock, he would have been inclined to leave the dog where it was. Obviously the schoolteacher liked her Princess.

Rebecca seemed lonely. What kind of idiot had her husband been, to leave a cozy home and a nice woman like that? On the other hand, maybe she was a widow. Yeah, that made more sense. Not that it should make any difference to him. A woman like that wouldn't have let him over her doorstep if she had known exactly what kind of man he was. He had learned pretty fast that respectable women didn't want to be anywhere near him once they found out what he had been doing for the past five years.

A sharp bark brought him back to the present. Slipping out of the car, he went around to unlock the back door and untie the leash from the handle. Bootsie hopped to the garage floor and danced happily around his feet, then tugged on the leash until he let her lead him out the side door. Panting noisily, she scampered along the flagstone path to the old gatehouse that served as the chauffeur's quarters.

He pushed open the back door. He never locked it—Witlock had keys, or other ways, to get into everything. Letting the leash drop, he stepped into the kitchen and flipped on the lights.

Bootsie made straight for the round-shouldered fridge in the corner, then barked imperiously until he had taken out a can of beer and poured a few mouthfuls into the bowl on the floor. While the dog slurped happily, Mike tipped the can to his lips.

Rebecca had well-shaped, generous lips when they weren't puckered into that schoolteacher sternness. Those lips had probably never touched anything as ordinary as a can of beer, though. He held out his arm and looked at the bandage she had wrapped around his wrist. He could almost be thankful to that stupid mutt for giving him a reason to extend his stay. Rebecca had said that she didn't get much company. She had even invited him to visit her again. But Mike knew that her interest had to be in the dog, not in him.

And that was good. Considering what he was mixed up in, he had no business starting something with any woman, no matter how warm her eyes looked or how gentle her hands felt. Besides, once he was finished with Witlock, Rebecca with her porch swing and her petunias was the last type of person he would want to become involved with.

The telephone on the wall shrilled suddenly. Mike swallowed, then set the can on the counter as he reached for the receiver. "Yeah? Hogan."

"Hello, Mr. Hogan. I trust you have fulfilled your mission?"

The oily voice effectively drove all thoughts of Rebecca from his mind. Mike glanced down at Bootsie. "The dog's here."

"Excellent. Bring her to the house."

The connection was broken. Mike stared grimly at the receiver for a moment until Bootsie whined and licked her muzzle. The dog nudged her empty dish, then rolled her eyes toward the can on the counter.

Mike ignored her silent plea and picked up the leash.

The main house was built of stone, with a slate roof and turrets that looked like medieval battlements. Large bay windows, with glass solid enough to deflect a bullet, graced the imposing facade. Floodlights illuminated the precisely trimmed lawns and the curving driveway. Mike nodded to a pair of men who leaned against the front steps.

The shorter man grunted, then hitched the strap of his AK47 further up his shoulder. "Evenin', Mike."

"How's it going, Guido?"

"Pretty quiet. Hey, is that Bootsie?"

"Yeah."

The other man snickered. "Another challenging errand, Hogan?"

Mike merely cocked an eyebrow and looked at the pale, thin man. He didn't need to say a word—the power implicit in his size usually spoke for him.

Under Mike's stare Trevor Dodge cleared his throat and inched closer to Guido and the AK47. "Hey, just kidding, Mike."

Tightening his hold on the leash, he walked into the house. His footsteps rang on polished marble as he led the dog through the black-tiled front hall. He walked past another guard, who stood by the staircase, through a pair of thick double doors that concealed a metal detector, then into the office at the heart of the stone mansion.

Worthington Witlock waited in a custom-designed leather chair behind a gleaming mahogany desk. He was wearing an old-fashioned smoking jacket with red satin lapels and a canary-yellow silk ascot tucked under his lowest chin. His face shone with traces of his custom-blended night cream. He would strike a stranger as an absurd, perhaps comical, figure. But no one laughed. At least, no one laughed for long.

Power and money. The combination was not to be taken lightly. Witlock's money came from a diversified portfolio of interests, from racehorses to art collecting, from trucking companies to hotels. The horses always managed to place exactly as he wanted, and the art occasionally was collected from unsuspecting sources. Some Witlock trucks were known to take unpatrolled back roads or load up at dark warehouses in the middle of the night. And the hotels did a thriving business in selling much more than an empty bed.

The power came from the money, and from the knack Witlock had of knowing the best way to manipulate people into doing exactly what he wanted. Often money was enough—that's why creative accountants like Trevor were on the payroll. Yet when necessary Witlock didn't hesitate to use simple, basic fear—that's why Guido was around.

But despite the power, the money and the fancy clothes, slime was still slime.

"Bootsie, my sweet!"

The dog sat on Mike's toes, her ears tilting forward.

"Take the leash off," Witlock ordered, wheezing as he pushed himself to his feet.

Mike squatted, holding the leash taut as he reached for the clasp. The dog didn't struggle. She simply turned her big brown eyes to his and twitched her nose.

"Come to poppa, Bootsie!" Witlock slipped a softly dimpled hand into the pocket of his smoking jacket and withdrew a cellophane-wrapped candy. "Look what I have for my bad girl. A humbug."

The dog padded forward, her tail swishing hopefully.

With great ceremony Witlock unwrapped the brown-and-white candy, then held it in his open palm. "Come on, Bootsie."

The dog stopped in front of her master and looked up, tongue lolling as her eyes brightened.

He pinched the candy between his thumb and index finger, dangling it over her head. "Beg, Bootsie. Come on, up on your feet."

Bootsie yapped once and obligingly balanced on her hind legs. A moment later Mike heard the dog crunch the candy between her teeth.

"Good work, Mr. Hogan."

"Thanks."

"The way you handled the search for my dear Bootsie was admirable. I wanted it discreet, and you gave me discreet."

Witlock had been insistent that no one else know that the dog had gone missing. In his business, it would be a matter of pride. The secrecy had made tracking the animal down much harder, and until the ad from Rebecca had appeared in the paper, Mike had been about to give up hope. "No problem."

"Yes, you did very well. I like a man who will do what he's told, but then you know all about the benefits of good behavior, don't you?"

God, he hated this man. "I guess I do."

"I also like a man who can keep his mouth shut. I feel very strongly about people keeping their mouths shut, Hogan." Unwrapping another humbug, he tossed the candy to his dog and moved back behind his desk. He levered himself into his chair. "Yes. I think it's time to discuss your future in this organization."

Mike felt his pulse thump. Finally he was making progress. "Sounds good to me."

"I like your attitude." The small eyes narrowed even further. "I hear you're good with cars. Could be I can find a use for you next month. How would you feel about a promotion?"

"That would suit me just fine."

"Naturally you'll be getting a substantial pay increase if you prove to be useful."

"Thanks."

"I'm very generous with my people, Mr. Hogan. That's good business." Leaning forward, he clasped his hands on the desk top. "You deserve to be rewarded for the way you found Bootsie. I think twice the amount you had to pay would be fair, don't you?"

Mike frowned. "What amount?"

"You found Bootsie with a woman named Stanford, didn't you? Wasn't that the name of the person who placed the ad?"

An uneasiness seeped into his limbs at the sound of Rebecca's name on those thick lips. She was a decent woman. She probably thought that people like Worthington Witlock only existed in her cops-and-robbers movies. "How did you know where I went?"

"Mr. Hogan, I know everything that my employees do."

Everything? With an effort he ignored the sick tightening in his gut that comment evoked. He kept his face expressionless. "Yeah, I got the dog from Mrs. Stanford."

"How much did she want?"

For a second he considered lying, but Witlock would probably find out and then the lie wouldn't have done any good for either Rebecca or himself. The faster he ended this conversation, the better. "Nothing."

"What? You mean she gave Bootsie back for nothing? Didn't she even want to be reimbursed for the ad?"

"No."

Witlock leaned back in his chair, the leather squeaking and the swivel mechanism groaning ominously. "Just an honest citizen?"

"That's right."

"My, my." He clasped his hands over his stomach. "Sounds interesting. Maybe I should personally express my gratitude for the care she took of my Bootsie."

"Mrs. Stanford didn't want anything."

"Everybody wants something, Mr. Hogan. And I don't like being in debt to anyone." His fingers fiddled with the knotted sash of his smoking jacket. "I always settle my debts. That's how I stay in business."

"What did you have in mind?"

"Maybe I'll pay a visit to this good citizen myself. See what her price is."

Tension crept along Mike's shoulder blades. Beneath the bandage that Rebecca had wrapped around his wrist, Bootsie's bite began to throb. This was a complication he hadn't anticipated. For some reason he couldn't imagine letting slime like Witlock come near the cozy bungalow with the weeping willow and the porch swing, or the delicate woman with the gentle touch.

But if he interfered this could ruin everything he'd been working for. He had to maintain sight of his goal. He didn't have time to be worrying about some prim little school-teacher....

Aw, hell. "I could take two hundred over for you tomorrow, Mr. Witlock. That's really part of my job."

The chair creaked as the man with the yellow ascot reached for another humbug. Bootsie looked up hopefully at the crinkle of the cellophane, but he popped it into his own mouth. His lips pursed as he sucked on the candy for a minute. He studied Mike shrewdly, his eyes almost disappearing above the folds of his cheeks. Then he nodded. "Make it three. You can deliver it after you take Bootsie for her appointment with Monsieur Aldo."

Chapter 3

The old swing creaked as Rebecca used her toe to push it into motion. Leaning against the wooden back, she lifted the collar of her blouse away from her neck, letting the breeze cool her skin. The sun would be burning its way past the willow tree in a few more minutes. She raised her hand to her eyes and regarded the tree critically. Those branches needed trimming. Maybe she could do that after lunch. Then she really should make a trip to the nursery to pick up some more flowers to replace the ones Princess had dug up. While she was out she could return the tapes to the video store. Then she could stop by the library and choose some more books for the rest of the weekend.

My, wasn't this a full life?

Rebecca sighed, then slid down on the swing until her ponytail hung over the back of the seat. No one could see her from the street if she didn't trim those willow branches, so what would it matter if her spine wasn't straight?

With her toe she kept the swing moving. Somehow she didn't want to be indoors today. The house seemed too lonely without Princess scrabbling around after the vacuum cleaner or snoring in the middle of the bed.

"Maudlin," she muttered to herself. First about her students and Ted, now about the dog.

It wasn't normal to get so attached to an animal in less than a week. Was her life simply so empty that she latched on to the first creature that showed her some affection? Not only was she getting maudlin, she was verging on pathetic.

Loneliness was a fact of life, so she shouldn't make more out of this than was necessary. Lots of people lived alone these days. Besides, when Ted had run off with his teenage stripper, it had been Rebecca's pride that had been hurt more than her heart. She had tried to make a good marriage, but eventually she'd had to face the fact that she had never been the kind of person Ted had wanted. He had called her cold, as well as a number of other more hurtful adjectives. He had resented her career, her values, even the house that she had bought before their marriage.

"Good riddance," she mumbled.

Her eyes closed as she listened to the rhythmic creak of the swing. Leave it to Ted to choose someone who was her exact opposite. He had never made a secret of how his wife failed to please him in the bedroom. The more he complained, the more difficult it had been for Rebecca to stomach his touch. Maybe it was all her fault, like he had said. But she couldn't be something she wasn't. It probably wouldn't have done their sex life any good even if she had dressed up in tassels and a G-string.

Incredibly, she felt a giggle escape her lips at the image of the respectable Mrs. Stanford strutting her stuff in the buff. Would she have to have music? Would she be able to get the tassels swinging in unison?

At that thought she laughed out loud. If she could laugh about it, she must be over him. Fine. So she could start calling herself *Ms.* Stanford. And maybe she should start considering what else she should do to fill up her life.

Opening her eyes, she watched the pattern of the willow leaves against the blue sky. It was a gorgeous color today.

It was the color of Mike Hogan's eyes.

Instantly his image sprang to her mind. That was easy. She had called it up often enough since yesterday.

It wasn't every day that a man like Mike showed up on a lonely woman's doorstep. Who could blame her if she thought about him a little more than was completely respectable? Of course, if she wasn't careful, thinking about him might turn into another one of her vices. Her lips curved wistfully as she remembered the unruly hair, the strong jaw and the chipped tooth. The flowers and the library books could wait a little longer, she decided as she drifted off into a daydream that was anything but lonely.

A plywood skateboard ramp had been set up in the driveway of the corner house. Eyes squinting in concentration, a red-haired boy zipped up the ramp, crouched over his board and flipped it neatly in midair at the top. Reversing direction, he made a wobbly landing halfway down the curved plywood. With one grubby fist raised in triumph he swiveled in a showy turn and coasted to a halt at the edge of the street.

Mike raised two fingers to his forehead in a silent salute to the boy's prowess, but it went unnoticed beyond the smoky glass of the tinted windshield. As the limousine turned the corner, the skateboarder, as well as the half-dozen kids who were gathered on the lawn, turned their heads like slow-motion spectators at a tennis match. Long black cars weren't an every-day occurrence in this neighborhood.

Bootsie must have realized they were getting closer. The bow that Monsieur Aldo had fastened on the top of her head was already trailing behind a pointed ear. Her tail moved back and forth so quickly it blurred. With her nose pressed against the side window, she gave intermittent, muffled barks, then slobbered on the glass.

Mike smiled. He might be hiding his feelings better than

the dog, but he didn't mind the idea of seeing Rebecca again, either.

The motor whispered quietly as the long black car turned into the driveway. Willow branches brushed the roof before the front bumper nudged the rear of the little Volkswagen and Mike shut off the engine. Bootsie was going crazy, turning around on the seat like a furry gray top.

"Hang on, mutt. We're here." Untangling the leash from the handle, Mike opened the door a split second before Bootsie hit the ground.

Rebecca was on the porch swing. Her hair was in a ponytail that hung down behind the seat back and her blouse was unbuttoned at the throat. Beneath the hem of her flowered skirt her long, slender legs were still pale from lack of sun. She was using the toe of one bare foot to push the swing back and forth. Even slouched on the seat she was still ladylike. The toe that propelled the swing was gracefully pointed.

Other people might not call her beautiful. The glasses, the plain hairstyle, the simple clothes served to camouflage her looks. Yet Mike found himself staring, entranced. He had imagined her like this, gliding languidly in that swing with her face relaxed and dreamy.

Get real, he told himself. She was way out of his league. The kindness she had shown him last night was the same as the kindness she had shown the dog. Besides, respectable women and cozy houses weren't for him.

"Rebecca?"

Her foot stilled. The toe lifted from the boards of the porch and glided along with the swing. Lazily she turned her head toward his voice. In the next instant her eyes widened and she sat bolt upright. "Mike?"

He couldn't help smiling at her look of surprise. "Yeah. I hope you don't mind—"

Bootsie's barking drowned out the rest of his words. Before the dog could strangle herself, he released the leash and she bulleted across the lawn and up the porch steps.

Rebecca grunted as the dog landed on her lap and tried to reach her face with her tongue. Laughing, she gave the animal a hug, then grasped her behind her front legs and pulled her away. "Princess. Or I guess I should say Bootsie."

"Princess suits her better," Mike said, shrugging out of his uniform jacket as he walked closer.

Looking past the squirming dog, Rebecca watched appreciatively as the man with the sky blue eyes approached. He moved with a swagger, despite the limp. He held his black jacket hooked on two fingers over his shoulder, and the shirt that strained across the wide chest was almost a perfect match for his eyes. "What a nice surprise," she said inadequately.

He halted in front of her. The breeze brought the scent of his soap and a tang of after-shave and just a hint of the man beneath the clean clothes. "I'm glad you were home."

"This is wonderful. I hadn't thought I would see either one of you again." Her voice had sounded breathlessly eager. Chagrined, Rebecca pressed her face to Princess's fur. Pathetic.

"I hope I'm not intruding."

"No, not at all."

"If you're busy or something, I won't stay long."

"I was just, uh, daydreaming." The fur was soft beneath her cheek. Lifting her head, she pretended to study the dog, but all she was conscious of was the gorgeous man at the foot of the steps. "She looks great."

"She just had a shampoo."

"The dreaded Monsieur Aldo?"

"Yeah. I have to take her every Saturday."

The greeting to Rebecca taken care of, Princess jumped from her lap and went off to sniff the flowers. A pink satin bow fluttered to the ground in her wake.

Rebecca wrinkled her nose. "She smells like a rosebush."

He shrugged. "That's what my boss wants."

His voice had changed subtly when he mentioned his employer. The naughty-boy good looks that had made such an impression on her last night, and had been haunting her in every free moment since, transformed into something else. Something almost…dangerous.

She blinked. The danger disappeared.

The stairs creaked as he climbed to the porch. "Thanks for taking care of me last night." He held up his left hand. The gauze she had wrapped around his wrist peeked out from beneath his shirt cuff.

"You're welcome. How does it feel today?"

"Okay." He twisted his arm to flex his wrist. "Like I told you yesterday, this wasn't the first time the mutt drew blood."

He was standing directly in front of her now, so it was hard for her to ignore the way his muscles ridged beneath his sleeve with his movement. Her fingers curled around the edge of the seat as she imagined touching his skin. "I hope your boss appreciated all you went through for him."

"It's what I'm paid for."

Her gaze slid past him to the driveway. For the first time she saw the monstrous black car that was parked behind her Beetle. "My goodness," she breathed. "What's that?"

"I had to use the limo today. The boss always wants Boot-sie driven around in style."

It really sank in then. Mike was a chauffeur. The coat he held so jauntily over his shoulder was part of his uniform. So were the black pants that had tightened over his thighs as he moved.

He earned his living driving around a rich man's dog.

It shouldn't make any difference, she decided. She wasn't a snob, was she? What did it matter what a man did for a living as long as it was good, honest work? And it wasn't as if she were about to marry him or anything. He had simply dropped by to let her visit with Princess. Besides, a man's occupation didn't guarantee his character. Ted was a computer programmer but he'd had the values of a tomcat.

With a smile she looked Mike square in the eye. "Well, as Clint would say, a man's got to do what a man's got to do."

A strange expression flickered across his face. "I think what he said was, 'A man's got to know his limitations.'"

"That was in Magnum Force, wasn't it? Are you a Dirty Harry fan?"

He shrugged. "They liked to play his movies, uh, where I was staying for a while."

"I rent them sometimes." She lowered her voice. "But don't tell anyone, okay?"

"Sure." He smiled his lethal smile.

Rebecca had never told anyone about what she considered to be her one vice. Not even Ted. But confiding in Mike had happened before she could consider otherwise. And seeing the smile again had been worth it.

She shifted to make a space for him beside her. "Why don't you sit down for a while?"

"You mean on that?"

"There's plenty of room."

He twisted his neck to check the bolts that secured the chains to the roof of the porch. "Are you sure it will hold me?"

"Of course it will. You mean you've never sat on a porch swing?"

"Nope. I never lived in the type of places that had porch swings." For a moment he hesitated, then he settled onto the seat beside her, laying his jacket across his knees and stretching one arm along the back behind her shoulders. With his foot he pushed the swing into motion. "Hey, this isn't bad."

"My parents had a swing on their porch, but they didn't use it often. Only on really hot evenings. I grew up a few streets over from here."

"Sounds cozy. Do you see them often?"

"No, they passed away several years ago."

"Sorry."

She smiled. "It's all right. I miss them, but even though they're gone, the people you love stay with you inside, don't you think?"

"Yeah, I guess," he answered vaguely. "Sounds like you've got roots in the neighborhood."

"Oh, yes. Are you from Chicago, too?"

"Yeah, but not from around here. You have a nice house," he said, glancing over his shoulder.

"Thank you."

"I like that willow tree."

Sunlight found its way through the thick branches to dapple patterns on her face. "It needs trimming."

"You keep the place pretty neat. The lawn and the flower beds and all. The tree doesn't matter."

"I remember last night you said something about preferring things a little messy, didn't you?"

He shifted. The arm he had slung behind her brushed her shoulders. "I said I like females a little mussed up. But I guess that could apply to trees, too."

Self-consciously she raised a hand to her hair. Strands from her ponytail had pulled loose and were hanging alongside her cheeks. With a quick movement she pushed the hair behind her ears. "It's warm, isn't it? It's going to get hot out here in a few more minutes once the sun comes around to the front of the house."

A bee rose from the flower bed and droned past lazily. Mike loosened his tie and undid the top two buttons of his shirt. It was nice here, on this shady porch in the middle of this sleepy neighborhood, but he shouldn't let himself forget why he had come. This wasn't a social call. "There's something I need to give you."

Her gaze focused on his mouth. "Oh?"

"My boss was really grateful for the care you took of Boot-sie last week."

"Oh." She looked down to her skirt and fiddled with a fold of fabric. "It was my pleasure. I guess he was glad to get her back, right?"

"Yeah. He wants to give you something for your trouble."

"That's not necessary."

"He insists."

"But—"

"Rebecca," Mike said firmly. "Some people don't understand the way you would do something just because you're a kind, decent person. My boss doesn't want to feel that he owes you anything." He turned his jacket over and felt around inside it for a moment, then pulled out a long white envelope. "He wants me to give you this."

Folding her arms across her chest, she shook her head. "It wouldn't be right."

"If you don't take it now, he'll come back himself when he learns that I didn't give it to you."

"Is this the reason you came over today?"

He slid the envelope onto her lap, then forced himself to lean into the opposite corner. When his fingers had brushed the warm cotton of her skirt, he had been tempted to leave them there. "I thought you wanted to see the dog."

"Oh. Of course, I'm grateful to you for that."

"Then take the envelope. Please?"

She uncrossed her arms slowly and reached for the object in her lap. "Well, if it will make him feel better I suppose I could. I can understand your boss's desire not to be indebted to anyone."

Mike didn't care whether this made Witlock feel better or not. He simply didn't want anything to bring Rebecca into contact with the type of people who filled his world.

"I guess it wouldn't be compromising my principles to accept a token like this." She peeked inside, then raised her eyebrows. "There's three hundred dollars in here."

"Yeah."

"For Princess? I mean Bootsie?"

"Believe me, my boss can afford it."

She frowned. "This doesn't seem right."

"Please, just take it."

"It wouldn't be honest—"

"Give the damn money to charity, then."

Closing the envelope slowly, she cleared her throat. "You're right. I'm being silly."

"No, you're not. There's nothing wrong with the way you want to be honest, Rebecca. A lot of people wish they had your strength."

"Strength?"

"To do the right thing."

"Oh, I have my faults. Just ask my ex-husband."

He blinked, startled. "You're divorced? I thought you were a widow."

"Why?"

"This place is so homey. And you're so sweet and ladylike I can't imagine any man giving you up."

She laughed. "Sweet and ladylike are a few of the faults he mentioned."

Deliberately he let his gaze roam over her face, then drop to her throat and the feminine shadows framed by the open collar of her blouse. "He must be nuts."

"No, he's Ted."

He chuckled. "You don't have any kids, do you?"

"I have over two dozen every year." Her eyes sparkled. "My third-grade class."

"Lucky kids."

"They keep me busy. Except for the summer."

"What about boyfriends?"

"Third-grade girls are too young for boyfriends."

He lifted his hand from the back of the swing and tugged lightly on her ponytail. "I'm talking about you, not your kids."

Her bare foot brushed the boards. "I guess I'm too old for boyfriends," she said hesitantly.

"You're right." He tickled the nape of her neck with the end of her ponytail. "I'd say you need men friends."

"The PTA would love that. They haven't had anything to gossip about since Ted ran off with his...since Ted ran off." She tipped her head forward until he released her hair, then turned to face him. "How did we get onto this subject anyway."

"What subject? You mean about you needing a man?"

Grasping the envelope in one hand, she waved it briskly, fanning the air across her cheeks.

"Getting warm?"

"Warmer all the time."

He grinned and tilted his head, enjoying the flush that brightened her skin. What would she look like without those glasses? How would that chestnut hair look curling across a pillow?

His grin slowly faded. How would those caramel-warm eyes look when she learned exactly what he was?

This had gone far enough. He was here to give her Witlock's money. There was no point getting more involved than that.

"Mike?"

He'd already been through this last night. This was the wrong time, and the wrong woman. He should keep away from her, for her good as well as his own. "I have to go," he said abruptly, getting to his feet.

"But you just got here. I mean, I don't mind if you and Princess stay a little longer."

"Thanks, but my boss expects me back at the estate."

"I understand," she said a little too brightly. "Thanks for stopping by."

He could hear the trace of puzzled hurt in her tone, but he steeled himself against it. Resolutely he pressed his tongue against his front teeth and whistled for Bootsie. Nails scraping on the wood, the dog bounded up the porch steps. Mike fastened on the leash, hesitated a moment, then looked over his shoulder at Rebecca.

She was still sitting in that swing, her hands clasped in her lap, her bare feet aligned primly together. More hair had come loose from the ponytail that had felt so silky in his hand. And at this moment he could think of nothing he wanted more than to go back to her side, slip his arm around her shoulders and taste the gasp of surprise she would make if he lowered his mouth to hers.

And that was precisely why he forced himself to turn and walk away.

He had fully intended to stay away, but during the next week he had to come back. Witlock had ordered Mike to bring Bootsie for three more visits.

What kind of game was Witlock playing? Was he still pushing Mike to see how much he would take? Was he still testing to see whether he'd follow orders? He had dangled that promotion over Mike's head the way he liked to dangle those candies for the dog. If there weren't so much riding on this job he'd be tempted to tell the man exactly what he could do with it.

Rebecca had sounded surprised and somewhat bewildered when Mike had phoned to check if she'd be home. He couldn't blame her, considering the way he'd left her on Saturday. But when he'd told her that he wanted to bring Bootsie over for another visit the pleasure in her voice had been unmistakable. And that was going to make keeping a safe distance from her all the more difficult.

The first time he eased the limo to a stop behind Rebecca's old Volkswagen he sat behind the wheel for a full minute, chewing at his toothpick and wishing it were a cigarette. Then he untied Bootsie's leash and watched as the dog raced across the lawn and into Rebecca's arms. Gritting his teeth, he took out a rag and spent the rest of the visit polishing the gleaming finish of Witlock's car. The second time was even worse. But the last time the inevitable finally happened.

It was another warm, sunny Saturday. As Rebecca opened the front door a shaft of sunlight fingered through the weeping willow tree, gilding her rich chestnut hair and giving the delicate angles of her face an unexpected, dramatic beauty. A stray breeze teased the full skirt of her plain blue dress, molding it against her slender legs while she gave him an open, uncomplicated smile.

More conscious than ever of the woman he was trying to avoid, Mike gave her no more than a cursory greeting, then sat on the top step of her porch and did his best to ignore her. Why couldn't she take the mutt inside? Why did she have to laugh and romp with it where he could hear her gentle voice and see her graceful movements and smell the clean, fresh scent of her when she passed close enough for his palms to itch?

Damn that Witlock and his stupid dog.

Rebecca threw a stick, exclaiming good-naturedly as the dog bounded through a bed of freshly planted petunias. Blowing a strand of hair from her forehead, she turned to Mike. "Would you like some lemonade? I made up a pitcher before you came over."

He clenched his hands. "No, thanks. I have to go soon."

"Well, maybe next time."

He took the toothpick from his mouth and cracked it between his fingers. "I won't be bringing Bootsie back, Rebecca."

She pressed her lips together and tried to keep her disappointment from showing. All week he had polished that car and chewed his toothpicks and had generally acted as if she didn't even exist. Today he had barely spoken with her. Of course he wouldn't be coming back. A man like Mike would have better things to do with his time than to sip lemonade with a lonely schoolteacher.

Rebecca threw the stick for Bootsie a few more times, then watched as Mike rose to his feet and pulled the dog's leash from his pocket. She had known this would happen. In a matter of minutes he would take his boss's dog over to that long black car and drive out of her life. And maybe that was just as well. She had a batch of library books to return. And now that Princess had been over again, there would be more flowers to replace...

In the next instant a little gray fur ball barreled into Rebecca's ankles, knocking her off balance.

"Watch out!" Mike called.

She stepped sideways, only to get her legs tangled in the stick Bootsie was enthusiastically returning to her. With typical canine logic the dog yipped and darted exactly where Rebecca was about to place her foot. She twisted, trying to avoid the impending fall at the same time she tried to avoid trampling the oblivious animal.

Mike caught her. Easily. His large hands clamped on either side of her waist and lifted her into the air. "You okay?" he asked. "The mutt didn't make you twist an ankle or anything?"

Shaking her head, Rebecca grabbed his arms for balance and hung on. She wasn't quite sure when her feet touched the ground once more. There were too many other far more compelling sensations claiming her attention. Sensations like the rock-hard biceps beneath her hands, and the strong fingers that slid to the curve of her hips, and the warmth of the long, lean body that pressed against hers. Or was she pressing against his?

"Rebecca?"

The word rumbled through Mike's chest. What was she doing? "Excuse me," she mumbled, mortified. Bracing her arms, she pushed away.

It seemed to take forever before he loosened his hold. Slowly his hands left her waist to skim lightly up to her shoulders. "Your husband was an idiot."

She couldn't have heard him right. "What did you say?"

"An idiot," he repeated. With one finger he raised her chin until she looked into his eyes. "For leaving you."

She gaped at him. "What?"

His finger traced her jaw, his caress amazingly gentle for such a large man. And for the first time in a week, he smiled.

Something did a weird little flip inside her at the sight of the sparkle in his eyes and the familiar chipped front tooth.

Something even more disturbing was happening where his skin was in contact with hers. Not really caring whether she stepped on the dog now or not, Rebecca released his arms and backed away from his touch. With shaking fingers she reached up to smooth her hair behind her ears.

Mike continued to watch her, an odd intensity in his expression. Then he shook his head and patted the front of his shirt distractedly. "Sorry," he mumbled. "That's none of my business."

"It's okay."

His forehead furrowed, as if he were waging some kind of silent, internal argument. "Tomorrow's my day off."

"This was an accident, Mike. I assure you, I didn't deliberately throw myself at you just then."

"No. I have the mutt to thank for that." His gaze dropped briefly to where Princess was lying on the lawn, happily adding more teeth marks to the stick. "Listen, if you're not busy, would it be okay if I dropped in tomorrow for that lemonade?"

"Do you mean you want to bring the dog for another visit after all?"

He hesitated, clenching his jaw until a muscle pulsed in his cheek. "No, I want to come by myself."

She was far too old for the silly burst of giddiness that swirled through her body at his words. And the thrill that lingered from the sensation of his touch was totally ridiculous. The man had ignored her for a week. Was she so pathetically lonely that she'd want to give him another chance?

And what would the good members of the Silverthorn PTA say if they knew that Mrs. Rebecca Stanford was entertaining a sinfully handsome chauffeur? She might be able to get away with hiding her Dirty Harry tapes behind closed shades, but there was no way that a man like Mike Hogan could be concealed.

But why should she want to hide? Underneath all the naughty-boy charm he seemed like a good man, no matter what he did for a living. She had seen his type before in the classroom. He was like the gum-chewing kid who perfected the desktop elastic launcher, then went on to win the Nobel prize for physics. One thing she had learned during her years as a teacher was that you could never be certain of another person's potential.

"Rebecca?"

She started. "Hmm?"

"Do you want to see me again?"

One look into his eyes and all the arguments didn't mean a thing. She nodded so hard her glasses slipped down her nose.

Chapter 4

"What would the PTA think of this?" Rebecca whispered to herself as she opened the front door the next day.

Mike must like his lemonade early. The dew had barely left the grass an hour ago, yet here he was, wheeling into her driveway and parking beneath the willow tree. One look at his vehicle and she realized why he didn't want to bring Princess with him.

"Good heavens," she breathed as the echoes of the powerful engine slowly died away. Her gaze was torn between the tall man swaggering across her lawn and the machine he had arrived on.

It was a motorcycle. A big motorcycle. With gleaming pipes cradling the back wheel, a long black seat with a chrome loop behind it and two helmets dangling from the handlebars.

"Hi," he called when he reached the steps. "Hope I'm not too early."

She watched him climb to the porch. He was as impressive as his transportation. His black leather boots thudded against the boards. Faded denim jeans hugged the contours of his strong thighs. A plain white T-shirt showed through the open zipper of a leather jacket. A black leather jacket. If it hadn't been for the endearing chip-toothed grin and the crinkles at the corners of his eyes, he would look like a hood.

"Hi yourself," she said finally. "And you're not too early. I'm a morning person."

"It's the best time of the day."

"My sentiments exactly."

"You look like a ray of sunshine in that dress." He stopped on the threshold and reached out to touch a fold of the yellow sundress that she wore, then put his hands on either side of the doorframe.

"You're..." She swallowed. "You look very different."

"It's my day off. I don't like uniforms."

"Well, you certainly look...different," she said inadequately. In the pale blue shirt and the tailored pants he had looked attractive, but like this? He was like a forbidden fantasy come to life.

"I don't suppose you have any coffee?"

Coffee? With his arms braced on either side of him like that, and the leather jacket gaping open over his wide chest, and the morning light silhouetting his powerful body, and the smell of man and leather assaulting her senses, why would she need a shot of caffeine? Her pulse was already pounding like thunder in her ears.

"Of course." She swallowed hard and stepped aside. "Come in. I could use a cup myself."

Mike thrust his hands into the pockets of his jacket as he followed her to the kitchen at the back of the house. His fingers ached to reach out and touch the silky folds of her dress again. Or to put his hands at the curve of her waist and feel her body pressed against his again.

What was he doing here? What was the matter with him? He'd only come back that first time in order to shield her from Witlock. He'd returned only because he'd been ordered to, yet he'd managed to resist this pull between them for a week. He had been prepared to walk out of her life for good yesterday, but then she had stumbled and he had caught her and he hadn't wanted to let her go. When he'd held her in his arms he hadn't given a thought to the risks he was taking or the trouble he could bring to her. He simply knew that he had to see her again.

This was completely nuts. This would never work. He was only going to be in Chicago long enough to finish his job. His future depended on it. Rebecca could have no place in the life he had planned and it was certain that he could have no place in hers. No, this had to be the last time he'd see her. For her good, as well as his.

"How about a bagel?" she called, her head stuck in the refrigerator. "I have some cream cheese in here somewhere too, I think."

He watched the outline of a shapely pair of buns push against the yellow dress and reminded himself to keep his hands in his pockets. "Sounds great."

She jerked up her head and whirled around. "Oh. I didn't know you'd followed me back here."

"I'm not used to being waited on."

With a nudge from her hip, she closed the refrigerator. "I spend a lot of my time in the kitchen anyway," she said, carrying a plastic container of cream cheese and a carton of milk to the counter. "I prepare most of my lessons at the table. Go ahead and sit down if you like."

He shrugged off his jacket and hung it over the back of a chair. Then he turned the chair around and straddled it, crossing his arms over the back as he surveyed the room. The table was round, made of maple. The cupboards gleamed with glossy white enamel. Flowered curtains framed the windows in the door and over the sink. He was struck by how welcoming, how cozy this house was. And again he thought that the departed Mr. Stanford was an idiot.

"The kitchen at home was my favorite room when I was growing up," she said, splitting open two bagels and placing them in the oven. "I remember spending lots of early mornings at the table whispering with my mother." She glanced at him over her shoulder. "We were the only early risers in the house."

"Did you have a big family?"

"No, I was an only child. I think I was a surprise to my parents, since Mom was in her forties and my father was nearing sixty."

His mouth twisted. "I was a surprise to my parents, too."

"A change-of-life child like me?"

"No, just a surprise."

"What do you mean?"

He leaned his chin on his hands. "My mother was fifteen, so she was very surprised. My father was so surprised he disappeared."

She turned to face him, her eyebrows tilting in sympathy. There was no shock or condemnation on her features, only concern. "Oh, the poor woman. It must have been so difficult for her to raise you alone."

"Maybe. She died before I was three."

"I'm sorry."

He lifted a shoulder. "I was too young to remember much."

"Still, you must miss her all the same."

"I guess you can't miss what you haven't had."

"You're trying to be brave, Mike," she said softly. "We can miss things we haven't had, just like we can dream of things and yearn for things we've never experienced."

"What do you yearn for, Rebecca?"

The coffee machine bubbled quietly on the counter behind her. Folding her arms over her stomach, she leaned against the edge of the sink. "That's a hard question to answer. I think I already have what I want. I'm happy being a teacher, and I'm happy living in this house."

"Even though you have to draw the shades when you watch your favorite movies?"

She smiled. "That's not fair. You promised not to tell."

"Do you still yearn for your husband?"

Her answer was immediate. "No."

"For any husband?"

She shook her head. "I'm not marriage material. Ted made that clear."

"You shouldn't bank on anything he told you. Obviously the man was an idiot. Maybe worse."

A chime sounded from the oven. Grabbing a pair of pot holders from a hook on the wall, she pulled out the bagels and slid them onto a plate. "Okay. Your turn."

"What?"

"Tell me what you yearn for."

The aroma of toasted bagels and melted cheese mingled with the smell of the coffee. For a moment he relaxed, and an unexpected answer to Rebecca's casual question slipped smoothly into his mind.

What did he yearn for? It was the impossible. It was everything she had. Roots, respectability, a good job, a home that was your own and that you could do whatever you wanted in.

And someone to share that home with.

Someone with warmth in her gaze and gentleness in her hands. Someone who would accept rather than judge. Someone who...

Get real, Hogan, he told himself roughly as he slammed the door shut on his fantasy. What did he know about any of the things she had? He wasn't home or husband material, and he didn't want to be. He was a loner, and he had been since the day he had been born. His earliest memories hadn't been of whispering over a kitchen table, they had been of crying to an empty apartment while his mother had gone out to another party. What respectability did a bastard have? What roots?

No, he already knew what he wanted. He was a loner. He traveled light.

"An empty highway and a full gas tank," he said finally.

She raised her eyebrows. "That's, uh, different."

"Just me and my Harley, rolling across the country."

"What about your job?"

"It's temporary."

"What would you do? Where would you go?"

He shrugged, pushing the chair away as he rose to his feet. "I'd do whatever I had to, and I'd go wherever I please. I've never seen the mountains, or the ocean. Once I finish here in Chicago I might take a trip to the West Coast and then maybe work my way up to Alaska."

"But what about a home?"

"My current job includes the chauffeur's quarters behind the garage. Otherwise, a room in a boardinghouse or an apartment that comes with some furniture suits me just fine. Doesn't tie me down."

"I can't imagine living like that," she said softly. Then she hastily cleared her throat. "Not that there's anything wrong with it."

"It suits me just fine," he repeated, moving behind her. In the small kitchen their bodies brushed tantalizingly close. "Where are your cups?"

"Excuse me?"

"For the coffee."

She pointed to the cupboard to his left. "Second shelf."

Reaching into the cupboard, he brought out two earthenware mugs and set them down onto the counter with more force than he had intended. What the hell did he think he was doing here, having coffee with a decent woman like Rebecca, talking about what he yearned for?

"Mike?" Her touch was butterfly soft on his forearm. "I'm sorry if I upset you."

Hang on to those mugs, he told himself. Otherwise his hands would be on this woman so fast she'd probably scream. "No, it was my fault. My grip slipped."

Across the street a lawn mower droned. Overhead, the willow branches moved listlessly in the muggy breeze. Rebecca followed Mike onto the driveway and listened in fascination as he described his bike.

"It's a Harley-Davidson," he said. The name meant nothing to her, but he pronounced it with so much pride that she smiled and nodded her head.

They had finished off the bagels and their coffee after more than an hour of surprisingly easy conversation. He was different today, no longer so distant. He was more open than he'd been even that first time he'd visited. It was as if shedding his uniform had allowed him to shed some of the tough-guy facade. She wasn't sure why she thought it was a facade, though. Perhaps a decade of dealing with children before the world had finished forming them into adults had given her a certain amount of insight.

Then again, perhaps she was simply trying to find some justification for the attraction she felt.

Oh, yes. She was attracted. What healthy woman wouldn't be? With each movement he made, his T-shirt and faded jeans outlined a body that could have been used as the model for a da Vinci sketch.

"I put it together from scraps mostly."

"What?" With an effort she concentrated on what he was saying. "Oh. You mean the motorcycle."

"Uh-huh. It was a long time ago." He ran his fingers over the rounded shape in front of the seat. "It took me months to find all the parts I wanted. I wrote away to the places listed at the back of motorcycle magazines for some and adapted a few from other makes. This gas tank I found in a junkyard."

"How did you know what goes where? I had to get the salesman to hook up my VCR for me."

"Hey, I used to take these apart and put them back together again when I was a teenager."

"It appears to be in good condition for such an old bike."

"I haven't had the chance to use it much until just recently. Some friends had been storing it for me." A lock of black hair fell over his forehead as he leaned down to rub some dust from a tail pipe. "It's good to have it back."

She focused on his unruly hair and tried to picture Mike as a teenager. "It must have taken determination and a good deal of mechanical knowledge to put scraps together into a machine like this. Have you ever considered opening your own business?"

He laughed shortly. "Rebecca, do you really think a bank manager would lend me the money to get started?"

"I don't know."

"Believe me, he wouldn't. Besides, I wouldn't want to be tied down with a home and the responsibilities of a business. I need my freedom."

"Just you and your Harley on the open road, right?"

"Right."

"It sounds…lonely."

He raised his head and met her eyes across the width of the bike. "You mean you're not?"

She rubbed her forehead. "I don't know why I said that. It was a stupid comment."

He patted his pockets for a moment as if looking for something, then glanced toward the house. "No, it wasn't. Being alone is a fact of life. Some people learn it earlier than others."

"It's funny. I was thinking about the same thing before you came over last Saturday."

His gaze was penetrating as it swung back to meet hers. "Yeah?"

"Yeah," she mimicked, smiling. "Why don't you stay for lunch, Mike?"

His lips twitched. "I thought we just had breakfast. If you eat all the time how come you're so skinny?"

Hesitantly she looked down at herself. Ted had always called her skinny, not enough woman to satisfy him. "I guess I am skinny."

"Hey." He came around to her side and reached out to tip up her chin. "I was teasing."

"It's okay. To paraphrase Clint, a woman's got to know her limitations."

His brows lowered in a frown. "Jeez, someone really did some job on you. I was only teasing." Gently his fingers grazed her throat, then traced the neckline of her dress along her collarbone. "Wet cats are skinny. Newborn colts are skinny. You're slender and graceful." His palms closed over her shoulders. "Under your lacy underwear you're all woman."

This time she gasped as she looked down, but nothing was showing that shouldn't. "How did you know...what makes you think that my underwear—"

"Is lacy?" he finished for her. His forehead smoothed out as his hands glided down her arms. "When you were bandaging my wrist your blouse got wet. That water made the cotton sort of transparent."

She should have been shocked, or embarrassed, or angry perhaps. But instead she felt a sudden tightening beneath her lacy bra. "You shouldn't have looked."

"Be thankful that's all I did." His thumbs stroked the soft skin inside her elbows. "You're a tempting woman, Mrs. Stanford."

Sexual attraction. She had read about it, had even experienced it to some degree in the early days with Ted, but nothing had prepared her for the way her knees went weak and her blood surged into the center of her body at Mike's gentle touch and husky words.

There was no doubt that he was attractive. Attractive? The man was gorgeous. He practically oozed sex appeal. From the first moment she had seen his crooked nose and chipped tooth and cocky grin she had felt that thrill of something forbidden. Even the hint of danger about him from time to time only strengthened the magnetism.

After the failure of her marriage, she had never thought this stirring excitement would happen to her. Yet hadn't she decided to quit dwelling on her loneliness and get on with her life?

Mike had already lost the battle with his reason. He had lost it from the moment he had felt her in his arms yesterday. How could he leave her now, with her body softening and her breath coming in shallow puffs through her parted lips? Right now Witlock and all the ugliness that waited for him beyond that weeping willow seemed like memories of a bad dream.

"I don't have any plans until later," he said, forcing his hands to stay locked safely on her elbows. "Maybe we could have lunch after all."

Her voice was distant, as if she weren't paying attention to what they were saying. "It's too early for lunch. We just finished breakfast."

"Then we have time."

"Time for what?"

"A ride."

She hesitated. "A ride? Where?"

"It doesn't matter."

Her glasses had slipped down. She peered over the rims into his face. "You mean on your bike?"

"Sure. Why not?"

Her eyes widened in shock. "I've never ridden a motorcycle in my life."

"Then I'm glad this will be your first time."

"But I wouldn't know what to do."

Tugging her forward, he placed her hands on his waist. The warmth of her palms seared through his T-shirt. "All you have to do is hang on to me."

She was silent. Slowly she turned her head and studied the bike, twitching her nose to push her glasses back up. "Where would I sit?"

"On the seat behind me."

"It looks so small. Where do I put my feet?"

"I'll show you."

Her hands dropped from his waist and she stepped back.

"To tell you the truth, I've always wondered what it would be like."

"Somehow that doesn't surprise me, coming from a person with the taste in movies that you have."

One corner of her mouth lifted. "You promised not to tell."

"Who would I tell?"

"Right. Princess Bootsie already knows."

"So? Want to give it a try?"

A pair of birds darted out of the willow overhead. From the street came the hollow rumbling whir of skateboard wheels. A soft breeze flattened Rebecca's yellow dress against her legs and lifted loose strands of hair from the knot on her neck. Who was he kidding? She was too nice, too respectable to be caught wheeling around town on the back of a Harley with a man like him—

"I can't go," she began.

"It's all right. It was a dumb idea."

"No, you don't understand," she said quickly. "I can't go until I change my clothes. Could you wait for me?"

"Uh, sure."

"Great." She grinned, then whirled around and raced for the back door.

Ten minutes later Rebecca locked the house behind her, then paused for a moment. Mike had put his black jacket back on and had propped a pair of sunglasses over the crooked bump on his nose. He was already sitting on the motorcycle, his long legs stretched out on either side. One helmet was propped on the gas tank in front of him, the other dangled from his fingers. At the sound of the door closing, he looked up and smiled.

Her stomach clenched and flipped over. That smile was dangerous. And in the danger lay an undeniable thrill. Was this why women fantasized about pirates and highwaymen? There should be a law against a man looking that sexy.

"Ready?" he called.

She tugged self-consciously at the waistband of her jeans

as she crossed the lawn. This was the pair she normally wore when she did yard work. They were baggy and unfashionable, but she realized that she needed something sturdy. She didn't have a leather jacket, but the old sweatshirt left over from her college days was thick enough to block the wind. Normally she wore skirts and prim blouses, because that's what she was raised to expect a lady to wear. Bundled up in these old clothes, she felt like a sloppy teenager. Next to Mike and his devil-may-care biker clothes, she felt about as sexy as a rolled rug.

He swung one leg over the seat and stood up to face her, the smile growing as she approached. "Here's your helmet."

"Do I have to wear one?"

"You do on my bike. Life's too precious to me to take dumb risks."

"Okay, if you insist." She took the helmet from his hand and tugged at the strap.

"Better let me help." With deft movements of his fingers, he unfastened the chin strap and leaned over to lift it onto her head.

"Ouch."

He took it off immediately. "What's wrong?"

"It's my hair," she said, reaching around to the back of her head and yanking out the pins that held her bun in place. "I should have thought of this."

Dropping the helmet at his feet, he turned her around so that her back was to him. "Let me."

His fingers were unbelievably gentle as he removed the last of the pins and handed them to her. "You have beautiful hair, Rebecca. Why don't you leave it down?"

"It tangles too easily."

"I'll braid it for you," he said. Before she could even think of stopping him, he had combed her hair through his fingers and separated it into three strands.

"You're a man of unexpected talents, Mike," she managed.

His knuckles lightly grazed her neck as he fashioned a loose braid. "In one of the foster homes I lived in there was a girl named Jeannie. She was part Cherokee or something, and had long black hair. I did her braid and she did my English homework."

"Sounds like a fair trade."

"Until the day she cut it short and dyed it blond."

"I guess you had to do your own homework then?"

"Not really. I got shuffled to another foster home where no one checked to see whether or not it got done."

How different his life had been from hers. She had been doted on and showered with the love of both her parents from the day she was born. They had always been there to guide her through school and afterward into a career and marriage. With the childhood Mike had had, it was amazing that he had turned out to be such a gentle, sensitive man.

Mike's hands stilled. He left them against the side of her neck for a long, drawn-out moment. Then he sighed and fitted the helmet back onto her head. "Is that better?"

"That's fine." She turned around and tipped up her chin as he fastened the strap. Her distorted reflection looked back at her from the lenses of his sunglasses.

He tapped lightly on the top of her helmet, then squatted down by the back wheel to point at a short metal bar. "You rest your feet on these. There's one on each side. Don't put your foot against the pipes, because they get hot."

"Got it."

"You sit up here," he said, straightening up and patting the back of the seat. "You can hang on to the bar behind you if you like, but you might feel safer if you put your arms around my waist and lock your hands together."

She eyed the gleaming machine once more. "How fast are you planning to go?"

He put on his own helmet, then propped his knuckles against his hips and grinned. "Don't tell me you're chickening out?"

"Not on your life. If you can try out my porch swing, I can

try out your motorcycle.'' Swinging her leg over the middle, she hopped onto the back of the seat.

He laughed. Then he settled himself in front of her and placed his hands on the handlebars. Leaning forward, he kicked something with one foot and the engine purred to life.

The vibrations startled her. They traveled through the frame of the bike into her thighs, as well as other more personal places. ''Good heavens,'' she murmured.

He reached back to pull her hands around his chest. ''Have you got your feet up?''

Quickly she put the soles of her sneakers onto the narrow pegs. Her thighs clamped around his hips. Why hadn't she realized what an intimate position this would be? ''All set.''

Mike twisted his wrist. The engine's purr became a growl. Then he toed it into gear and they wheeled around under the willow tree and headed for the street.

The kids on the corner had set up the skateboard ramp again. A freckled redhead who had been one of her students four years ago coasted down the plywood slope and stopped at the curb. He stared, openmouthed, as the motorcycle came closer.

''Mrs. Stanford?'' he squeaked.

It was Andrew Barring. He had been a pleasant student, despite the fact that his father was on the school board and his mother was the president of the PTA.

Mike slowed down. ''You're pretty good with that board, kid. I saw you last week,'' he said as they coasted past.

''Th-thanks,'' he stuttered.

She had a fleeting glimpse of rounded eyes and a mouth still drooping open. Then Mike gunned the engine and she had to lock her hands in front of him as the bike roared down the street.

Now she'd done it. News of her Sunday morning motorcycle ride would be all over the Silverthorn School grapevine if Andrew told his mother.

She closed her eyes and sighed. She had already decided

that Mike wasn't the type of man who could be hidden. He might not work in a glamorous job, but there was nothing wrong with honest work, even if it was chauffeuring a rich man's dog. And why should she want to hide? She had nothing to be ashamed of. This was merely a friendly ride.

Tightening her grip on Mike's jacket, she risked a glance over her shoulder.

Three more baseball-capped skateboarders had joined Andrew at the curb and were following the progress of the Harley with undisguised adolescent admiration.

She groaned.

"Are you okay?" Mike called as they slowed for a stop sign.

"Uh, sure. Just fine."

The engine idled like distant thunder. "Any particular place you'd like to go?"

Firmly Rebecca put thoughts of the Barrings to the back of her mind. "Anyplace. As long as we're back by lunch."

He chuckled. "Okay. Hang on."

It was a ride she would never forget. In all her thirty years she had experienced nothing that even came close to this. Mike handled the powerful machine easily, making the bike growl through gear changes with relaxed twists of his strong wrists. He used his shoulders for balance, calling back to Rebecca to lean into the turns with him as they took corners at speeds that left her breathless. Still, she knew he was always in control. He guided them through the streets she had known since she was a child, though today they seemed different. From her perch behind his broad shoulders, even the familiar trees and houses and white picket fences seemed exciting.

The sun was warm on her back, the wind cool on her face as they eventually left the city. Although the highway wasn't empty and she had no way of knowing whether the gas tank was full, the sense of total freedom was exhilarating. No wonder Mike dreamed of doing this.

"Now I understand," she called above the noise of the wind.

"What?"

"Why you want to ride across the country. This is great."

His shoulders shook with laughter. "Yeah? Just wait till you spend ten hours bouncing around on this thing. You wouldn't want to sit for a week."

A semi went by and she ducked her face behind his back to avoid the dusty air current in its wake. Her fingers slid on the thick leather of his jacket until she gripped her hands together just above his waist.

The ride wasn't the only thing that was exciting, she admitted to herself with a rueful smile. Being this close to Mike was a thrill all by itself. Each time his toe flicked the gear lever, she could feel his thigh flex against hers. When he leaned into the corners, she felt the strength of his body draw her with him. Crazy. It was crazy to think about that while traveling at sixty miles an hour with nothing but fleece and denim between her skin and the blurring asphalt.

Her smile widened. Maybe it was crazy, but it sure was fun. It beat the heck out of returning library books and planting petunias.

The countryside rolled past with the freshness of spring instead of early summer. The shades of green were more vivid from this perspective, the scents sharper. At times Rebecca even imagined she could feel the changes in texture of the air against her cheeks. Finally, though, they topped a hill and Mike slowed to pull onto the shoulder. The noise of the engine dropped as he extended his legs on either side of the bike, the heels of his heavy boots scraping the gravel. A moment later they had stopped.

A pair of cars whizzed past on their left. Mike twisted to face her. "We'd better head back."

She was surprised at the depth of her disappointment. "Already?"

"I'd say it's almost one."

"You're kidding! How could the morning go by so fast?"

He lowered his sunglasses to look at her over the rims. "Did you like it?"

"Yes," she answered immediately.

"Not getting tired or sore yet?"

She laughed. "Nope."

He responded with one of his killer smiles. "Then how about if we take the long way back?"

Settling herself more securely behind him, she reached out daringly to push up his glasses. "That suits me just fine."

Gravel spurted from beneath the back wheel as Mike twisted the throttle. The Harley leapt forward and they were back on the highway. She probably would be sore tomorrow, and her face would be windburned and her hair a tangled mess, but snuggled so close to Mike's strong, solid body with the memory of his smile sending warmth to her cheeks and the rumble of the engine thrumming subtly through her bones.... Lord, she didn't want this ride to end.

Chapter 5

Mike couldn't believe how he had let the day slip away from him like this. Although he never wore a watch, he usually could tell within five minutes what time it was. During the past five years, Mike had become an expert on the passage of time.

He brought the Harley to a stop beneath the weeping willow and shut off the engine, levering the kickstand into place as he slid from the seat.

Rebecca was still glued to the back of the bike, her cheeks flushed, her eyes shining. The sweetest smile he had ever seen stretched across her lips.

"Thank you," she said. "I can't remember when I've enjoyed myself more."

If that were true, then her husband must have been impotent, as well as an idiot. He offered his hand to help her to her feet. "Steady, there."

Her knees wobbled for a moment before she regained her balance and took a step away. "Now I really do owe you lunch."

"It's late."

"I won't take long. I can make a salad, and—"

"Rebecca, I can't stay."

The smile slipped, then stiffened. "Of course. This is your day off. You probably have plenty of things you want to do."

Oh, yeah. There were plenty of things he wanted to do, starting with taking her into his arms and kissing that brave, vulnerable smile from her lips.

His hand wasn't quite steady as he reached up to unfasten the strap beneath her chin. Placing his hands on either side, he lifted the helmet from her head.

The braid he had fastened had come loose. Without thinking, he eased his fingers into her hair to unravel the rest of it. Chestnut curls stroked his wrist, whispering sensuously over his leather sleeve.

He wanted this woman, wanted her with a sudden fierceness that surged through every inch of his body.

"Well, thanks again for the ride," she said, taking another step away. Her hair floated freely over her shoulders, framing her face in delicate waves.

His hand clenched into a fist, then dropped to his side. "Anytime."

She wiped her palms on the thighs of her stiff jeans, subdued her hair by tucking it behind her ears and tugged self-consciously at her shapeless sweatshirt. With a brisk movement she checked the watch on her wrist. "My goodness, it is late. I'd better get to the library before it closes. My books are a day overdue."

Reality was reaching out to both of them, drawing them back into their separate lives, their impossibly different lives. His movements slow, Mike turned to fasten the extra helmet to the chrome loop behind the seat. "Yeah, I have an appointment that I'm already late for."

Her smile looked brittle enough to crack. "Drive safely."

He nodded, wishing for a cigarette.

"Say hello to Princess for me."

"Sure."

"And if you're ever in the neighborhood..."

"Sure."

She held out a hand. "Well, goodbye, Mike."

He enclosed her slender fingers in his hardened palm. "So long, Rebecca."

They stood there motionless for a full minute, neither one wanting to take that final step away.

Mike wished there was a dog around that could make her stumble into his arms.

So did Rebecca.

"You know I won't be staying in Chicago, don't you?"

"I know. The empty highway and full gas tank."

"I'm not in a position to start anything serious with a woman."

"I understand. This has been fun, but I know that's all."

She had gotten under his skin. Had he thought that he could spend the day with her and then leave it at that? If he had thought that he was lost when he had touched her, that was nothing compared to how he felt now that he had heard her laughter on the wind and felt her body press tightly to his back. He yanked off his sunglasses, his gaze locking with her caramel warmth. He had been existing in a state of self-denial for five years, and he had been strong enough to handle what life had thrown at him. Yet he didn't have the strength to deny his need for this woman.

The words tripped out too quickly to take back. "If I'm in the neighborhood next Sunday, would you mind if I came by?"

Her delicate hand squeezed his. "I wouldn't mind that, Mike. I wouldn't mind it at all."

Thirty minutes later he was in a very different part of the city, back into his side of reality. There weren't any weeping willows or front porches here. The windows, those with any glass left, were covered with steel mesh or iron bars. Kids the same size and age as that redhead with the skateboard looked old and hard as they stood in loose groups on the street corners. The breeze rolled an empty can across the road and fluttered bits of paper debris as Mike steered into an alley, killed the engine and let the bike coast to the back door of a warehouse.

It raised immediately, the heavy door sliding on well-oiled tracks. "Where the hell have you been, Hogan?"

Mike pushed his Harley inside and waited until the door lowered once more before he turned toward the man who had spoken. "Relax. I'm here, aren't I?"

Prentice moved into the square of sunlight that struggled through a grimy window. He was wearing an olive drab shirt with the sleeves cut out, a bright red bandanna on his head and a four-day growth of blond stubble. Other than that his features appeared completely unremarkable. That's what made him so good at his job.

"Have you made any progress?" he demanded.

"Yeah, I'm getting closer." Mike patted the front of his jacket and glanced around. "Have you got a smoke?"

"No. I thought you quit."

"Right." He slipped his hands into his pockets. "Witlock's going to give me a promotion. He wants to move me into the organization."

"Good work. Now we'll get somewhere."

"Yeah, he's impressed with the way I chauffeur his dog," he said bitterly. "And he likes people who keep their mouths shut. He reminded me what happened to the last chauffeur."

"That was unfortunate. We've got to be careful. No one, absolutely no one, can know about this. I wouldn't want to jeopardize everything we've worked toward—"

"Not to mention my hide, right, Prentice?"

"Naturally. You're a valuable member of the team."

He snorted. "Team? You made me an offer I couldn't refuse."

Prentice fidgeted with the collar of his olive drab shirt as if looking for a tie to straighten. "Any more information you can give me?"

"Whatever he's planning is going down next month. From the sound of it he needs a driver. I don't know the details yet, but it's my guess this is going to be something out of the ordinary."

"If it's big enough it might be just what we need. He's still being too slick for us to get him on his regular rackets."

"Then let's hope it's big."

"Do you still have the number I gave you?"

Mike tapped his forehead. "In here."

"Call anytime, day or night, if something unexpected comes up." He glanced at the Harley that Mike still straddled. "Can't you find something less conspicuous to drive around on? I could hear you coming a block away."

"This was part of our deal, remember? I got this bike out of storage when you got me out, and it goes with me when this is over." His jaw tensed, his voice lowered to a growl that would rival the Harley. "I'm only in this for one thing, Prentice. I'll see this through because I want the payoff you promised."

"It's already in the works. When we get Witlock, you get what you want." He moved to the window and glanced outside. "Next Sunday we meet at the church."

"What are you going to be? The priest?"

His body straightened from the insolent slouch he had been using as if he were already beginning the transformation. "Good idea. I'll expect you around eight in the morning. Use the side door."

With a curt nod Mike signaled his agreement, then kicked the starter and coaxed the bike back to the alley.

From the time he had first met him, he didn't like Prentice. But then, Mike had never liked cops.

For the next five days Mike was kept busy with the maintenance of Witlock's cars, tuning the engines and boosting the performance a touch above street legal. Today he was giving the fleet their weekly waxing. The fender of the limo already shone like a mirror, but Mike continued to rub the gleaming black finish until his arm began to throb.

Sunday and his day away from here couldn't come soon enough. The pressure was starting to get to him. Prentice had said he was a member of a team, but he knew the real word for what he was. An informer. He walked a tightrope between two sides, not belonging to either. He didn't want to be waxing cars or jumping when Witlock whistled. He didn't want to be involved with Prentice and his dirty schemes, either. He wanted to be back on the highway again with the wind on his face and the pavement rolling on in front of him, beckoning him toward the next horizon, and the horizon after that.

And Rebecca clinging warmly to his hips with her breasts pressed against his back and her hands at his waist…

"Hey, Hogan."

Guido was leaning against the open door of the garage, his gun propped against the wall. Leisurely he used the blade of a short knife to pick at his nails.

Mike wrenched his thoughts away from Rebecca and went on the alert. He was always wary around Guido, even though it was because of his connection with him that he had been able to get hired on by Witlock in the first place. Guido was never one to be openly antagonistic or vindictive. No, the swarthy, mustachioed guard carried out any order with equal detachment, from picking up fried chicken to encasing someone's feet in cement and dropping them off the yacht club pier. Balling the cloth in his hand, Mike leaned back against the fender he had buffed. "Morning, Guido. How's it going?"

Heavy brows lowered. "I've got that toothache again."

"Maybe you'd better see a dentist."

"I hate dentists. They hurt." He flipped the knife shut and shoved it into the front pocket of his khaki pants. Guido liked to dress in army surplus clothes, although the military had gotten rid of him long ago when they had discovered that he was too homicidal, even for them.

"Maybe it's only your sinuses."

He brightened at that prospect. "Yeah." Picking up his gun, he moved into the garage. After a frowning survey, he walked over to an empty oil drum and sat down. "I heard you'll be coming in with us next month."

"The boss mentioned that possibility."

"Hey, didn't I tell you I'd fix you up good when you got out? This chauffeur stuff is nothing."

Mike shook out the cloth and tossed it onto the car. "I'm looking forward to something more interesting."

"It'll be big. The boss has been doing a lot of planning in his office for this one." As casually as if he had been changing the cassette in a tape player, he reached into a pocket of his khaki pants, withdrew a long ammunition clip and snicked it into his gun. "We've never done an armored truck before. Trevor says—"

"Shut up!"

Guido jumped off the oil drum and spun around, gun poised.

Aristocratic features twisted into a characteristic sneer, Trevor Dodge walked through the garage door and crossed the cement floor to stand directly in front of Guido. Instead of a rifle, Trevor slung a camera strap over his shoulder. Instead of army fatigues he wore a button-down collar and a preppy sweater with a tiny animal embroidered over the pocket. Someone who didn't know him might mistake him for a yuppie tourist.

With an index finger, Trevor knocked the gun barrel away. "Don't point that thing at me, you crazy moron."

"Hey. You got no reason to call me names."

"I apologize. You're not crazy."

The insult was lost on Guido. "I was telling Hogan about next month's job."

"I heard. But he's just the chauffeur." His long nose turned toward Mike. "Isn't that right, Hogan?"

Mike narrowed his eyes in warning. He knew that Trevor liked to think of himself as Witlock's right-hand man. While the chauffeur was at the bottom of the pecking order of the men who worked on the estate, Trevor viewed himself as perched at the top. Next to the boss.

Guido hooked the strap of his gun over his shoulder. "But the boss says—"

"He doesn't need Hogan as long as he's got me," Trevor said.

Scowling, Mike straightened to his full height, rounded the front of the limousine and walked forward. Deliberately he flexed his arms as he rolled his sleeves a bit tighter above his elbows. "You know, you're really starting to annoy me, Trevor."

Pale eyes flicked to the tendons that stood out on Mike's hands and the muscles that corded along his forearms. Swallowing quickly, Trevor backed toward the door. A few minutes later Guido followed.

It wasn't until Mike was completely alone that he allowed the tension to ease from his body. Leaning a shoulder against the open garage door, he took a deep, cleansing breath of fresh air. He hated being around people like Witlock, and he hated having to act like them. He took another deep breath and rubbed a hand over his eyes. Sunday couldn't come soon enough.

The past week was one of the shortest that Rebecca could remember. Usually her summer vacations dragged by, with each lonely day blending fuzzily into the next. But this week had seemed to shimmer with the memory of last Sunday, and tremble with anticipation of the Sunday to come.

Leaning over the sink in her bathroom, Rebecca stared shortsightedly at her reflection in the mirror, then slipped her glasses back on and ran a brush through her hair. No bun or ponytail today. With nimble fingers she separated her hair into sections and wove the damp strands into a French braid.

Her eyes sparkled as she stepped back to judge the effect. Chestnut tendrils escaped the braid to curl around her face. Even without makeup her cheeks were flushed and her lips moist. She felt a bubble of giddiness rise in her throat as she thought about the day ahead.

What would her mother have said?

She shook her head. Her mother had been a wonderful, warm woman who had wanted nothing more than to see her daughter, the light of her life, settled into a safe home and a safe marriage. The rules of behavior and respectability she had insisted on had been her way of trying to insure her daughter's safety.

"The narrower the road, the less chance of going astray." That was one of Rebecca's father's favorite sayings. He had died the year she had started college. She had wanted to quit then, but her mother had insisted that she owed it to her father to complete her degree and become the teacher he had wanted her to be.

Because of a lifetime of expressing her love and gratitude to her parents by obedience, she had completed her degree and become a teacher. As it turned out, she was happy with the career she had. Yet that same sense of obedience to the rules had probably led her into her disastrous marriage, as well.

Her fingers tugged lightly at the waistband of the new jeans she had bought last week. The salesclerk had assured her that they fit perfectly, but she had never worn such a formfitting garment before. She turned, peering over her shoulder and stretching onto her tiptoes to see the back view. The topstitching on the seams and the pockets seemed to emphasize the curve of her buttocks and hips. Her waist appeared narrower, her legs longer. "I shouldn't wear these," she told herself. But she didn't take them off.

Turning back to the mirror, she smoothed her candy-pink T-shirt over her breasts, making sure that no shadow of lace showed through the cotton. Perhaps her mother wouldn't have minded the T-shirt as much as the jeans. It was comfortable, and covered as much as a blouse did. Besides, she would be putting a jacket over it before she went riding with Mike.

At the thought of Mike the flush on her cheeks deepened. Warmth glowed in the pit of her stomach as she remembered the broad shoulders in front of her and the narrow hips beneath her knees. A tingling sensation began in her chest, spreading slowly outward.

"Good heavens," she whispered when she glanced down at the front of the candy-pink cotton. Perhaps she had better wear a blouse after all.

From outside the house came a deep rumble. Rebecca sighed with disappointment. They had predicted thunderstorms for later in the day, but she had hoped that Mike would be able to take her out before the storm hit.

The rumble ceased abruptly. It was followed by the thud of boots on her front porch and a pounding on the door.

It hadn't been thunder. It had been the Harley.

It must have been a trick of the lighting, Mike thought as the door swung open and Rebecca smiled up at him. Her face was bare of makeup, but it was radiant. Her hair, braided loosely behind her head, seemed to crackle with energy. And her eyes were luminous.

All the way over here he had tried to convince himself that she couldn't possibly be as good as he remembered. How well could he know someone after sharing nothing but a few minutes being bandaged over a bathroom sink, or gliding on a porch swing, or having bagels and coffee at a kitchen table? Yet there had been that ride, too.

She was all he could think about as he had left the gates of Witlock's estate. It was only her face he pictured when he met the blond and suddenly portly "priest" at the church and passed on the week's worth of information. The minute he stepped over Rebecca's threshold and the door swung shut behind him, he felt Witlock and Prentice and the tangle of his life fade like smoke on the wind. He inhaled the first fully free breath he had taken in a week and it was all because of Rebecca.

She drew him. He'd heard that opposites attract, but somehow this was more than sexual.

"Well? What do you think?" she asked shyly.

Think? He had stopped that function the moment he had seen her. "About what?"

"The new outfit. I realized the wind wouldn't pull so much if I had tighter clothes. I have a jacket to put over this, too. It isn't leather, but the denim should be thick enough to provide some protection…"

He was no longer listening. His gaze took her in from the length of her deliciously curved legs to her slender neck and caramel-warm eyes. "You're beautiful," he said softly.

She looked away. "I wasn't fishing for compliments."

He raised his hands to her face hesitantly, then cradled her cheeks in his palms. "I mean it."

"Thanks. I guess anything would be an improvement."

Mike frowned at the vulnerability in her gaze. "Hasn't anyone ever told you that you're beautiful?"

It seemed as if she wouldn't answer. The corners of her lips trembled briefly as she tried to recapture the smile she had greeted him with. Then her breath escaped on a sigh. "No," she answered simply.

"What about Ted?"

"What does he have to do with this?"

"Didn't he ever tell you—"

"I don't want to talk about Ted." She pulled away from him, backing into the living room.

"Why would you marry a man who never told you that you were beautiful?" he asked, following her.

She hesitated, crossing her arms over her chest and still not meeting his gaze. "Our families had known each other for a long time. It was always assumed we would get married."

Slowly he closed the distance she had put between them. "I'm sorry. It isn't my business, is it?"

"I'm sorry I snapped at you like that. But why are you always mentioning my ex-husband?"

"I've been curious about your marriage because I can't imagine anyone leaving you." Carefully he brought his hands back to her cheeks. Her skin was warm silk. "But I have no right to ask, because I haven't told you anything about my past, either."

She rubbed her cheek lightly against his palm. "My life's no secret. Ask any member of the local PTA and they'd be glad to tell you all the gory details."

Did he really want to know? That would mean getting close. Sharing. Learning to understand what made Rebecca the woman she was.

"I was a failure as a wife," she said briskly.

"You? I can't believe that." He stroked his thumbs along the delicate skin at her temples.

"Believe it. Ted's off in Las Vegas with the nineteen-year-old stripper he left me for. Evidently she is much more successful at satisfying a man than I was. So thank you for your compliment. Would you like some coffee?"

The pain was there under her brisk words. He felt a flash of anger at the man who had so recklessly thrown away a chance with such a warm and giving woman. Yet at the same time he felt a twinge of pleasure that her husband *had* left. She was alone, like him. And if no one else had ever called her beautiful, then he wanted to make up for that.

His words hadn't seemed to convince her. Perhaps his actions would. Mike smiled and tightened his hold on her face. Before he could reconsider what he was doing, he tilted his head and lowered his lips to hers.

He didn't push her. He moved his mouth gently, giving her a chance to grow accustomed to the feel of him. His fingers slid down to her neck, capturing the pulse beneath her skin.

A vein throbbed hard against the base of his thumb. Was she frightened of him?

Deep in her throat she made a sound. It was soft, hushed, almost reverent. A moan of yearning. She stepped closer until her toes nudged his, then wound her arms around his neck and parted her lips.

He hadn't wanted to take the kiss further, but how could he refuse her sweet invitation? His hands moved to her shoulders, then over her back as his tongue traced the contours of her mouth. She was so sweet, so giving. He wanted to lose himself in what she offered and let the world disappear. Closing his eyes, he deepened the kiss.

Rebecca swayed against him, feeling his hands splay across her shoulder blades as his tongue plunged into her mouth. Was this really her, kissing in her living room on a Sunday morning? Were these really her hands, tangling in Mike's stubborn black hair and learning the shape of his ears and the texture of his cheeks? Was that really her body feeling the jolts of electricity everywhere she rubbed against his?

Undoubtedly there was a thrill in the forbidden. She was behaving contrary to everything she had been taught was right and proper. Yet this *felt* right. She had been wanting to do this since he had walked in her door. The anticipation she had been feeling all week was nothing compared to the tingling thrills that followed his touch.

The kiss ended as gently as it had begun. He pulled away slowly, moving his hands back to her face and replacing his lips with the tip of an index finger. As his sky-blue eyes gradually opened and focused once more, his fingertip traced the moisture from her mouth.

She dropped her hands to his sleeves and hung on to the thick folds of leather at the bend of his elbows. "Mike, I don't usually do this sort of thing…"

"I know." The tiny lines at the corners of his eyes deepened. "That's why I enjoyed it so much."

"Mmm. I think I'd better go and fix that coffee."

"I have a better idea."

"I'm sure you do, but—"

"Rebecca." He laughed. "For a schoolteacher you have a devious mind."

"Schoolteachers are full of ideas, didn't you know?"

"We'll have to explore all of them someday." Denim rasped as he boldly pressed his knee between hers. "It would be interesting to see how they compare to mine. But that's not what I meant."

Releasing his sleeves, she sidestepped awkwardly. "Oh?"

"Don't sound so disappointed. I'll kiss you again if you like."

"No. I mean I liked it, but I wasn't expecting…" She trailed off as a grin spread across his face. Putting her hands on her hips, she faced him squarely. "Just because you're six foot two—"

"Three," he corrected, grinning unrepentantly.

"And have biceps like rocks and look sexy as heck doesn't mean that I need any charity kisses."

"You think I'm sexy?"

"You're missing the point."

"You're missing a lot more," he said, deliberately lowering his voice to its deepest register.

"Why did you kiss me?" she demanded. "Was it because you felt sorry for me?"

His grin wavered. "Sorry for you? Why would you think that?"

"I guess I came across as pretty pathetic, right? A divorced woman all alone without even a dog for company?"

The amusement faded from his expression. He took a step toward her, then stopped and shoved his hands into the back pockets of his jeans. "What the hell are you talking about?"

All her insecurities seemed to rush to the surface, clamoring to be dealt with. "Is that why you took me out on your bike last week? A man like you wouldn't normally waste his time on someone like me. There must be dozens of women who are a lot better at…who know what to do…who can please you better than I could.''

"A man like me? Is that what you said?'' He swore under his breath. "You don't know anything about me.''

"Then tell me. Why did you come back, and why—''

"Why did I kiss you?'' he finished for her. "Because you're a warm, desirable woman and you've haunted my thoughts and my dreams for two weeks. And when you opened the door this morning and welcomed me inside all I could think of was how beautiful you were to me.'' He paused and inhaled shakily. "You're the only good thing in my life right now, but I know I've got no business being with a fine, respectable person like you. Not me, not with what I'm doing.''

Stunned, she stared at him. In his own way he was as vulnerable and insecure as she was. "It doesn't matter what you do for a living, Mike,'' she said softly. "You're a good man inside.''

He snorted. "You don't know me.''

"I'd like to.''

"Why?'' He turned her own words on her. "Are you feeling sorry for me?''

"No. To be honest, I feel strongly attracted to you and I have from the beginning. And the more I learn about you, the more I'm certain that you're someone I want to know.''

Her words hung in the air between them as they each paused to digest everything that had been said.

Slowly the tension eased. With a sigh deep enough to make the leather of his jacket creak, Mike broke the silence. "A picnic. That was the idea I was going to mention before all this started.''

"A picnic?''

"Yeah. I thought we could make a few sandwiches and go out somewhere. Spend the whole day together. Outside. I like being outside.''

She took several deep breaths, then lifted her hand to push up the glasses that had slipped down her nose.

A picnic, he had said. Spend the whole day together. Rebecca felt her heart skip into the same pounding rhythm that had accompanied the kiss. What if he wanted more than simply a ride on his bike? He didn't know that she was incapable of giving him more. At least, Ted had always said she was incapable. And with someone as blatantly masculine as Mike, how would she be able to face the disgust in his eyes when she disappointed him, as she was bound to?

What was she thinking? For heaven's sake, it was only a kiss.

A sudden knock at her front door kept her from replying. With a guilty sense of relief she smoothed her palms over her jeans and moved to answer. It was just as well this conversation had been ended. Even now she couldn't believe the things she had actually said aloud. She had called Mike sexy. And she had told him about her marriage. And she had told him she was attracted to him....

Attracted? Since when did she have such a penchant for understatement?

Mike took his hands from his pockets and slowly clenched them into fists. She was the one good thing in his life, all right. He shouldn't have kissed her, just like he shouldn't have come over here today. But doing the right thing was something Mike was seldom accused of.

His knee twinged from the tension that hardened his muscles. Reaching down, he massaged it roughly, then limped after her as she made her way to the door.

A redheaded woman stood on the porch. At her side was the freckled skateboarder from down the street.

"Mrs. Barring," Rebecca said. "And Andrew," she added. "This is a surprise."

The woman was almost as tall as Mike. She kept a bread-dough plump hand on the boy's shoulder and smiled like a cat at a mouse hole. "Good morning, Mrs. Stanford. It's a lovely day, isn't it? I do hope we won't be getting the thunderstorms they predicted."

Rebecca tugged at her T-shirt. "What can I do for you, Mrs. Barring?"

Leaning slightly to the side, she made a point of looking Mike over from head to toe. "Oh, I'm sorry. You have company. Perhaps I should come back later."

With a sigh Rebecca opened the door wider and stepped back. "This is a friend of mine, Mike Hogan." The glance she shot at him was hesitant. "Mike, this is Mrs. Barring and her son Andrew."

The boy twisted his head to look at the driveway. "Is that your bike?"

Mike nodded, then shoved his hands back into his pockets. "Yeah, it's mine."

"Wow. Cool."

"That's enough, Andrew." The woman was still inspecting Mike, her mouth tight, her eyes narrowed. "You're not from around here, are you, Mr. Hogan? We don't usually see your sort in this neighborhood."

He had seen that look all his life, so he should be used to it by now. His jaw tightened as he narrowed his eyes and returned the perusal.

"Mrs. Barring," Rebecca said, "we were about to go out, so if there's something you wanted…?"

Her gaze slid back to Rebecca. "I wanted to bring over this letter." From the pocket of her voluminous dress she produced a crumpled envelope. "It was delivered to our house by mistake the other day."

Rebecca took the letter, glanced at it briefly, then frowned and focused more carefully. She was silent for a moment. Finally she raised her head and put her hand back on the doorknob. "Thank you for your thoughtfulness, Mrs. Barring. I know you must be busy, so I won't keep you any longer."

Mrs. Barring's eyes widened at the tone of dismissal. She didn't move. "Andrew said that he thought he saw you on the back of some motorcycle the other day, but I told him he couldn't possibly have been right."

Rebecca's delicate jaw clenched briefly. "Well, he was. It's a Harley Davis, and we were about to go out on it again, so if you'll excuse me?"

"Mrs. Stanford, I really think you ought to—"

"Goodbye, Mrs. Barring," she said firmly.

The woman barely had a chance to blink before the door was closed in her face.

Rebecca stared at the door for a full minute, then whirled around, threw the letter to the floor and headed for the kitchen.

Puzzled, Mike followed.

She opened a cupboard, withdrew a loaf of bread and placed it stiffly on the counter. "What kind of sandwiches do you like?"

He leaned a shoulder against the fridge and frowned. "What's the matter?"

"Did you see that woman?"

"Yeah."

"Do you know why she came here?"

"She said she wanted to bring you a letter."

Rebecca grabbed a knife from a drawer and slammed it down beside the bread. "The letter was addressed to 'Occupant.' It was only an excuse."

"What do you mean?"

"She's a nosy busybody. She thinks that because her husband's on the school board and she's the president of the PTA that she's got a right to keep track of everything I do."

Mike remembered the way the redheaded kid had stared at the limo. And at the bike. Understanding was quick. "She came to see who you were keeping company with."

"They've had a field day with my marriage and my divorce. I guess Mrs. Barring hoped that she'd be able to find something else to gossip about."

"I'm sorry. It's my fault, isn't it?"

She didn't appear to hear him. Striding to the refrigerator, she barely let him get out of the way before she yanked open the door. "I'm a good teacher. What I do outside the class-room isn't anyone else's business."

"I should have realized that I'd damage your reputation if people saw someone like me—"

"Someone like you?" she repeated, pausing in the angle of the open door. "It doesn't matter what you do for a living, as far as I'm concerned. Do you think I'm a snob?"

"No, I never thought that."

Frowning, she bent to rummage through the gleaming shelves. After a moment she withdrew several plastic food containers, closed the door with her hip and moved back to the counter.

"Do you want me to leave?"

"What?"

"If I've made things awkward for you, maybe I should leave."

"I thought we were going on a picnic." She waved a but-tery knife at the slices of bread she had spread out in front of her. "I don't care what that self-righteous cow thinks, I have a right to choose my own friends."

"Self-righteous cow?"

Her hand stilled. "Oh. That was a terrible thing to say, wasn't it?"

He tried to suppress his grin. The description had been dead on the mark. "Terrible," he agreed.

Carefully she placed the knife down. "I don't know what came over me. I don't usually lose my temper like that."

Some of her hair had escaped from her braid. Her cheeks were flushed, her eyes wide and gleaming. There was a deep well of passion beneath the surface of this woman, Mike de-cided. Passion that her idiot husband had probably never sus-pected, let alone tapped. "It's Davidson," he said.

She met his gaze slowly. "What?"

"Harley-Davidson, not Davis. My bike."

"I doubt whether Mrs. Barring knows the difference." She smiled tentatively. "Do you like mustard or mayo with ham?"

He hesitated. The visit from the neighborhood busybody should have reminded him he could only mean trouble to Rebecca. He should make some excuse and leave. Now. Before it was too late.

His sigh was inaudible. "Mustard."

Her smile was incredible. "Fine."

Chapter 6

Lake Michigan gleamed restlessly. Gulls swooped and flapped along the water, their screeches carried away by the wind. The shore rose gently to a low hill at the boundary of the park where Rebecca leaned back on her elbows on the plaid blanket and stared up through the shifting canopy of leaves above her. Clouds were beginning to roll in. The air was charged with the expectancy that precedes a storm, but she felt no hurry to leave. It had been a wonderful day.

She turned her head. Mike sat at the base of an oak tree, his back against the trunk, one leg stretched out in front of him, the other bent so that his wrist rested on his knee. He rolled a toothpick between his thumb and index finger, a substitute for the cigarettes he had told her about giving up. She had laughed with delight when he'd agreed to demonstrate how he could use his tongue to move the toothpick along his lip or tilt it at a jaunty angle. When she had taken one to try it herself, Mike had attempted to hide his amusement, but after she had dropped the fifth toothpick in the grass because she was giggling too hard to keep her lips closed, he had lost control and hooted with laughter.

He had a wonderful laugh, although she seldom heard it. Deep and full chested, it was filled with a sense of something unexpected. Even though he was quiet now, his face was still relaxed. The harsh lines and angles that could make him appear hard had softened as the day wore on.

"This is a beautiful spot," she said contentedly.

"Yeah." His hair lifted from his forehead in the strengthening breeze, and his eyes were focused on the horizon.

"I'm glad you brought me here. It's good to get out of the city, or at least to a park so you can pretend you're out of the city."

He nodded, then rested his head against the tree. "Watching the horizon, feeling the wind on your face, listening to the gulls…they're simple pleasures, but they should never be taken for granted."

A squirrel leapt from a branch overhead, then scrabbled down the trunk of an adjacent tree. Lazily Rebecca followed its movement, then turned her gaze back to Mike. They had finished their sandwiches hours ago, yet he seemed satisfied to simply sit and watch the water. He looked completely at ease, as if he belonged out in the open like this, unconfined, free.

She had tasted that sense of freedom with him and had reveled in it. A warm flush, unnoticed by her companion, stole into her cheeks as she remembered her uncharacteristic outburst this morning. And the kiss that had precipitated it. Oh, but he kissed like an angel. Or a devil. Perhaps it was the combination of both that was so fascinating. There was such vulnerability in his eyes at times that she wanted to reach out to him, wrap him in her arms and cuddle him like a lost child. Then the next moment those eyes would glint with such masculine challenge that she would want to take him into her arms for a completely different reason.

What was happening to her? Was she finally turning into

the worst of clichés, the man-starved lonely schoolteacher? She grimaced.

"What are you thinking about?"

He was no angel, if he chose this moment to ask that question. "Uh, not much," she mumbled.

He was no longer looking at the horizon. "Is something wrong?"

"Uh, of course not."

There was nothing vulnerable little-boy about him now. He shifted against the rough bark of the tree, stretching both legs out and crossing his ankles. With a sigh he raised his arms and locked his fingers behind his head. "Those clouds are getting thicker."

"I suppose we'd better go back," she said, trying not to stare at the perfect contours of his flexed arms.

"Yeah. I guess. Is that lady going to give you a rough time?"

"What lady?"

His lips twitched. "The cow."

"Oh." She remained silent for a moment while she considered the consequences of the brusque dismissal she had given Mrs. Barring. "I don't think so. She isn't that bad. And simply because my friend wears a black leather jacket and rides a wicked-looking motorcycle doesn't mean that I'm about to corrupt the morals of my grade-three class."

"You think of me as your friend?"

"Well, yes. Don't you?"

The squirrel chattered and jumped back to the oak tree. Mike tipped back his head to watch its progress for a while before he replied to her question with one of his own. "What do you think a friend is, Rebecca?"

"Someone to talk to. Someone to do things with."

"Like picnics?"

"That's right."

"Anything else?"

"Sure. Friends…care what happens to each other."

His sky-blue gaze locked with hers. "I care what happens to you."

"So I guess we're friends."

"Yeah." Leaning forward, he reached out to brush her hair from her cheek. "The wind's picking up. We should get going."

His fingertips were warm on her skin. His palm was work toughened yet gentle as he smoothed his hand along her jaw. Rebecca felt her pulse trip. "They predicted rain," she said.

"Yeah." He moved his thumb across her lower lip, pressing lightly, testing the softness.

"I, uh, put the rest of the lunch in the knapsack already."

"Good," he said absently, pushing away from the tree to kneel at her side.

She was still half reclining, her elbows propped behind her. Against the background of the shifting leaves, Mike's face hovered over hers. Moving slowly, he braced his arms on either side of her.

He's going to kiss me, she thought, anticipation surging through her body. Her breath caught. Her fingers curled into the scratchy wool of the blanket. Eagerly she arched her neck to bring her head closer to his.

She wants me to kiss her, Mike thought, watching as Rebecca's eyelids lowered and her lips parted. The afternoon was practically over. In the distance, thunder rumbled almost below the threshold of hearing.

Restlessly she moved, bringing her hip against his knee. Even through the layers of denim, the contact was electrifying.

She was so sweet, so good. So trusting. How could he do this?

Shifting her weight to her left side, she raised her right hand tentatively. Like butterfly wings her fingers grazed his chin.

How could he not?

He dipped his head and captured one of her fingers with his lips. Holding her gaze, he bit gently on the fingertip, then sucked it into his mouth.

Her eyes widened. "Oh!"

"Is it all right for friends to do this?"

"What exactly are you doing?" she asked shakily.

"Good question." He released her finger and leaned closer until her face blurred. Her breath was hot on his lips. The muscles in his arms trembled as he remained braced above her. Gradually the touch of her breath was replaced by something more solid. Had he moved? Or had she? Did it matter?

He increased the pressure on her mouth and her hand slid around to the nape of his neck. He leaned closer. His chest nudged her down until her spine touched the blanket. Through the thin T-shirt she wore, he could feel her nipples harden.

Suddenly greedy, Mike opened his mouth over hers, thrusting his tongue inside. She was so sweet and warm and welcoming. He stretched out to lie beside her, his body responding to thoughts of the act his tongue mimicked. He had been right. Passion ran deep in this woman.

Thunder rumbled again, closer this time. If she heard it she didn't react. Instead she returned the kiss with enthusiasm, moving against him so that her breasts flattened and rubbed across his chest.

Mike released the clip from the end of her braid, combing his fingers through the luxurious strands. His eyes closed in pleasure. Her fresh scent surrounded him, brought by the wind that teased the hair he touched. His mouth moved to her cheek, tasting her, trailing to the delicate angle of her jaw. Then he nuzzled toward her ear until he drew the hot lobe between his lips.

Her fingers clutched his shoulders. Wriggling her hips, she made a sound that was far from ladylike.

He rolled to his back, bringing her on top of him. His hands skimmed over her shoulders, down to her waist and fastened on either side of her hips. When her seeking lips found his once more, he captured them in a kiss that rocked him to his soul.

Damn, how he wanted this woman. Right here. Right now. The hell with tomorrow and the rest of the world.

Groaning, he lifted his hand to the side of her breast.

At the bold touch Rebecca gasped into his mouth, then shifted so that her breast filled his palm. Oblivious to everything except the pleasure he was giving her, she reveled in the sensations he was awakening.

How far would they have gone? How far would she have let him go? They would never know. In the next instant the thunder crashed directly overhead.

Mike wrenched his mouth from hers and opened his eyes. The sky beyond the sheltering oak boughs had darkened to the color of slate. Small branches whipped like banners, their leaves trembling. The storm was about to break.

With a muttered curse, he moved his hands back to her waist and rolled them to their sides. "We've got to go."

She blinked rapidly, disoriented. Her wire-rimmed glasses were touchingly askew. "Mmm?"

He glanced past her shoulder. A squall line was advancing across the lake like a dark curtain. Sitting up swiftly, he helped her come to her knees. "Come on."

A series of expressions danced eloquently across her face. Disappointment, resignation. Then chagrin. "Oh!" She raised a hand to her mouth. "Oh, my goodness."

He pushed to his feet, then leaned down to grasp her wrist and bring her alongside him. "Ditto."

She wavered for a moment, her hands splayed against his chest, before she raised her chin and took a hurried step away. "Oh, my. I don't usually—"

"You don't usually end your picnics with a roll on the blanket, right?"

"No." She pressed her hands to her flaming cheeks. "I'm so embarrassed."

"You can blame me. I'm a bad influence." A fat raindrop splatted on his cheek. "Come on, we're going to get soaked."

She looked around them just as another peal of thunder vibrated overhead. "I guess we should have left before this."

"We were kind of busy." He retrieved his jacket from the base of the tree and held it out to her. "Here, put this on."

More raindrops splashed around them. Shaking her head, she slipped into her denim jacket. "No, you keep it. I'll use the blanket," she said as she snatched it up, folded it diagonally and wrapped it around her shoulders, fashioning a makeshift poncho. Stooping to pick up the knapsack, she turned to face him.

If he'd had the time, he would have paused to admire the way she looked, with her hair pulled loose from its braid, blowing free around her flushed face, the corners of the blanket clutched bravely in front of her breasts, the dark clouds flashing with lightning behind her. Was this passionate, elemental woman the same one who had appeared so dainty and feminine gliding on a porch swing?

What would it be like to spread that blanket out once more, to have the rain glisten on her skin and the wind carry her cries, to have her naked to the wrath of the storm and to release her passion by giving her his own?

"Mike?"

Dangerous thoughts. Shrugging on his jacket, he draped his arm across her shoulders and led her to where he had parked his bike.

Rebecca unlocked the back door and stepped into the kitchen. "Come inside. I'll get some towels."

Mike stood in the doorway, his black jacket dripping on the floor, his jeans soaked through and clinging like a second skin to his thighs. "Are you sure you want me to come in?"

She dropped the wet blanket over the back of a chair and crossed the floor to take his hand. "Yes, I'm sure. You need to dry off before you go home or you'll catch pneumonia."

"I thought the rain was just what I needed."

She drew him inside, then went back to close the door. "What do you mean?"

"A cold shower."

On the ride back from the park she had promised herself she would stop being embarrassed about what had happened. They were adults, weren't they? They hadn't done anything wrong. She decided to let his comment pass. "I could put your clothes in the drier if you like, but I don't have anything that would fit you in the meantime." She pulled out a chair and sat down to unlace her sneakers. "I threw out all of Ted's stuff after he left. Besides, he was a lot smaller than you."

He hadn't moved from the center of the floor where she had left him. Slowly he undid his jacket. "Maybe I could wipe this off."

She removed her wet socks, then padded barefoot to the linen closet in the hall. This was the right thing to do, invite him into her house and offer to dry his clothes. It had nothing to do with wanting to have him naked. No, nothing.

Her hand trembled as she reached for a stack of fluffy white towels and she bit her lip. Maybe she was the one who should be taking a cold shower.

It took all of her self-control not to gasp when she returned to the kitchen. Mike was carefully wiping the moisture from his leather jacket. But he wasn't using a towel, he was using his T-shirt.

Her fingers tightened into the nubby terry-cloth towels she held in her arms. His back was to her. With every movement he made, his skin gleamed and the lean muscles beneath the surface rippled. She could see the perfect symmetry of his powerful shoulders and the strong ridge of his spine. She swallowed hard. Could he hear the way her heart pounded in her throat? "You could have used a towel."

He paused, then glanced over his shoulder. "I didn't want to get your things dirty."

Look away! she told herself sternly. Instead she let her gaze take in everything, from the way his hair curled in short, damp tendrils at his nape to the way his wet jeans rode low on his hips. Unclenching her fingers, she set the towels down on the table. "You can use these. I'm going to go and change."

There is a big, gorgeous, half-naked man in the kitchen, she told herself. A man who had been kissing her senseless less than an hour ago, whose long, hard body had been cradling hers while his palm had cradled... Why was she leaving? Why wasn't she pressing herself back into his arms?

Was she afraid? Perhaps she was. It was easy to let herself get swept away by his sexual magnetism when he touched her, but now that they were back in her normal surroundings she felt those insecurities stir up once more. She'd had little experience with men, apart from Ted, and she hadn't needed his complaints to know that had been a disaster. And Mike was so much more...man.

"Coward," she whispered to herself as she sprinted down the hallway to the sanctuary of her bedroom.

Fifteen minutes later Rebecca had toweled her hair and re-plaited it into a loose braid. Her jeans and sweatshirt hung over the shower curtain rod in the bathroom. She hesitated a moment, then pulled on a pair of linen slacks and an oversize cotton shirt. Rolling up the sleeves as she went, she walked back to the kitchen.

Mike had draped a towel around his shoulders. His jacket hung over the knob of the back door, his boots rested on the mat. He was straddling a chair, his arms crossed over the back, a mug held loosely in his hand. "I hope you don't mind," he said, holding up the mug.

He had made coffee. The aroma wrapped itself around her in welcome as she stepped through the doorway. "No, of course I don't mind. It smells inviting."

"I'll get you some." He rose immediately and poured her a cup, then took it to the table and pulled out the other chair.

"Thanks. Maybe you'd be more comfortable in the living room."

"I'm still damp." He gestured to the denim that clung to

his thighs. "I'll go as soon as the rain lets up, if that's okay with you."

Nodding, she sat across from him and lifted her cup. The coffee was strong enough to clear her sinuses. She inhaled sharply, then forced down a mouthful out of politeness.

Mike stretched his right leg out in front of him and massaged the knee. "The thunder's stopped already."

"Does your leg bother you?"

"Not really. It just gets stiff sometimes."

"Those wet jeans probably aren't doing it any good."

"Are you saying you want me to take my pants off?"

Coffee slopped over the side of her cup. "No, of course not."

"Relax, Rebecca. I was teasing. Despite what you might think of me, I'm not about to jump you."

Surprised, she glanced up at him. "No. I trust you, Mike."

"Even after what happened in the park?"

"I think…" She cleared her throat. "I think we were both equally responsible."

"You really are a decent woman, aren't you?" He reached out to wipe a drop of coffee from the corner of her mouth. "I've never met anyone like you before."

"I've never met anyone like you before, either. It's not surprising, though, considering the difference in our backgrounds."

"Yeah, we sure are different."

She put her cup down, then propped an elbow on the edge of the table. "You told me a bit about your childhood last week. From the sound of it, you saw a lot of the ugly side of life from the time you were very young."

"The foster homes I grew up in weren't exactly the Brady Bunch."

"It's a shame you were transferred around so much."

"It was my own fault. I wasn't an easy kid to get along with."

"But despite that you turned out all right."

He frowned and put his cup down with a thud. "You don't know that."

"Sure I do. I can see the type of man you are."

"You don't know me, Rebecca."

She waved a hand impatiently. "You keep saying that. You remind me of some of the kids I've had who try their best to act tough, tossing spitballs and cultivating pet worms, but deep down inside they have the sensitivity of a poet."

He leaned over, putting more force into the massage he gave his knee. "I stopped being a kid a long time ago."

In silence she watched him as he flexed his leg a few times then continued to rub his knee. The tendons on the backs of his hands stood out from the pressure he exerted.

Concerned, she leaned forward and touched the tips of his knuckles. "It does hurt, doesn't it? Your knee?"

"I'm okay," he said.

She pulled her hand back. "How did you hurt it?"

His fingers stilled. "It's a long story."

"I've got the time." Tilting her head, she listened to the rain at the window. "So do you."

He hesitated. Then with a sigh he sat up and folded his arms over the back of the chair once more. "It happened during my last year of high school," he began. "I never did very well in school. It didn't interest me when I was a kid, and no one made me go when I didn't want to."

"Except for the time when your foster sister helped you with your English homework. Jeannie, wasn't it?"

His voice softened. "Yeah. Except for then. Most of the time I don't know how I managed to scrape through from one grade to the next. Maybe the teachers just didn't want to keep me back." He smiled wryly. "I was always kind of big for my age."

"Mmm. I bet."

"Well, by the time I was in high school, the only courses that interested me were mathematics and shop. One year I had a shop teacher who let me take apart a Corvette." He shook his head. "When we put it back together we had some parts missing, so we took it apart and did it again. I progressed to motorcycles from there. Less parts."

She laughed softly. "Go on."

"Well, this shop teacher convinced me to go out for the football team. Because of my size and my speed—running fast came in handy in my neighborhoods—I ended up doing pretty well. I didn't really care that much, until some college scouts came to one of our games. They offered me a scholarship."

He fell silent, his forehead creasing.

"And? Did you go to college?"

He shook his head. "During the last game of the season, the championship game, I wasn't careful. We were winning. I had broken the record for the yards I carried the ball and was feeling cocky and let everyone know about it. A few of the guys on the other team didn't like it, so they took me out."

"Took you out?"

"I was dumb. I didn't see it coming. They waited until the game was over and met up with me in the showers." He rubbed his eyes briskly. "I heard later that there was some big money lost on the game. And maybe I had been spouting off a bit too much about my scholarship. Anyhow, a knee snaps pretty easily when some guys hold your leg across a pair of benches and a fullback jumps on top of it."

Rebecca shuddered and clamped her hand to her mouth, an image of the vicious attack coming vividly to her mind. Mike had been naked, helpless and outnumbered and they had held him down and extended his leg and...and...oh, God.

"That shop teacher tried to go to the police, but I'd told him it was no use since it was my word against theirs. The cops told him the same thing. It didn't make any difference anyway. The scholarship was gone. The leg never did heal properly. I was in and out of hospitals so much that I barely managed to get my high school diploma."

She reached across the table and grasped his wrist. "Oh, Mike."

"Don't feel sorry for me."

"There's a difference between pity and compassion. I'm your friend, Mike. I didn't know you then, but I still care about what happened." Her grip loosened. With her fingertips she stroked his arm lightly. "I wish I could take the pain away."

He shrugged stiffly. "It happened a long time ago."

"How old were you?"

"Eighteen."

"You were so young."

"It was seventeen years ago, but I had stopped being a kid long before that."

"Have you ever thought about finishing your education, of going to college?"

"What for?"

Yes, she thought. What for? Was she trying to change him? Was she really too much of a snob to have a friend who was merely a chauffeur to a rich man's dog? Slowly she withdrew her hand. "That's none of my business, is it?"

A muscle in his cheek jumped as he watched her. "There's another reason I didn't go to college, Rebecca."

A change seemed to come over him, although he hadn't moved. His back tensed, his lips thinned. The clear blue of his eyes seemed to dim as if a shutter had been drawn across them.

She shifted uneasily. "You don't have to tell me any more if you don't want to."

"But I need to. I told you that you don't know me, and it's true. The busted knee was only part of what happened."

She jumped up. She didn't want to hear this, she was sure of it. His manner had suddenly become harder, almost dangerous. "I'm going to get some more coffee."

"You never finished the first cup."

"I, uh, it's gone cold."

He didn't buy the excuse. Rising from his chair, he followed her to the counter. There was nothing of the endearing little boy in him now. With his bare chest and grim expression, his raw masculinity was almost palpable. He grabbed her arm. "Why don't you want to listen?"

She felt small and suddenly helpless. He kept saying that she didn't know him. Was he right? Was she only seeing what she wanted to see? "I guess you're making me nervous," she answered honestly.

Immediately he relaxed his grasp, sliding his hand down to her wrist. "I'm sorry."

"You've explained how you hurt your leg. You don't have to tell me any more."

"Yes, I do. I owe it to you."

He sounded so serious. Unwillingly she nodded. "Okay."

"After my leg was ruined, I felt pretty sorry for myself. And angry. Even if I'd never made it to the professional leagues, I had hoped that if I went to college I'd at least get a decent, respectable job. As it was, I figured that I was cheated out of my one chance to get ahead."

"You were so young. Of course you'd feel that way."

He took her hand in his. "I did a lot of things that I'm not proud of. I got in with a bad crowd."

"Lots of teenagers do that—"

"Rebecca," he said, his voice sharp. "Don't defend me until you know it all. When I say bad, I mean bad."

His fingers were tightening painfully over hers. She forced herself to speak calmly. "What did you do?"

"We started out stealing cars."

Rain drummed against the window as a sudden gust of wind rattled the panes. The kitchen was warm and bright, still familiar with its flowered curtains and the homey smell of coffee. Rebecca couldn't quite believe what she had heard. "What?"

"Joyriding, mostly. We'd drive until the gas ran out and then dump it."

Okay, he had been young and hurt and angry. Plenty of teenagers got into minor scrapes like that. With her sheltered upbringing, she had never personally known anyone who did anything worse than rack up overdue fines at the library, but that didn't mean—

"Then we started to strip them down and sell the parts."

Desperately she tried to justify that in her mind, as well. Poverty did odd things to people. Without the proper guidance Mike was misled. Or perhaps he had been bullied into taking part.

"I thought I was pretty smart," he said bitterly. "With my knowledge of mechanics I could strip the car down and have the parts shipped out of the garage we were using before the owner even knew the thing was missing. I never got caught, either. By the time I was twenty I was running one of the best hot car-parts businesses in the city."

A car thief, she thought numbly. It had been more than youthful rebellion or troublemaking. It had been organized, premeditated crime, and Mike had been an active and willing participant. This must have been the edge of danger she had sensed about him from the start. Mike had been a criminal.

Had been? Her blood chilled. If he still was a criminal, he wouldn't be working as a chauffeur, would he? If he was that bad, she wouldn't be drawn to him like this, would she? Could she? Carefully she withdrew her hand from his, crossing her arms over her chest. "Go on."

"Some of my people did get caught, but there were plenty of others willing to take their place. It was no surprise that I ran into a lot of the kids I had grown up with. But then one day I found out that one of my new recruits was Jeannie."

"Your foster sister. The girl who helped you with your English homework."

He snorted. "Yeah. She came to me for help that time. She needed money."

"She must have fallen on hard times."

"I hadn't seen her since I was a kid. I almost didn't recognize her at first, she had changed that much."

"How?"

His jaw worked for a moment before he answered. "She was a drug addict."

Her eyes filled. "That's awful."

"It made me take a good look at myself and the things I was doing."

She grasped desperately at the change in his tone. "And that's when you went straight?"

"It wasn't that simple. I wish to God it could have been." He turned away. "I managed to get a straight job, and for a few years things were going okay. I thought Jeannie was getting treatment, but she hadn't really quit." His voice wavered. "And then everything fell apart."

She stared at the rigid line of his shoulders. Her hand rose, then stopped before she could touch him. He had distanced himself without moving an inch.

"I went to prison, Rebecca. I spent the last five years of my life in prison."

Her head spun. Something was wrong with her breathing. Mike? Who loved the wind and the sound of the gulls? Who spoke about freedom and simple pleasures? In prison?

He braced his hands on the edge of the counter and stared blankly out the window. "I hate cops. They didn't do anything to the guys who stomped my knee. They didn't do anything to stop the drugs that killed Jeannie. But they were quick to hand out their justice when they found me standing over the body of the bastard who put the needle in her arm."

Slapping her hands over her ears, she backed away. She didn't want to hear any more. This was too real. This wasn't the safe make-believe of the movies.

Slowly he turned to face her. With one hand he pulled the towel from around his neck and coiled it tightly around his knuckles. "They had me cold, Rebecca. I had threatened him in public. They caught me holding the gun that had killed him and charged me with second-degree murder."

She shook her head, trying to stop the words she feared were going to come. Because once they were spoken, nothing could be the same again. She had been a fool. She had been deliberately deceiving herself. "No. Please, Mike. Don't say any more."

"They found me guilty."

"No!"

"I got fifteen years but I got paroled in five," he finished. "How does it feel to know you've been kissed by a convicted killer, Rebecca?"

"Oh, God." She moved her hands to her mouth, pressing her fingers against her lips. Revulsion shot through her body. She had let him kiss her and touch her. She had bought new clothes, she had ridden his motorcycle, she had slammed the door in the face of the president of the PTA. She had acted like a fool, like a desperately lonely fool. She had ignored all the lessons of her normal, secure childhood and had risked her reputation. For him.

She had been wrong. Wrong.

Had she thought the aura of danger around him was exciting? This was no longer a harmless flirtation. He was real. His danger was real.

He stared at her in silence, motionless, apart from the muscle in his cheek that twitched with a pulsing tightening of his taut skin. He looked as if he wanted to say more. But then he dropped the towel on the counter, slipped on his damp shirt and walked to the door. "What's the use," he said, all emotion drained from his tone. "I knew this was a mistake from the start."

She watched him go even though there was still a part of her that wanted to call him back. This was too much to take in, too much to handle. She was numb from the horror of the life he had described, shocked by the brutal reality of his past. He had been a car thief. He had been in prison. He had killed—

No!

But thirty years of ingrained values and a firm sense of right and wrong couldn't be swept away that easily, no matter how sympathetic or how physically attracted she felt toward him.

He stepped into his boots and shrugged on his jacket, then paused with his hand on the door. For an instant, just an instant, their eyes met. And in that instant she was tempted to forget about a lifetime of values and fling herself across the room and into his arms and kiss the hurt from his clenched jaw and...

The door closed behind him. Strong, and lonely, his footsteps were swallowed by the storm.

Chapter 7

The place had never looked so good. The willow tree was trimmed. The lawn was like a putting green. The walk was swept clean the moment a stray leaf dared to blow onto it. Kneeling beside the flower bed at the front steps, Rebecca plunged the trowel up to its handle in the soft earth, scooped out a hole, then reached for another petunia.

Busy. She had kept busy since Mike had left on Sunday. Numbly she had cleaned her house, washed the curtains, polished the furniture, vacuumed the rug, scrubbed the oven, packed her winter sweaters away in tissue paper and even dusted the tops of the door frames. When the inside jobs had run out, she had attacked her yard with manic fervor. She had to keep busy. At least this was something she knew she could handle.

What she couldn't handle were her feelings about Mike. Not yet. Not until she gave her mind a chance to sort through everything that had happened.

How could she have been so wrong? She didn't want to be.

She had thought that she knew him. She had thought she could be his friend.

And those were part of the feelings she couldn't handle. She had wanted to be more than a friend. The man excited her. He made her toes curl and her juices flow like no one ever had in her life before. In his arms she hadn't felt frigid or unfeminine. There was nothing of the prim and proper lady about the way she had responded. The kisses they had shared still burned in her memory. His touch on her body had been gentle, almost reverent. His hands were so sensitive....

His hands had killed a man.

She sprinkled fertilizer into the hole, thrust in the flower, patted the earth back into place and moved on her knees to the next spot.

How could she have been so completely wrong? She had been so certain of her initial impression, so positive that he was basically a good man deep down inside, how could she have been so wrong?

He had stolen cars. Willingly. Profitably.

He had taken a life and had gone to prison.

But he had been young and hurt and understandably bitter. He had straightened himself out, had voluntarily quit stealing. He had...

He had killed a man.

She stabbed the trowel into the earth again. His story was beyond anything she could have imagined. Why did he have to tell her? Oh, why couldn't he have simply let things go on the way they were? Yet the way he had told her, had forced her to listen, made her think that he was expecting her to turn away from him, wanting her to turn away from him.

And that's precisely what she had done, hadn't she? She had wiped her hand across her mouth as if she could erase the memory of their kisses and she hadn't said a word to stop him from walking back into the rain.

Blinking hard, she tossed a handful of fertilizer into the next hole and jammed in another hapless petunia.

This wasn't how it was supposed to be. Nothing had prepared her for the clash of feelings that rolled inside her. She always did the right thing. All her life she had done the right thing and had respected the laws of society, even the unwritten ones. She had dutifully followed the narrow path, as her father had advised, and so far she hadn't gone astray. She knew right from wrong.

Then why was everything suddenly becoming blurred?

Dragging the box of flowers along with her, she moved over once more. After she was finished with the garden, she was going to drive to the video store. She was in the mood for something simple, where it was easy to tell the good guys from the bad guys, where right and wrong had no shades of gray.

Mike popped the ring on the beer and poured a quarter inch into the dish at his feet before tipping the can to his lips. Bootsie woofed and scrabbled across the floor, skidding to a stop beside him and lapping happily.

"Is that the only reason you hang around here, you dumb mutt?" he said, propping his foot on the seat of a chair and leaning over to cross his arms on his knee.

Bootsie looked up. Drops of liquid clung to her muzzle. With a swipe of her tongue she cleaned them off, then stuck her nose back into the dish.

"I guess it is."

She nosed the empty dish across the floor until it knocked against the bottom of the round-shouldered refrigerator. Plumping down on her hind legs, she looked back at Mike, her tongue lolling.

He shook his head. "That's enough, girl. I don't want to make you sick."

With a huff the dog came back to his side, her tail wagging experimentally.

Mike hesitated, then reached down and ruffled the fur behind the pointed ears.

Bootsie rewarded him with a wet tongue.

"Jeez," he muttered, wiping his fingers on his pants. "You're pathetic. Someone gives you some attention and you figure they care about you."

Undaunted, the dog yapped once, then sat down on his foot.

"You just never learn," he said, placing his hand gently on the silky ruff at the back of her neck.

He knew he wasn't only talking about the dog.

Damn that Rebecca. He had thought she was different, but he had seen that look come into her eyes at the end, that revulsion she wasn't able to hide.

What did he care? He hadn't wanted her approval or her friendship, he'd wanted her body, plain and simple. That was all. He knew better than to let someone get close. He had learned early not to open up his feelings to anyone. Tough. That's what he'd had to be in order to survive.

What did he care? There was no future in what he had felt for her. He was in Chicago only long enough to finish this job and then he was going to hold Prentice to his promise and get on with the life that had been put on hold five years ago when he had picked up that gun.

The beer can clunked his teeth as he took a quick swallow. He didn't often let himself think about that night, and he had long ago given up trying to tell people about it. Rebecca hadn't wanted to listen, either. She had slapped her hands over her ears before he'd had a chance to tell her the rest.

Besides, even if he had told her how he'd found that man already dead, even if she'd believed him, it wouldn't have made any difference. As far as the law and society and people like that redheaded skateboarder's mother were concerned, neat little concepts like guilt or innocence, bad guy or good guy were for the movies, not for real life.

Bootsie whined and nudged his hand. He frowned and crossed his arms.

Real life was a mother who swatted him when he cried, who was too wrapped up in herself to care whether he was hungry or cold or lonely when she went partying. Real life was a three-year-old child refusing to talk to the social workers who'd had to break down the apartment door the night his mother finally didn't come home. It was having the hope of a college scholarship shattered by a bunch of petty animals. It was seeing a sister turn her back on his pleas and continue on her path of self-destruction. It was slamming your fists against a cement wall until they bled.

No, he knew better than to try to get close to anyone. And if Rebecca believed he really was a cold-blooded killer, well then that was fine. That would eliminate the possibility of ever seeing her again. He hadn't been able to keep away from her, but his record and her prissy values would keep her away from him.

"Hey, Hogan." The shout had come from outside the screen door.

"Yeah?"

Guido's bulky form appeared silhouetted in the opening. "The meeting's set for seven."

"I heard."

"Things are picking up, eh?" He pulled open the door, the hinges screeching suddenly. "You got any more beer?"

"Sure." He walked over and popped a can from the plastic ring, then tossed it to Guido.

The guard caught it in a meaty hand. "Thanks."

He had served three years of his sentence when he had met Guido—in the pecking order of prison, a convicted murderer like Mike got plenty of respect. For over a year they had been cell mates. When Prentice and his crew decided to go after Witlock, they contacted Mike, hoping his connection with one of Witlock's people would get him into the organization. Mike's well-known dislike of the police was another factor in his favor, helping to put him above suspicion according to Prentice's way of thinking.

"Do you know any more about the plans?" Mike asked.

"Not much. Trevor's been all over town taking what he calls reconnaissance photos, so I guess they're still laying the groundwork.'' Under the army fatigues, a heavy shoulder lifted in a shrug. ''Well, I gotta make my rounds. Thanks for the brew.''

He listened as the guard's heavy footsteps faded. Swiveling his head, he took stock of the place. It wasn't much, but it was an improvement over a cement cubicle with bars for one wall. Without warning, his thoughts veered to the bungalow with the weeping willow and the porch swing. Now that was a home. The image of Rebecca as she had opened the door for him on Sunday morning came vividly into his mind. Now that was a woman.

And he could have neither. He didn't want either.

He drained his beer, crushed the can in his fist and hurled it across the room.

The tall man stood by the edge of the water, the ends of his tie whipping sideways in the breeze. At his feet sprawled the man with the bandaged nose, his fingers splayed inches away from the rifle that had been used to terrorize a city. The words were the same as before, but the meaning now was completely different. It was no longer a game, guessing whether the tall man with the magnum had fired six shots or only five.

''Do you feel lucky? Well, do you, punk?''

The psycho laughed maniacally and reached for the rifle.

Dirty Harry pulled the trigger on the sixth bullet, the one he had known all along was still in the chamber.

Rebecca stared at the screen in silence as the movie credits rolled past. The man with the bandaged nose had killed that little girl and had hijacked a school bus. He *deserved* to die.

Didn't he?

But if Harry deliberately killed him, didn't that make the hero a bit of a villain himself?

How could she have thought that these movies were simple? The line between right and wrong was blurred. What if some-one did the right thing for the wrong reason? Did that make it better than someone who did the wrong thing for the right reason?

Lifting up her glasses, she rubbed her eyes wearily. How could she decide these things herself? Centuries of philosophers hadn't come to terms with this kind of dilemma. How could she?

She was just an ordinary woman with ordinary needs. Could it be possible that Mike *was* a good man, in spite of what he had done in his youth? Could her heart have been that wrong about him?

Her heart? Since when was her heart involved? It was sex, plain and simple. At least, she assumed what she felt was a result of sexual attraction. What else could it be? He was everything her mother had warned her about. In her sheltered upbringing, she'd never even met someone like Mike before, let alone been the target of those twinkling eyes and that cocky grin.

Restlessly she rose to her feet, fluffing the cushions she had leaned against and realigning the corners of the coffee table with the front of the sofa. Maybe it was just as well he had left like that, without another word or a backward glance. Their relationship couldn't have led anywhere. They were too different. Besides, he had already made it clear that he had never intended to stay. Now that she knew about his prison record, she understood his desire for freedom and the open road. He was a loner. He was just passing through.

Princess was gone. Mike was gone. The rest of her summer still loomed emptily in front of her. Before she started getting maudlin, she should find herself a hobby. She certainly shouldn't be spending her time agonizing over Mike.

It was unlikely that she would ever see him again.

Things were moving fast now. After weeks of being left dangling, Mike was finally part of the inner circle. His mind was humming like a high-speed recorder as he memorized the words being said around the mahogany table and the faces of the people who said them.

It was an ambitious plan. Someone in Witlock's far-reaching web had learned of a shipment of cash and bearer bonds that was to arrive at the airport in two weeks' time. The security would be too tight until the money and the bonds were loaded into the armored truck, but once on the ground and moving through the streets, the truck would be an easy target.

Easy for a man like Witlock, that is.

Mike slouched in his chair, his gaze scanning the glossy black-and-white blowups and the detailed maps that littered the table's surface. The plan was brilliant in its simplicity. Orchestrate a traffic jam, maneuver a tow truck against the armored truck, drag it into an alley and into the back of one of Witlock's eighteen-wheelers. Not much concern was given to the fate of the security men at that point, since the money and bonds would be in Witlock's hands one way or another.

Or so he thought. His expression impassive, Mike glanced around the table. Prentice would turn this information into a perfect trap. With luck they would catch Witlock red-handed, not to mention the rest of his organization. His eyes rested on Trevor. Mike suspected that Trevor Dodge would be the first to crack under questioning. His testimony, along with the evidence the cops would be able to find in Witlock's bullet-proof office, would put this sleaze out of business for a long time.

And then… And then Prentice would give him what he had promised when he had met him in the warden's office that morning three months ago.

The police would get Witlock, and Mike would get his freedom.

When it came to manipulating people into doing what he wanted, Prentice was as adept as Witlock. Mike had been sentenced to fifteen years. He would have been up for parole in seven, but Prentice offered to get him out in five on the condition that Mike help them nail Witlock. The official reason that was given for his early release was good behavior. That

was fitting. Prentice had known that in exchange for his freedom Mike would do practically anything, even if it meant
driving dogs and waxing cars, or working with people he
hated. Or risking his life.

Things were moving fast now. Two weeks. If Prentice could
set things up, this could all be over in two weeks. Mike felt
a tremor of excitement. He could almost smell the open
road....

The meeting broke up with scraping chairs and noisy back-
slapping. Witlock levered himself to his feet and shuffled over
to Mike. "Come to my office, Hogan. We have something
private to discuss."

He fell into step beside him. "Sure, boss."

They passed through the metal detector doors. Witlock
picked up a large envelope from his desk and tossed it to Mike.
"You might be interested in checking out your insurance policy."

He caught the envelope, surprised by its weight. "Insurance
policy?"

Witlock's fat cheeks creased into an indecently cherubic
smile. "I've placed a good deal of trust in you now, Hogan.
I like to make sure I can count on you."

Mike's palms began to sweat against the coarse brown paper. "I thought I'd proven that by now."

"You have." The smile revealed a glinting gold tooth.
"Look inside and you'll see why."

Forcing his fingers to remain steady, Mike lifted the flap
and reached within. He touched smooth paper. His forehead
creasing, he drew out a stack of black-and-white photographs.

"Trevor does excellent work, don't you think?"

Mike couldn't breathe. He felt as if a fist had just slammed
into his gut. "How did you get these?"

Witlock lowered himself into his chair and leaned back,
steepling his fingers on his stomach. "I make it a practice to
know what people want, Hogan. And when an opportunity
presents itself, I take advantage of it."

Mike glared at him, for the first time not bothering to veil the hate he felt. "You set me up. That's why you wanted me to take the dog over for visits."

"Now, now, Mr. Hogan, it's nothing personal. When I saw how you reacted to the mention of Mrs. Stanford's name I thought I'd push you two together a few more times and see what developed." He wheezed, then smacked his lips in a way that made Mike's stomach roll over. "I can't blame you. That schoolteacher's quite a hot little number."

Mike's gaze was drawn back to the photograph on top of the pile. The details were fuzzy because of the telephoto lens and the poor lighting, but the couple on the blanket was still easily recognizable. Anger, white-hot and sizzling stabbed through him. Anger at Trevor, for sneaking around and spying on him, anger at Witlock for ordering it, at Prentice for involving him. Most of all, he was angry at himself. He should have known. He should have realized the risk he was taking. He should have been able to control his desire for that woman.

Oh, God. What had he done?

The pictures crumpled in Mike's fist. He wanted to scream in frustration. He wanted to hit someone. "Leave her alone."

"I fully intend to leave her alone, Hogan. I'm a businessman. What good is an insurance policy if it's cashed in too soon?" The smile grew crafty. "As long as you continue to work out as well as you have, we won't have a problem."

Rebecca laid the book on the bedside table and frowned. It sounded as if someone were at her back door. Grabbing her robe from the bedpost, she belted it tightly and tiptoed barefoot into the kitchen.

Someone was there, all right. A large shadow blotted out the moonlight on the other side of the glass panel. Approaching cautiously, she grasped a corner of the curtain and peeked outside.

"Mike," she breathed.

Evidently he had seen the curtain move. He tapped on the glass with his knuckles. "Rebecca? Let me in."

Let him in? It was almost midnight. She hadn't seen him since he had strode out of this very room almost a week ago. Her pulse thudded. "Go away, Mike."

"I have to talk to you," he said, his shadow moving closer to the glass.

"It's late."

"Jeez, I know it's late. Will you just open up the door?"

"I don't know if I want to see you."

"It's important." He paused. "Really important."

She drew her lower lip between her teeth and fastened the top button of her nightgown. A week ago, before he had told her about his past, she might have considered opening her door at midnight to him. But now? "Come back tomorrow."

He thumped a fist against the door, making the curtain sway. "Either you open it, or I will."

"Don't threaten me, Mike."

Silence. "Okay, Rebecca. I know you don't want anything to do with me, and I wouldn't be here if there was any other way. But I have to talk to you."

She wavered indecisively.

"Please, Rebecca."

Taking a deep breath, she switched on the light and unlocked the door.

He stepped inside immediately, then closed the door behind him and leaned against it.

The change from the last time she had seen him was startling. Dark circles smudged the skin beneath his eyes, as if he hadn't been sleeping for the past week. Coarse black stubble skimmed his cheeks, darkening the grooves beside his mouth. His lips thinned into a grim line. His entire body seemed to radiate tension.

She took a step back. "What's wrong?"

"You have to leave."

"Why? What are you talking about?"

"Leave this house. Leave Chicago."

"What?"

"Have you got anywhere you can go for a while? Some relatives you can stay with?"

"No. I don't have any relatives. All my friends are on vacation." She frowned. "This is crazy. I'm not going anywhere."

He pushed away from the door and grabbed her upper arms. "Rebecca, for God's sake. I'm trying to protect you."

"Protect me? What on earth do you mean?"

"Protect you from Witlock, my boss."

"I don't even know your boss. Witlock, you said? And why should he want to hurt me?"

Dropping her arms, he paced across the room. "I didn't want to involve you in this, Rebecca. You have to believe me. I thought there would be no harm done if we saw each other a few times, because I had always intended to be long gone before anything happened." He paused, running his fingers through his hair, leaving it sticking up in unruly tufts. "It's my fault. I've always been on my own, so I never thought they could get to me through someone else. I've never had to think of anyone else."

"Mike, calm down, you're not making any sense. Just start at the beginning and tell me what's wrong."

He turned to face her. In the silence of her kitchen his leather jacket creaked with his movement. "Witlock is dangerous. He's found out that I was seeing you, and he's threatening to hurt you if I step out of line."

"But you're just...I mean, you're his chauffeur. Why would he need to threaten anyone? If he didn't like your driving he could simply fire you."

"I'm not just a chauffeur. And threatening people is all part of Witlock's business. He's a crook, Rebecca, a criminal. He makes that car-theft ring I once had look harmless by comparison. He gets his wealth from theft, graft, extortion and prostitution, just to name a few of his interests. And I'm right in the thick of it.''

She staggered backward, her fingers clutching the lapels of her dressing gown. She felt a buzzing in her head, just as she had a week ago. Too many facts were coming too fast. "Your boss is a criminal? You're working for a criminal?"

"Why do you think I was so anxious to get his damn dog back to him? Worthington Witlock is not the kind of man you want to cross."

"Why, Mike? Why would you get involved with him after trying to go straight and then spending all that time in prison? Surely you could have gotten a real job somewhere."

"There are things you don't know, Rebecca."

"What things?"

His jaw hardened. "I can't tell you."

"This is too much," she moaned. "Too much."

"It's my fault you got mixed up in this. I never meant for it to happen. I'm sorry."

"You're sorry? You come into my home, make me like you and think of you as my friend. Then you turn my world upside down with that story about your past and I scramble to make excuses for you in my mind and still try to believe in you...." She paused, striving for control. "And all the while you were involved with a criminal? The dog I took in belonged to a criminal? And that money you gave me? I used a criminal's money to buy flowers and rent videos. How could you let me do that?"

He clenched his fists, his arms rigid. "I told you that you didn't know me."

She stared at him, disappointment misting her eyes. "No, I guess I didn't know you. I was deceiving myself, wasn't I? There still is a big difference between right and wrong and you've deliberately chosen to take the wrong path."

"Think what you want. Doesn't make any difference to me."

She had a crazy impression of a lost child trying to be brave.

She shook her head. No. No more seeing things that weren't true. "So after you served your sentence you went right back into the life-style you had tried to give up."

"I've got my reasons. You don't need to know. It's for your own good. You're already too involved as it is."

Yes, she was too involved. She had been too involved from the moment she had first seen this man standing beneath her front porch light. "I'd like you to leave now, Mike."

"Look, I know you're angry, and you have every right to be, but listen to reason. I'm trying to warn you that you're in danger. You have to go somewhere safe until we can get you some protection—"

"Get out." She pointed at the door, her finger shaking. "Now."

"Are you going to leave town?"

She drew herself up, squaring her shoulders. "If this man is as bad as you claim, then I'd be better off simply calling the police. I'm not going anywhere."

"Rebecca, let me help you."

"I think you've done enough already."

He swore and closed the distance between them with two swift strides. "I won't let them hurt you." He caught her hand and pressed her palm to his chest. "Whatever you think of me, I can't help the way I feel about you."

"Mike, I..."

"If we were two other people, if I wasn't mixed up with Witlock and all these dirty deals, maybe things could be different."

Oh, how she wished that were true. But she was through spinning lonely schoolteacher fantasies about the recklessly exciting man with the sky-blue eyes. This was too real.

His size, his strength, his sheer masculine presence was overwhelming. Heat flowed from his chest to her palm, her fingers began to curl against the smooth cotton of his shirt. Her blood pounding, she raised her gaze to his face. "Why can't you go to the police? Turn yourself in. Maybe you could make a deal or a plea bargain or something.''

He inhaled sharply, shaking his head. ''Don't even mention that. To anyone. Like I said, Witlock isn't the kind of man you want to cross. He makes the guys that did my knee look like a bunch of Boy Scouts.''

Her heart clenched. She looked back to her hand. Of their own accord her fingers had spread, as if to absorb as much as possible from this point where their bodies touched. His grip on her wrist was possessive, his tanned skin firm against her delicate paleness. They were standing close enough for her breasts to brush the zippered edges of his open leather jacket with each breath she took. She shifted and her bare toe grazed the tip of his heavy boot, sending a vivid stab of sensual awareness up her legs.

Even now. Even with everything she knew about him, everything that repelled her, she couldn't stop the betrayal of her body.

Why did life have to be so complicated?

He fitted his other hand to her nape, his fingers sliding into her hair.

She knew that he felt it, too, the sudden, mindless, impossible pull.

His head lowered.

What was wrong with her? Hadn't she listened to what he had said? Hadn't she learned anything from the pain and turmoil of the past week?

Warm and vital, his breath caressed her cheek.

With a cry she jumped back. ''No!''

His eyes sparked, the challenge unspoken.

''No. This is wrong.'' She took another step away. Ruthlessly she drew her lower lip between her teeth and bit down.

He reached for her, then closed his hands in midair and brought his fists down on the kitchen table. He waited, staring at his knuckles until the last of the vibrations faded from the wood. "Hell, I know this is wrong. It's what got us into this mess in the first place."

With trembling fingers she tightened the belt of her robe and refastened the knot. "Tell your boss he's made a mistake, that you're not seeing me anymore. Tell him you don't know me."

"That won't work. He's got pictures."

"Pictures? You mean photographs?"

"Of that day in the park."

No, she couldn't take any more. Everything was getting turned around. Even the spontaneous pleasure of that reckless embrace was now twisted. Their passion should have been private. But their passion shouldn't have happened, just like she shouldn't have continued to see Mike or let him into her kitchen at midnight or into her heart…

"Rebecca, I don't have much time before I'll be missed. Are you going to leave or not?"

"No."

The table rattled as he pushed himself away. He walked to the door, his leg stiff. He should have known she would react like this. Getting her out of town would have been the quickest and easiest solution, but when had things ever been easy?

He should have kept on going tonight. That's what he should have done. Thrown his clothes and his toothbrush into his duffel bag, opened up the throttle of the Harley on the darkened streets and then ridden until dawn. It would be years before either Witlock or Prentice caught up to him. That had been his plan all along if the job hadn't worked out.

But now there was Rebecca. Sweet, sheltered Rebecca who even now likely didn't realize how serious her situation was. How could she? As far as she knew, he was as much of a criminal as Witlock and would give his boss no reason to make good on his threat. She didn't know, and he wasn't free to tell her, the real reason he was working for Witlock. She didn't know how he lived each minute with the risk of discovery. In exchange for his freedom he had been willing to risk his life.

But he wasn't willing to risk hers.

A precious minute had passed while he had stood there hesitating. Resolving to find some other way, he reached for the doorknob. "Lock the door behind me when I leave."

"I will. What are you going to do?"

He lifted his head. "Whatever it takes, Rebecca."

The first phone booth was a block and a half from her bungalow. Mike brought the Harley to a halt bare inches from the swinging glass doors. He dug a quarter from his pocket, dropped it into the slot and punched in the number he had memorized.

It was answered on the second ring. "Yes?"

"Prentice. We've got trouble."

"Hogan! What's going on?"

"I want you to get a woman named Rebecca Stanford out of town. Take her to a safe house or put her in protective custody until Witlock goes down."

"What are you talking about?"

Tersely he relayed what he had learned earlier that night at the mahogany table, and then he explained Witlock's idea of an insurance policy. When he had finished, Prentice's reply wasn't what he had hoped for.

"We can't touch her," the cop said.

"Then at least let me tell her what's going on."

"That's out of the question. Revealing the operation to a civilian at this stage would be totally irresponsible. We don't know how she'll react. And if Witlock even smells the police anywhere near her he's going to know whose side you're on."

"Sometimes I wonder about that myself," he gritted.

"If we openly provide her with protection it would mean swift retribution for you."

"And that would jeopardize the investigation."

"I'll keep an undercover team standing by, okay? We're too close to finishing this to risk you blowing your cover now. If she's merely insurance, then Witlock won't want to do anything to her as long as you keep playing your role. The minute things start to come together I guarantee we'll be able to get to her before Witlock. Personally I doubt whether he'd follow through on the threat to the woman. He's figured he's got the key to make you do what he wants. He's an expert on manipulating people.''

''Sounds just like you, Prentice.''

Silence. ''Look, I'll see what I can do without tipping anyone off, will that suit you?''

''I want a twenty-four hour watch on her. She gets full protection. If Witlock or one of his goons gets within ten yards of her, I'm taking care of it myself.''

''Hey, wait a minute.''

''This is nonnegotiable.''

''Calm down. I'll handle it. Just don't do anything to blow your cover—'' he paused significantly ''—or our deal. Remember, Hogan. One word from me and you're back inside.''

Mike's hand tightened on the receiver, his knuckles white. He glanced at the quiet street, at the darkened houses and the peacefully arching trees. He thought of the horizons he had yet to see.

He slammed the receiver down and banged his forehead against the glass wall.

Chapter 8

The blind fell back into place with a clatter of plastic slats. Tucking a wisp of hair into her ponytail, Rebecca stepped away from the window with a frown. Three days had passed since Mike's midnight visit. Apart from the neighborhood kids and the group of hard-hatted workmen who were ripping up the pavement at the end of the street she hadn't seen a soul in all that time.

"Maybe he made a mistake," she murmured to herself as she smoothed the gathers of her flowered dress. "Or maybe he's already left town."

She walked to the door, then paused with her hand on the chain. As more time went by, Mike's story about Witlock seemed harder to accept. After he had left she had gone straight to the telephone. She'd had the receiver in her hand and had dialed the first number of the police station before she had realized she had no proof that she had been threatened by anyone. Only Mike's word. The police were already over-worked. They wouldn't do anything about some vague possibility of danger, especially since she had no intention of giving them any details about Mike.

Why should she believe him anyway, now that she knew what he was? Why should she continue to trust him?

And why should she miss him so much?

With a sigh she slid the chain from its slot. Even though she'd begun to doubt that there really was any danger, she had been careful. She had locked her doors securely each night, had jammed wooden bars into the window frames to prevent them from being opened, and had ventured no farther than her yard. Nothing had happened. She hadn't heard a thing from Mike, either. Maybe the problem had passed. Or maybe he had overreacted. She had probably overreacted, as well, considering the late hour and the raw state of her emotions when she had seen him. Crime and violence were part of Mike's world, not hers. This was her home. It was solid, respectable and ordinary, just like her.

She checked that her yard was empty, then stepped into the sunshine. The noise of the jackhammers clanged in short staccato bursts from the foot of her driveway. Hitching the strap of her purse over her shoulder, she walked past the willow tree to assess her chances of getting her car out.

"This is a disgrace. They have been doing virtually nothing for the past three days." Mrs. Barring advanced on her. With her jutting prow of a bosom and the billowing ivory housedress, she was under full sail. "I intend to speak with the mayor."

"Hello, Mrs. Barring. How are you?"

"Yes, hello, Mrs. Stanford." She came to a halt in a swirl of ivory rayon. "You must be very concerned with the way they've blocked off your driveway. Why, no one can get in or out of here unless they were to drive on your lawn."

Rebecca craned her neck to see the bottom of the hole that had been dug in the street. "I haven't needed to go anywhere."

"I've been watching them, and I've never seen such a lazy bunch of incompetents in all the years I've lived here."

At least she's found another target for her scrutiny, Rebecca thought. "I shouldn't have too much trouble with my car. The Volkswagen's not too big."

"Humph. Excuse me? You there."

One of the workers looked up as Mrs. Barring approached. He leaned his forearms comfortably on the handle of his shovel, the tails of his checkered flannel shirt flapping in the breeze. Dirty blond hair poked out from under his hard hat. "Nice day."

"What exactly are you doing here?"

He angled his hat up with the tip of his thumb. "Got to repave this whole section. I hope the weather holds."

"Repave it? Why weren't we informed of this?"

"And who are you, ma'am?"

"Mrs. Anthony Barring. My husband is the chairman of the school board—"

"That's not our department. We're from public works."

She scowled and waved an arm at the pitted street. "How much longer are we expected to put up with this?"

The blond workman looked over his shoulder. "Hey, O'Hara."

Another man who apparently had nothing better to do than lean on his shovel looked their way. "Whad'ya want?"

"The lady here wants to know how much longer we'll be."

"No one tells me." O'Hara grinned. "Why don't you ask the guy in charge?"

The blond man shrugged and turned back to Mrs. Barring. "Sorry for the inconvenience, ma'am."

She whirled around and returned to where Rebecca was mentally charting the path that would do the least damage to her lawn. "Well! I'm certainly going to phone someone about this. With those barricades at the end of the street, practically no one has been able to visit this neighborhood in days." She paused, her eyes narrowing. "Is that why we haven't seen your Harvey Davis, Rebecca?"

"Harley-Davis," she corrected absently.

"I assume you broke it off with that man."

"What?"

"Good for you. I was afraid that after the way Mr. Stanford behaved so shamelessly that you might be easy prey for some—"

"Excuse me, Mrs. Barring, but I really need to get some groceries. What's your opinion of the best way to steer around that hole?"

As she had hoped, the change in topic redirected the woman's attention. With Mrs. Barring offering suggestions, Rebecca managed to maneuver her small car onto the street. The Volkswagen rattled and lurched over what was left of the pavement. The workmen, now apparently on a coffee break, waved as they pulled aside the barricade.

Breathing a sigh of relief, she drove quickly to the nearest supermarket. She hurried down the aisles, but no one approached her or even made eye contact as she took her purchases to the checkout. She was beginning to feel a little foolish. Hiding out in her house for three days and checking through her blinds for suspicious characters was bad enough. Did she really think that vicious criminals hung out at the local grocery store?

Her arms filled with paper bags, she was almost back at her car when the black Mercedes pulled into the parking slot beside her.

She fumbled in her purse for her keys.

"Pardon me."

She glanced up. An aristocratic-looking man had emerged from the black car and was standing in the angle of the open door.

Shifting her bags, she aimed the key at the lock by touch. "I'll be out of the way in a minute."

That was when she heard the bark. It was high-pitched,

anxious. She recognized it immediately and turned back toward the Mercedes. "Princess?"

A second man sat in the driver's seat. He was dressed in army fatigues. In one hand he held tightly to the leash of a squirming gray dog. In his other hand he held a knife.

Her grip on the bags tightened. She heard an eggshell break. No, this wasn't Princess. This was Bootsie. The dog belonged to Mike's boss. Witlock. The criminal.

It was really happening. Mike hadn't lied. They were here, in her neighborhood, in broad daylight. They had been waiting for her. And now they were threatening an innocent animal. "Don't hurt her," she whispered.

"Guido has no desire to hurt that dog, Miss Stanford," the first man said smoothly. "And he won't, as long as you smile and get into the car with us."

She glanced around, the whole scene taking on a bizarre unreality. This couldn't be happening. But shoppers were wheeling their carts right past her. The only people who appeared to take notice were a pair of workmen in a dusty pickup truck. "No."

"I thought you liked that dog, Rebecca."

Her mind worked frantically. They were willing to hurt the woman they thought was Mike's girlfriend in order to keep Mike in line, but... "That's Witlock's dog," she said, her voice amazingly controlled considering the way her pulse was rattling like one of the jackhammers she'd been listening to. "No, you're bluffing. You wouldn't hurt your boss's dog."

A frown of irritation flitted across his forehead. The breeze tugged at but couldn't move his perfectly styled hair. "You're too smart to hang around with a gimp like Hogan." Swiftly, silently, a silver gun appeared in the palm of his hand. It glinted obscenely in the cheerful sunlight. Concealed from anyone else's view by the half-open door, it pointed straight at her heart. "Get into the car. We're not going to hurt you. Mr. Witlock just wants to have a chat and get better acquainted with you."

The hair on her arms stood on end. She had read of people saying their flesh crawled, but she had never experienced it until now. Something in that man's tone sent chills racing down her spine.

"Hi, Mrs. Stanford," a youthful voice called. "Need any help with your groceries?"

She glanced over her shoulder. It was Andrew Barring, his baseball cap twisted backward with a handful of red curls peeking through the gap over the band. He waved as he coasted closer, his skateboard rolling hollowly between the parked cars.

"Get into the car. Now."

Princess, no, Bootsie barked frantically and twisted against the leash, her diamond-studded collar coming perilously close to the blade of the knife. Andrew swerved nearer. Across the parking lot the two men got out of the pickup and were walking toward them.

And in the distance came a rumble like approaching thunder.

Except there were no clouds.

"Come on, come on," the man with the gun sneered.

Desperately Rebecca looked to the street. A lone biker was weaving determinedly through the light traffic. At this distance she couldn't make out his features, with the helmet over his forehead and the sunglasses concealing his eyes. Still, on some subconscious level she had recognized him immediately.

"Mike," she breathed.

"What the—" The man whipped his head around and swore. "Hell, Guido, I thought you said he'd be busy for the morning."

Bootsie yipped suddenly, then snarled. A hoarse exclamation came from the front seat. "Hey! The mutt bit me!"

The gun wavered for an instant.

Taking a deep breath, Rebecca threw her weight against the car door, slamming it into the man's shins.

With a cry of pain he collapsed onto the seat.

She didn't hesitate for a second. A pair of oranges and a package of potato chips bounced out of her bags as she whirled around and sprinted for the street.

The workmen from the pickup broke into a run, heading straight for the Mercedes, but the car was already squealing out of the parking lot in the other direction.

Andrew stepped on the back of his skateboard, flipping it up to catch it in one hand. His mouth hung open as Rebecca raced past. "Mrs. Stanford?"

The Harley swerved over the curb, roaring past the station wagons and housewives with their shopping carts. Eyes invisible behind his mirrored sunglasses, mouth pressed into a grim line, the leather-jacketed biker skidded to intercept Rebecca. With one leg extended to the pavement for balance, he pivoted the powerful machine.

"Mike!"

He stretched out his hand.

She glanced down at her arms. Ludicrously, she still clutched her groceries. Her car keys still dangled from her fingers. This couldn't be happening.

But it was.

She dropped the bags onto the pavement. She tossed her keys to the gaping Andrew. Then she slung her purse over her shoulder, hitched up her flowered skirt and grasped Mike's hand.

He half pulled, half flung her onto the back of the bike. Her sandals struck the exhaust pipes for a burning instant before she managed to find the pegs she had used before.

"Hang on!"

Her fingers clutched the thick leather folds at his waist.

He opened the throttle. The Harley leapt into motion.

Pressing her face to his back, Rebecca closed her eyes against the wind.

She didn't know where they were going. She hadn't even thought to ask.

Mike didn't know where they were going, either. All he

knew was that he had to get her away. He had guessed some-thing was in the works this morning when Guido and Trevor had left together. Prentice had promised to protect her. Against his back he felt her shudder. Yeah, right, the cops had done a great job of protecting her.

He'd caught a glimpse of Prentice in that parking lot as he and some other cop had been running after the Mercedes. He'd warned him that their cute little road crew masquerade wouldn't work, but they were more concerned with the success of their investigation than with the safety of one woman, or one man. Mike was deep into Witlock's organization now and they wanted him to stay there until they could set up the sting that would bring everything to an end. Prentice had looked furious when he'd realized that Mike had come for Rebecca.

So had Trevor. Mike thought with satisfaction of the look of surprise on Trevor's face when she had smashed that door into his shins. She had looked so prim and proper in her wire-rimmed glasses and that short-sleeved dress with the tiny flow-ers all over it. God, what a woman.

Flicking the gear lever with his toe, Mike shifted down to take a corner. Rebecca's body moved with his, leaning into the curve. Her thighs tightened around his hips as she tucked the loose edges of her skirt securely underneath her to keep the fabric from getting caught in the wheel.

They couldn't simply keep on riding. Not like this, not the way she was dressed. Mike checked his surroundings and re-alized he was only a few miles from the abandoned warehouse that Prentice had used for a meeting place. He gunned the engine, checking his side mirrors as he zipped into one alley and down another. Prentice had complained about the noise of this machine, but once it was moving, there wasn't much that could catch it. Mike had been sloppy that Sunday Trevor had followed him, but not this time. All the lessons he had learned during those final years of his car business came back to him now. Using the city itself for cover, he worked his way closer to the warehouse. Within seconds he had found a door he could jimmy and he eased the Harley into the cavernous interior.

The door closed securely behind them, Mike circled around twice, sweeping the headlight into the shadows to make sure they were empty before he shut off the engine. Vibrating echoes lingered like the dust motes that sifted through the air. Mike took off his helmet, levered out the kickstand and slipped off the bike, then turned to help Rebecca.

She had faced down Guido and Trevor. She had gamely tossed down her groceries and hopped onto the back of a moving bike. She had ridden across town with no helmet or heavy clothing or notion of what was going to happen. Now, finally, her adrenaline wore off.

With a cry she launched herself into his arms.

Mike caught her willingly. Splaying his hands across her back, he lifted her from the floor, holding her tight to the front of his body. "It's okay," he murmured. "You're safe."

She pressed her face into his neck, her cheek against his collar. "I was so scared."

"I know you were."

Her breath hitched on a half-swallowed sob. "Oh, Mike. It was awful. At first I didn't know what was happening, but then I saw Princess and that man with the knife and then the first one pulled a gun—"

"Trevor had a gun on you?" He set her back on her feet, his fingers gripping her shoulders.

"It was just a small gun, not a .44 Magnum or anything, but he was pointing it—"

Fiercely he pulled her against him once more. "We have to get you away from here."

"I should have left when you told me." Her arms stole around his waist. "But I thought I was being careful."

He stroked her back, her buttocks, her bare arms, anything he could touch. "I'll keep you safe, Rebecca."

Her hands slipped inside his jacket, smoothing around his

ribs to his spine. Then she raised onto her toes and touched her lips to his.

He took the kiss she offered. He gave her what she wanted, what she hadn't even known she had wanted. His mouth possessed hers, tracing the contours, probing the secret depths. His stubbled cheek was sandpaper rough, sensitizing skin that already burned.

Gasping, she pressed her face to his neck, inhaling the scent that was cotton and leather and basic, virile man. The bristles of his beard caught in her hair as he bent closer, his breath hot on her ear.

It must have been a reaction to the danger she had just gotten through, or to that mad ride through the city streets. Her blood seemed to sing through her veins as she responded to his bold masculine power.

The concrete floor gritted under the thick soles of his boots and the delicate leather of her sandals as Mike backed her out of the feeble pool of sunlight toward the shadows that hugged the wall. Odors that were oily and musty, unidentifiable traces of things that had once been stored here, stirred as they moved. The backs of Rebecca's heels struck something wooden and hollow. An instant later Mike fastened his hands on her waist and lifted, sitting her on what she distantly realized was an old packing crate.

He grasped her knees, bringing them on either side of his hips as he stepped between her thighs. His palms slid beneath her skirt, his fingers gently possessive as he touched the sensitive flesh. Dipping his head, he pressed his lips to her throat.

A pigeon fluttered through a broken window high on the wall. Its wings slapped rapidly until it scrabbled to roost on a rafter. A distant siren whined.

Rebecca raised her arms to Mike's shoulders, leaning into him as his mouth traced the neckline of her dress. His tongue flicked the swell of a breast, sending tingling tendrils of sensation to the tip.

He pressed closer. His thumbs skimmed her hips. Grasping her buttocks, he pulled her tight against his groin.

Her breath caught. The feel of him, so large, so hot, so blatant, shocked her out of the sensual haze. What was she doing? *What was she doing!*

He moved his hips. Just a little. Just a hint of a motion.

It made her quiver.

She pressed her hands to his chest. "Mike."

His teeth closed gently over her collarbone.

She groaned and braced her arms. "Mike, no."

His fingers tightened.

The pigeon launched itself from its roost, flapping noisily out the window. Rebecca forced herself to focus on the dingy warehouse. And on the reason she was here. "No, Mike. This is crazy. We can't do this."

Slowly he straightened up until his gaze locked with hers. "Do what?"

She inched backward, retreating from the intimate position of their lower bodies. "This. You and me."

His jaw clenched. "You seemed willing enough a minute ago."

"I'm sorry."

"So am I."

"I'm sorry," she repeated inanely. "I don't usually—"

He grabbed her suddenly and swung her to the floor. "You don't usually make out in abandoned warehouses. Yeah, yeah. I know that, too."

Her legs weren't steady enough to support her. She grasped the edge of the packing crate.

Mike rubbed his hands over his face. Hard. "Aw, hell."

"I'm sor—"

"Don't apologize again. I should know better than this. You wouldn't be in trouble if I could have kept my hands off you in the first place." He took a series of deep breaths, then backed away.

Her heart tripped. She tried to force her pulse back to normal, but what was normal?

"We've got to make plans."

Plans. It all came crashing back on her then. Swaying, she put her other hand on the crate. "I should go to the police. I can ask them for protection."

He laughed harshly. "Believe me, they're no help. If Witlock wants to get to you, he will. No, the only way to keep you safe is to get you out of town. We're doing things my way now."

"But where could I go?"

"Somewhere far enough that no one will bother you. Somewhere no one would know to look."

"But how—"

"I'll take care of that. I got you into this mess. I'll get you out of it." He looked at her for a moment. "First thing we have to do is get you some clothes. That dress isn't safe on the back of a bike."

"What?"

"You need some jeans and heavier shoes. A thick jacket for the wind."

She glanced at the motorcycle that gleamed silently in the center of the floor. She thought of how she had clung to him on the way here and how she had flung herself at him when they had arrived. And how difficult it had been to stop. "Mike, I can't simply leave."

"Well, I'm sure as hell not taking you back to your house. Don't let the way you got away from Trevor fool you. If it had been Guido holding the gun, you would have been in that car before you could blink. No, we're getting you out of here. I'll slip out and buy what you need for the trip. Then as soon as it's dark we'll hit the interstate."

"What about my car? It's still in that parking lot. And my house? Who's going to take care of the flowers and the lawn?"

"Jeez, woman, you barely avoid getting abducted in broad daylight and you're worried about your petunias?"

A flash of anger stiffened her spine. "Don't you make fun of me. And don't expect me to simply drop everything and leave. I have a home. And responsibilities."

"That can all be taken care of."

"How?"

He paced unevenly, rubbing the back of his neck with one hand. "I'll figure something out once we leave."

"Then how long would I have to stay away?"

"My job should be over within the month and I'll be leaving Chicago for good. With me gone, you won't be any use as insurance, but if there's any more trouble the cops should be able to help."

She frowned. "But you said they wouldn't be able to stop Witlock."

"Not now. By next month things should be different. I'll make sure of it before you come home." He reached into the back pocket of his jeans and pulled out his wallet, thumbing through a thick wad of bills. "This should do until I can get you settled."

Revulsion swept through her as she looked at the money. That was Witlock's money. "Mike, why don't you quit your job now? If you can get me away safely, why can't you do the same for yourself?"

He tensed. "I have unfinished business here, Rebecca."

She kept forgetting. He would do something brave and noble like rescuing her from a gang of criminals, but she kept forgetting that he was one of them himself.

Roughly he shoved the wallet back into his pocket. "I know it's a stretch for you, but you'll have to trust me on this, Rebecca."

She crossed her arms tightly over her chest. "Do I have a choice?"

"You didn't have to take my hand when I pulled into that parking lot. Trevor and Guido were already leaving." He strode forward quickly, grasping her elbow. "Despite your objections, you know this is the best option you have."

The contact of his hand on her skin was electric. She jumped backward, her gaze snapping to the shadows behind her. "This won't work. After what you wanted to do on that packing crate two minutes ago—"

"We didn't do anything near to what I wanted, Rebecca." His eyes bored into hers. "And you can't pretend that you didn't want it, too."

She whirled around, walking quickly across the floor until the motorcycle was between them. He was right. About everything.

His fingers curled into his palm. "Look, Rebecca, it's not as bad as it seems. When this is over you can go back to your house and your petunias and all your third-graders like nothing happened."

"What about you?"

"Empty highway and full gas tank, remember?"

Yes, she remembered. He had told her that from the start. Why hadn't she listened? "About what happened here…" She cleared her throat. "I mean, with the two of us…"

He paused. "What about it?"

"It can't happen again."

A muscle in his cheek jumped. "I already know I should keep my hands off you."

"It would be best."

"Fine."

"I'm not the type of woman—"

"Who kisses strangers or necks in parks or would be willing to jump into the sack with an ex-con. Fine. Here's a news flash for you, Rebecca. Contrary to what you think, I am capable of controlling my baser instincts."

"I'm not the type of woman who could have a…a casual fling."

"A fling? There are plenty of names for the act, but I've never met anyone who called it that."

"As long as we understand each other."

"You've made yourself perfectly clear."

"Good."

His heels thudded on the cement floor as he strode to the door. "This is going to be one hell of a trip."

Chapter 9

The beam from the headlight spread across the pavement like the sweep of a blind man's cane. Rebecca still didn't know where they were headed. All she knew was the stretch of road in front of them.

Transport trucks roared out of the darkness, the air currents of their passing grasping at the Harley. Rebecca tightened her grip on the loop of metal behind her and hugged the seat with her thighs. A knapsack that Mike had picked up at the same store where he'd bought her clothes was strapped to the other side of the bar. A loose buckle on the outer pocket chinked repeatedly against the metal, whipped by the wind.

This couldn't be happening. Mrs. Rebecca Stanford, third-grade teacher, respectable, bespectacled, deserted divorcée, was riding cross-country on a Harley with an ex-con, hiding from a crime boss. Her flowered dress and sandals were crammed into the knapsack. The running shoes Mike had supplied fit amazingly well, but the jeans were too tight and the heavy sweatshirt was too loose and the denim jacket didn't have the demure embroidery on the collar that the one in her closet at home did. This one was sturdy and serviceable, just what the average third-grade teacher needed for riding cross-country on a Harley with an ex-con.

She didn't know whether to laugh or cry.

For the first forty miles she worried. Was this wild plan going to work? Would Mike find somewhere safe for her to stay? Would she get back in time to prepare for the new school year? Would she even have a job left once Mrs. Barring started talking to her husband? What about the school board and the PTA? And what about Mr. Witlock and his gang? And which one should worry her more?

For the second forty miles she ached. The leisurely Sunday rides she had taken with Mike hadn't prepared her for the reality of long-distance travel on a two-wheeled vehicle. Although the Harley was a big bike and the powerful motor ate up the miles of highway almost effortlessly, it was a strain to sit stiffly on the seat like this. The vibrations from the engine thrummed through the soles of her sneakers all the way up to her teeth. While her shoulders throbbed, her backside was rapidly becoming numb.

Somewhere outside Bloomington she put her helmet close to Mike's and raised her voice above the noise of the wind. "Don't you want to stop soon?"

He turned his head slightly until she could see the curve of his cheekbone. "What?"

"Don't you want to stop?" she yelled.

"What for?"

"Aren't you tired?"

He shrugged. "I want to get as far away from Chicago as we can."

She shifted carefully, adjusting her grip on the metal bar behind the seat. "I understand."

"Are you all right?"

"Sure," she lied. "Just fine."

The roar of the engine dropped to a throaty rumble as Mike slowed and pulled off onto the shoulder. Without a word, he lifted one hand from the handlebars and reached back to grasp her knee.

"What are you doing?" she shrieked.

"Relax, Rebecca," he said, pulling her leg snugly against his hip. "You'll be more comfortable if you lean on me for a while. You can't stay stiff like that forever."

"But we shouldn't be touching each other."

He put his hand back on the handlebar. Now that they had stopped there was no wind to cover up the four-letter word he muttered.

She winced. "I thought it would be better—"

"This doesn't count. Or do you think I'm planning to molest you on a moving bike?"

"Of course not, but—"

"Put your arms around me."

"What?"

"Hang...on...to...me," he growled. "Like you did before. Lean against my back."

She felt like a fool. The last time she had been on his bike, she hadn't hesitated to hold on to him. She had probably left nail marks in his leather jacket. Jerkily she brought her hand forward and splayed her palm over his chest.

"Now the other one," he ordered.

She complied wordlessly. It must be her imagination. Surely she couldn't feel his heart beating through the leather.

"Good," he said. "Now slide your butt closer."

"Excuse me?"

"You heard me."

Gingerly she inched forward until her legs fitted snugly against his sides. In another minute they were back on the highway. With her arms holding on to him for support, she had to admit that the vibrations of the bike were more bearable.

"Better?"

"Yes," she called. "Thanks."

For the next forty miles she worried again. This time about something else entirely.

She had been crazy to think that this would work. How on earth was she going to handle the effects of this man's nearness? Pressed intimately to his back like this was sending her much-abused pulse soaring. Why hadn't she thought this through more carefully? Had there been some other choice that she had overlooked?

By the time they pulled into an all-night gas station outside of Springfield, Rebecca was more confused than ever. Her conscience, her values, her heart and her still-vibrating body were all screaming at her from different directions.

So when Mike eased himself off the bike and stretched his cramped muscles, she didn't know whether to avert her eyes or admire him openly or run as fast as she could for the nearest bus station.

"Dawn's breaking already," he said, leaning over to unscrew the cap from the gas tank.

She turned. Beyond the glare of the buzzing light overhead she could see the first blush of sunrise in the east. "Do you think we've come far enough yet?"

"No, not yet. We'll try to find a place to lay low for the rest of the day."

They found a small motel a few miles from the gas station. Mike roused the night clerk, then wheeled around to the back out of sight of the highway. He had two keys.

"You're in here, in Number Eight," he said, unlocking the door of the room in front of his bike. He followed her inside to look around for a moment, then set their knapsack at the foot of the bed and handed her the key. "The place isn't fancy, but it looks clean. I'll be right next door in Number Nine if you need anything."

She grasped the key in her palm. "Thanks."

With a grunt that might have been a "you're welcome," he waved toward the knapsack. "I bought you a toothbrush and stuff while I was getting those clothes. It's in the bottom of the pack.''

"Thank you. I'll pay you back."

"Forget it." He held their helmets in one hand, grasping them by their chin straps as he fiddled with the buckles. "I've been thinking about the way you were worried over your car and your house before we left."

"I couldn't help it. I know what you think—"

"No, listen. I remembered that back in the parking lot you tossed your keys to that redheaded skateboarder. His mother's the neighborhood busybody, right?"

"Mrs. Barring?"

"That's the one. Once the kid told her what happened there's a good chance that she took care of everything without being asked."

She considered what he said. "You might be right. That's exactly the kind of thing she would do."

"Anyway, you could call in a few days to check, let her know what you want done."

"Thanks for suggesting it."

His leather jacket creaked as he lifted a shoulder. "Just because I've never had a home doesn't mean that I can't understand what yours means to you." There was no self-pity in his voice. He sounded like a person who had come to terms with his situation a long time ago. "Make sure you bolt the door and use the chain when I leave."

A transport whined past on the highway and reality struck her anew. She was such a long way from home, from anything familiar. Except for this enigmatic man she was completely alone. She swallowed against a sudden, disturbing tightness in her throat.

"What's wrong?"

She tried for a casual shrug but couldn't quite pull it off. What was wrong? The list would be shorter if he asked what was right. "I guess I'm a little scared."

Tentatively he reached out to brush a strand of hair behind

her ear. "No one knows where we are. We'll be fine for the day."

"I'm sure you're right. It's just…"

His fingers gently grazed the edge of her jaw. "I won't let anything happen to you, Rebecca. I swear it."

She had an unreasonable urge to close her eyes and press her cheek against his broad, callused palm. Instead she tightened her grip on her room key and took a step back.

His hand fell. "We better get some rest."

Pressing her lips into a tight line, she nodded.

He closed the door firmly behind him. It wasn't until she slid the chain into its slot that she heard his footsteps move away.

She blew out her breath hard enough to ruffle the hair on her forehead, then slipped off her sneakers and sat on the edge of the bed. A minute later she heard the creak of bedsprings and two muffled thumps from the adjacent room, probably Mike's boots hitting the floor. This was the first time they had been separated since they had pulled out of that warehouse, but she imagined she could still feel the imprint of his body against hers. Leather and denim had been between them then. Now there was a wall, one thin wall.

With a sigh she leaned over to pull the knapsack onto her lap and groped inside. A small plastic bag at the bottom proved to contain the toothbrush Mike had mentioned. It also contained toothpaste, a comb and a cardboard sleeve of hairpins, as well as small bottles of shampoo and skin cream. To her surprise, the toothpaste, shampoo and cream were the brands she used. How had he known? She glanced at the wall, a puzzled frown on her face. He must have remembered seeing them that first night when she had bandaged his wrist in her bathroom.

There was a larger package under the first. Curious now, she quickly pulled it out, then stared at the white fabric that bunched in her hands. It was a nightgown. Supple, softly brushed cotton, it was modest from the buttoned neck to the ruffled hem. And it was almost identical to the one she'd had on the night he'd first asked her to leave town. She hadn't realized he'd observed her so closely. And she wasn't sure how she felt about it.

He had bought her the clothes out of necessity, but the nightgown and the cream weren't necessities. They were more like…gifts. Why had he done this, after the things they had said to each other back in that warehouse?

Sometimes Mike seemed so sensitive and acted so tender. How could he be…what he was?

She plucked off her glasses and rubbed her temples. Her life had always been so predictable. Now she didn't know what to think, or what to feel or where she would be tomorrow.

It was almost two when she awoke. Afternoon sunlight streaked through the crack in the drapes and probed into the quiet motel room. She had slept almost eight hours straight, she realized groggily. With a groan Rebecca rolled off the bed and padded to the window.

The first thing she saw was the back of Mike's head. He was sitting on the parking lot curb in front of her room, his shoulders flexing beneath his T-shirt as he rubbed a rag along some shiny thing on his bike. She let the curtain swing back into place, then had a hurried shower and dressed. She was still fastening the buckle of the knapsack when she opened the door.

At the sound, he twisted to look up at her. Healthy muscles rounded under the sprinkling of black hair on his arms. Bronzed cords stood out on his neck. His cheeks had that smooth sheen of freshly shaved skin. In the sunlight his hair gleamed with blue highlights. A toothpick tilted rakishly at the corner of his mouth. "Hello, sleepyhead," he said softly.

At the intimate timbre of his voice her pulse sped. Whatever else he was, there was absolutely no disputing the fact that he was a devastatingly attractive man. "Hi." She cleared her throat. "Have I kept you waiting long?"

He gestured toward his bike with the rag he held. "I'm just cleaning off the pipes." Rising to his feet, he leaned on the seat and crossed his ankles. "We might as well get something to eat before we start out."

She pulled the door closed behind her, then paused. "Thank you for the things you bought me. It was very thoughtful of you."

"You're welcome."

"And thank you for the nightgown."

For a moment the lines beside his mouth deepened as he almost smiled. But then his expression hardened and he turned away. "I figured you weren't the type of woman who would sleep in the buff."

They chose a restaurant well off the interstate. It was the dimly lit, plastic-coated-menu kind. Mike ushered her to a booth near the back and sat so that he faced the door. They were dressed like the majority of the sparse clientele. No one appeared to take any notice of them. Even the waitress who brought their order of chicken-fried steak and baked potatoes slapped their plates on the table and then ignored them.

"I made some phone calls this morning," Mike said, slicing into his steak. "I've arranged for you to stay with some people I know. I trust them to keep you safe."

Rebecca hesitated, her fork halfway to her mouth. "Where?"

"Independence. We should get there by the morning. We won't be making as good time now since I want to stay off the interstates."

She glanced uneasily toward the restaurant entrance, then leaned forward. "Do you think Witlock will try to follow us?"

"I'm still being cautious, but no, I don't think he'll try to follow us. He knows I'll be back. I told him."

The baked potato that had tasted so delicious now felt like cold porridge on her tongue. "What?"

"That was another one of the phone calls I made."

"Why did you call him? What did you tell him?"

"I told him I didn't appreciate his cashing in my insurance policy early. He said it was a misunderstanding, that Trevor had acted on his own initiative." He cut another thick chunk of meat and chewed thoroughly. "That might be true. Trevor's had it in for me since I started working for Witlock. Anyhow, it doesn't make any difference whose idea it was to rough you up yesterday. The fact that they tried makes it easier for me to go back."

"You'll have to explain this. I'm not up-to-date on mob protocol."

"They broke their word first."

"So?"

"Since Witlock claims it wasn't his idea, he can't blame me for getting you out of town."

"Does that mean I'm safe now?"

"No. They'll use you again if they can. It won't be safe for you to go back until this is over and I leave Chicago for good. That part hasn't changed. But at least I haven't ruined my chances for finishing my job with them."

He talked about these criminals as if they were normal, reasonable people. And he obviously had no desire to break away from them. Now even the steak was beginning to lose its flavor for her. "Who are the people in Missouri?"

"A guy I knew back before I did my time. He moved out of Chicago when his brother opened up a business in Independence."

"Uh, what kind of business?"

He didn't answer her immediately. Taking a slow sip of coffee, he leaned against the back of the booth. "They work with cars."

Cars? Mike used to steal cars. This dinner definitely wasn't going to sit well during the upcoming motorcycle ride. Was he taking her away from one group of criminals only to plunk her down in the midst of another?

He frowned and pushed his plate aside, leaning his forearms on the table so he could lower his voice. "I can see what you're thinking by the way you're puckering up your mouth like the rear end of a lemon."

"I don't know what you mean."

"You're worried about what kind of friends a man like me would have, aren't you?"

Sometimes she wished he wasn't so perceptive. Shifting uncomfortably, she began shredding the paper napkin that she'd spread over her lap.

"I think you and Sly are going to get along just fine," he said, a smirk twisting one corner of his mouth.

She had to trust him. That's what it came down to. Hadn't he already demonstrated his concern for her welfare? He said she'd be safe with this man and his brother, and Independence should be far enough from Chicago. Taking what was left of the napkin, she wiped her lips. Was her mouth really puckered like a lemon? "You said he knew you before you went to prison?"

"Uh-huh. I met Sly and his brother seventeen years ago."

"Then I'm looking forward to hearing what you were like as a teenager."

His smirk faltered. "You don't want to get Sly going on that. You'll be bored within a day."

"We'll see. Is 'Sly' short for 'Sylvester'?"

"Don't call him 'Sylvester.' He hates it."

"I'll keep that in mind."

He patted the front of his shirt, looking for the phantom cigarettes as he always did when he was rattled.

She reached into her purse and pulled out a package of gum. The wrapper was crumpled but not broken, so she offered a stick to Mike. "Here. Will this help?"

"Sure you don't have a smoke in that bag?"

"Positive. Tell me about what you did after you went straight." She ignored his scowl and continued. "What kind of job did you get?"

He hesitated, then unwrapped the gum and popped it into his mouth. "I worked in garages, taking cars apart and putting them back together. Basically the same thing I'd done before, only I made a lot less money."

"You must have been good at it, working with cars, I mean."

A ghost of a smile touched his lips. "The best."

"Tell me about it. Where did you live? What did you do in your spare time?"

To her surprise he started to talk. In his straightforward, no-nonsense way he told her about some of the people he worked for and the odd places he lived. He told her about putting together his bike and taking long, solitary rides. Again, there was no trace of self-pity when he described his life, but Rebecca couldn't suppress the twinge of sympathy she felt for him.

She still didn't know what to think of this man. She hadn't come to terms with her reaction to him, either. The attraction she felt was only sex, wasn't it? Or loneliness? How could she be developing feelings for a man who was a criminal and an ex-con? His world repulsed her. Or was she using all of that as an excuse, a shield, so she wouldn't have to deal with what was happening between them?

What was happening between them?

His jaw flexed as he worked the gum. In the dim lighting of the restaurant the angles of his cheekbones were shadowed, giving him a lean and hungry appearance. She studied the stubborn chin and the strong line of his throat and remembered how he had bought her that nightgown and had tried to ease her worries about her house and had soothed her fears with that tender caress.

And she remembered how he had smelled when she had pressed her face to his neck.

At least two feet of space and a plate-strewn Formica tabletop separated them. Yet instantly she was back in the warehouse, pressed against Mike's rigid body, kissing him, running her hands up his back.

The silence stretched out between them. Crockery clinked at a booth near the door. From the speakers over the counter came the whine of some country singer lamenting a lost love. Behind Mike's vivid blue gaze his thoughts were as impenetrable as his sober expression.

Mike clamped down hard on the gum. He hadn't known it would be this bad. Even after driving all night, he had barely slept after they had arrived at the motel, because each time he had closed his eyes he had remembered the way she had fitted herself so sweetly against his back. At every bump in the highway she had rubbed against him, her fingers holding tightly to his chest. The warmth of her legs against his thighs, combined with the subtle vibrations of the engine…how the hell was he going to endure it for another night?

But he was committed to this now. If he wanted his freedom, he had to be sure that Rebecca would be removed from any danger. His third phone call this morning had been to Prentice. The cop hadn't even asked whether Rebecca was all right. The first question had been whether Mike was still in good with Witlock.

Prentice had come as close as the cop ever would to apologizing for the way they had let Trevor and Guido get to her. He'd also had the good sense not to push Mike about leaving her in police custody now that he'd gotten her out of Chicago—Prentice already knew the way Mike felt about cops.

Sly would take good care of Rebecca, Mike was sure of it, even though it had been plain from the look on her face that she thought the worst of him. Not that he could blame her, considering the way he'd given her nothing but trouble. For a minute there he'd been tempted to tell her about Prentice and his deal, just so she'd quit looking so disappointed when he mentioned going back to Witlock.

But he knew better than to open up to her again. She could

think what she wanted. What did he care? It wouldn't make any difference in the end.

It was better this way, for both of them. Besides, Prentice was so obsessed with his secrecy and masquerades that he had once again refused to give Mike permission to reveal their plans to Rebecca. And as long as she thought the worst of him, she would keep pushing him away. When it came to keeping his distance, he needed all the help he could get.

"It's getting late," Rebecca said hesitantly. "Perhaps we should be going."

He watched the way her lips moved as she spoke. She never wore lipstick. Her mouth was naturally rosy. Lush. Kissable.

"I'll meet you outside," she said, rising from the table and walking toward the rest rooms.

He watched the sway of her hips as she moved, the graceful stride that was unconsciously seductive in its guilelessness, and he remembered how easily his hands had fit around her waist and lifted her. He noticed that the sweatshirt he had bought her sagged loosely to one side of her shoulders, revealing the edge of a lacy strap that she would be mortified to know was showing. And he remembered how her skin had tasted. And how warm the flesh of her thighs had felt against his palms.

With a muttered curse he stood up and put some bills on the table to pay for their meal, then went outside to where the Harley was parked. They hadn't even started out and already his body was twisting into knots.

She joined him a few minutes later, taking the helmet he held out to her and fastening the chin strap easily. When she straddled the seat behind him she hesitated for a moment. Then she slid forward and locked her hands around his chest.

He felt like jumping off the bike and running as fast as his bum knee would allow. He felt like turning around and taking her into his arms and kissing her senseless.

He did neither. Leaning forward, he kicked the bike to life and guided them back to the highway.

If he had thought last night was bad, that was nothing compared to what he was enduring now. The hours crawled by, no matter how hard he pushed the throttle. They crossed the Mississippi and were past Hannibal before he allowed them a brief rest. Rebecca hadn't complained, but Mike could tell she was uncomfortable and fatigued. He could tell, since his body was acutely sensitive to every nuance of hers.

Darkness enclosed them, broken only by the occasional passing car or the sleepy small towns. By now, as soon as Rebecca brushed against him, Mike's entire nervous system seemed attuned to her. He could smell the herbal shampoo she used, along with the scent of the same motel soap he had lathered over his skin in the shower. Had it lathered over her skin, as well? Had it rinsed off in bubbly swaths and left her naked body glistening beneath the water?

It's your own fault you're in this condition, he told himself. If it hadn't been for him, she wouldn't be mixed up with Witlock. He was responsible for this mess, so he owed it to her to curb his libido until he got her safely settled. He deliberately replayed the end of their last kiss, dwelling on her rejection of him, in an effort to fight the growing urge he felt to pull the bike into some darkened field and carry her to the ground. And he tried to counter each gentle memory of her with the reminder that there was no place for a woman like her in his future.

When the wind blew up and the clouds obscured the stars on the western horizon, Mike wasn't disappointed by the threat of rain. He didn't think he would have been able to make it to midnight anyway. A week with next to no sleep combined with Rebecca's tender torture…surely it was unhealthy for a man to be in a state like this for such a prolonged length of time.

The lightning started suddenly. Jagged flashes played across the sky, followed by rumbling that was felt more than heard. Mike slowed the bike and called over his shoulder, "I'm going to pull off and look for somewhere to stay the night."

"Already?"

He gritted his teeth as she pressed closer in order to hear his reply above the wind. "Yeah. Already."

The first drops of rain were rifling against them when a fluorescent sign glowed mercifully through the gloom, proclaiming a vacancy. Near the limit of his endurance, Mike turned into the driveway and coasted to a stop in front of the office.

Of course, there was only one vacancy.

He stared at the key in his hand, then glanced at the yawning clerk. "You sure you only have the one room?"

"Yup."

What would be worse? Having Rebecca wrapped around his back or having her in the room with him? Mike pondered his choices. She would have a prissy schoolteacher fit when she found out they would share a room. On the other hand, judging by the buzzing in his ears and the slow blurring of his vision, he was in no shape to drive any further.

At that moment thunder crashed directly overhead and the clouds opened, deciding the matter for him. Running outside, he steered the bike under the overhang in front of the motel room and killed the engine.

He had expected an argument.

He wasn't disappointed.

"What do you mean, we're sharing the room?" she said as soon as he had set their helmets and knapsack on the floor.

He closed the door firmly, tossing the key onto the low dresser. "This was all they had."

"We had agreed it would be better—"

"Jeez, Rebecca," he said, shrugging out of his jacket and brushing off the raindrops. "I know that."

"Then why—"

"This was all they had," he repeated. He rubbed his palms over his face, hearing the rasp of stubble. "And with this storm, it wouldn't be smart to go any farther tonight."

"But it's still early, compared to yesterday, I mean this morning."

He looked at her over the tips of his fingers. "I can guarantee you wouldn't have been happy with the results if we had kept going."

She paced the length of the room once, then propped her hands on her hips and whirled to face him, her caramel-colored eyes filled with confusion. Chestnut wisps escaped her loose braid and lay softly against wind-kissed cheeks. The neckline of her sweatshirt drooped low on one shoulder again, revealing a good two inches of bra strap this time.

She looked too damn good.

He sighed and rubbed his eyes. "There are twin beds."

"I noticed."

"Well, what do you want, Rebecca? Do you want me to go outside and sleep on the bike?"

"Of course not."

"Or maybe we should string a clothesline down the middle of the room and hang a blanket over it. Would that make you feel safer?"

She shook her head. A succession of emotions flickered across her face too quickly for Mike to make out what she was thinking. Finally she lifted her hand to her nose as if to fortify the barrier of her glasses. "I'm sorry for being so difficult," she said stiffly. "I should have realized how tired you must be."

"Yeah, right."

"You've had to manage the bike while I've merely been a passenger."

"Believe me, I noticed."

"Those circles under your eyes are even darker tonight."

"Not sleeping tends to do that."

Her eyebrows tilted, concern softening her expression. "Weren't you able to rest during the day?"

With rigid fingers he raked his hair back from his forehead. "Forget it. Look, I don't like the idea of sharing this room any more than you do, but there's no other choice. So we might as well make the best of it."

"All right." She glanced at the twin beds. "Which one do you want?"

Which one? The one with her in it. "Take your pick. I think I'd better go have a shower."

Chapter 10

Rebecca stared at the closed bathroom door. He might be an ex-con and everything else her mother had warned her about, but Mike was still human. With the rough black stubble covering his jaw and the dark smudges beneath his eyes, he appeared worse now than when he had arrived at her house that night last week. Ever since they had started traveling, he had been looking more and more tense. Today had seemed the worst. Each time she had shifted behind him she had felt his body stiffen. A few times when they had passed over a bump she'd heard a muffled groan. If he hadn't been sleeping well he must be nearing collapse. Arguing about the single room seemed childish and petty.

"We're both adults," she told herself in her best nononsense schoolteacher voice. "This is no big deal."

Through the bathroom door came the sound of water drumming against the shower stall. Then the squeak of bare feet on tile. Then the muffled sound of water hitting skin. A vivid, startlingly clear picture of what was going on behind that closed door sprang instantly into her mind. Good Lord, he was naked in there. The broad back and wide shoulders that she had been looking at for two nights were probably wet and glistening. Those large hands that had been gripping the handlebars were probably lathering the soap and spreading it across his chest and down his belly and...

Cheeks flaming, she turned away. This was ridiculous. She was the one who had insisted they couldn't be intimate. And Mike had agreed. Maybe she was the one who needed the shower. A cold one.

Snatching the room key from the long dresser beside the door, she grabbed her purse and ducked outside. The rain was still coming down as if heaven had turned on a fire hose. Dodging past the parked Harley, she ran across the parking lot to the lighted windows of the coffee shop on the other side of the motel office.

Things weren't any better when she returned.

"Where have you been?"

Rebecca took a deep breath and closed the door behind her. She had thought that she had stayed away long enough to give him time to finish his shower. Yet he hadn't even finished getting dressed. "Uh, I went out."

His hair was as wet and black as the night outside. Slicked back from his forehead, it still bore furrows from a comb. His brow bore deeper furrows from his frown. "You shouldn't have left without telling me."

"You were in the shower."

"You still could have told me. I hadn't locked the bathroom door."

She couldn't let herself think about that or she would have to turn around and run back into the rain. "I thought you would have appreciated the privacy."

He pulled away the towel that had been draped around his neck and tossed it onto the bed beside him. He wore no shirt. Or socks. "Do you have any idea how worried I was?"

It was difficult to concentrate on what he was saying. "I was only across the parking lot."

His jeans rode low on his hips, revealing a strip of pale skin that hadn't been touched by the sun. If his near nudity bothered him, he showed no signs of it. Quite the contrary. He strode across the short distance between them as if totally unaware of his lack of clothing. "Don't do that again."

The paper bag she held crinkled in her fingers. "Do what?"

He grasped her upper arms. Hard. "Don't leave like that."

"You're overreacting."

"Why did you go out?"

"I was hungry. I got some hamburgers." She twitched her shoulders against his tight grip. "What are you so angry about?"

"I was worried about you. You should have told me."

"Well, I'm all right so you can stop—"

"And I don't want to be." He released her arms and shoved his hands into his pockets. "I don't want to be worried about what happens to you. I'm not used to this."

"*You're* not used to this?"

"I've always been alone, and it's simpler that way." His jaw tensed as he took a step away. "I didn't know where you could have gone when I came out of the bathroom and saw you weren't here. It's dark, we're in the middle of nowhere and it's raining. What was I supposed to think?"

She couldn't tell him the truth. She couldn't tell him that the fact of being merely a dozen feet away from his naked body had sent her out into a rainstorm. "I'm sorry."

"Just because we've made it this far without any trouble doesn't mean that we can relax."

"I said I was sorry. There's no need to shout."

He took a deep breath, then blew it out slowly in an obvious effort to calm down. "Like I told you once before, I'm not used to having to think about anyone else."

"I know. Your life has been very different from mine."

"From the day I was born I've been alone."

"You were so young when your mother died."

"My mother was fifteen when she had me, did I tell you that?"

She placed her purse and the bag of food on top of the dresser and leaned back against the door. "Yes, I remember."

"She used to go out every night. She never bothered with little niceties like baby-sitters. The neighbors complained when I cried, so she used her hands to teach me to be quiet. If she hadn't been killed in that car accident, the social workers would probably have taken me away from her anyway."

Shock kept her silent. He had never told her these details before. She had never imagined anything so horrible. Losing a parent during childhood was bad enough, but having to experience neglect and abuse... Sympathy welled inside her as she listened.

"Some of the people in the foster homes I was in probably tried to reach me, but I got a reputation as a troublemaker and they learned to leave me alone. Jeannie was different. I let myself care for her. But she was lost to me long before the drugs finally killed her." He took his hands from his pockets and ran them through his hair, obliterating the neat furrows. "So I've always been alone, Rebecca. I don't know any other way."

She took a step toward him. "Oh, Mike."

"I don't want to worry about you," he said, settling his palms on her shoulders. "And it makes me angry to realize how much I do."

The revelations about his childhood were still whirling in her brain. She didn't even consider moving away from his touch. "I understand."

"Do you?" He stepped closer. "Do you really understand how I'm feeling right now?"

Her vision was filled with his chest. It was so broad, with damp black hair glistening across the subtle swells on each side of his breastbone. The tight curls softened into a downy line that narrowed over the taut ridges of his abdomen and disappeared under the loose waistband of his jeans. The scent of fresh-scrubbed male drifted to her senses. And she had an almost overwhelming urge to lean forward and lay her cheek against his skin. "I'm sorry I worried you."

"I shouldn't have yelled. It's not your fault."

Her gaze lifted to the pulse that beat at the base of his throat. "Sometimes when we're anxious about something we react with anger even though we're not actually angry."

"I need to be sure you're safe, Rebecca. That's the whole idea of this trip."

"I only wanted to run over to the coffee shop before it closed." She looked into his eyes, struck yet again by the pure, vibrant blue. "At the last place we had separate rooms. You wouldn't have known whether or not I had gone out."

"I knew every move you made."

"But—"

"Motel walls are thin, Rebecca. And I didn't sleep much."

With a start she remembered the way he had been sitting in front of her window this afternoon, polishing the chrome on his bike. Had he been watching over her?

His thumb moved to the neckline of her sweatshirt where it had pulled to one side, rubbing across her exposed skin.

At the contact of flesh against flesh, a shock trembled through her body. "Maybe we should eat before the hamburgers get cold."

"They'll keep."

"I bought some sodas, too."

"I have a better idea."

She shivered.

He placed both palms against the door beside her head and leaned closer. "Are you cold, Rebecca?"

Her pulse thudded as she felt the warmth of his breath on her cheek. "My shirt's wet. I forgot to put my jacket on when I went out."

"You should change into something dry."

"You've been very considerate—" Her words ended on a gasp as he moved his hands to her waist.

"Considerate?" His fingers slipped beneath the hem of her sweatshirt, trailing across the bare skin of her midriff. "I've been a goddamn saint."

Another shiver traveled through her frame. "Mike, what are you doing?"

Using his thumbs, he pulled the damp fleece fabric upward. "Taking off your wet clothes."

She clasped his forearms. "This isn't a good idea."

"No, probably not."

Muscles like steel bands flexed beneath her hands. She locked her knees and pressed back against the door in an effort to steady herself. "We already decided we shouldn't do this."

"No, we shouldn't," he agreed readily, spreading his fingers over her rib cage, letting the sweatshirt fall over his wrists. "You're warm, Rebecca. Your skin is soft and warm here." His thumb skimmed an inch below her breast. "And here. Are you like this all over?"

In her mind she knew all the reasons why they should stop. Yet her mind seemed so very far away from the reaction humming through her body. Her hands slid from his arms to his chest. To push him away.

The back of his knuckles caressed the valley between her breasts. "Yes, you're soft and warm here, too." With his fingertips he traced the lace at the top of her bra.

The hair on his chest was springy, curling against her splayed fingers. Beneath her right palm his heart pounded.

"Which one are you wearing? Is it the one with the lace all over?" He rested his palm on her breast, then moved the heel of his hand across the tip. "Ah, it's a silky one. It feels as smooth as the skin on your thighs."

She gasped, feeling a tightening, burgeoning fullness follow his touch. Push him away. Now. Don't move your hands to his shoulders like that. Don't tilt your face toward him like that.

He moved swiftly, covering both her breasts with his hands, pressing her back against the door with his body. "You've rubbed these against me for two nights now." He squeezed gently. "You don't know how many times I've wanted to know what you felt like without a layer of leather between us."

She shuddered. Her fingers dug into his shoulders.

"Do you know what it's been like for me? Do you have any idea?" He inserted his knee between her thighs. "Do you know how close I came to turning onto some back road and stopping that bike so I could do this?"

The thrill of his words, the spell of his virile body held her speechless. Her lips parted. All she could do was hang on.

"But you're not that type of woman, are you?" His voice dropped to a throaty whisper. "You wouldn't want to park in some farmer's field and make love on a Harley, would you?"

Wouldn't I? she wondered.

"Do you know how we'd manage that?"

Hazily she shook her head.

"First you shuck off those jeans." His knee rubbed rhythmically against the inside of her thigh. "Then you straddle me instead of the seat."

The image was immediate, electrifying. Rebecca's throat went dry while wet heat spread into the most intimate parts of her body. It was like nothing she had ever felt before. Her lungs heaved, her heart pounded. The scent of Mike's clean skin now mingled with a heavier, darker scent of arousal. Rain pounded against the window. Thunder trembled in the distance.

His hands moved, cupping, circling, kneading. His knee rose, his eyelids drooped sensuously. "Are you thinking about it, Rebecca? Is that why I feel those hard nubs pushing against my palms?"

Thinking about it? Lord help her, she was picturing it in every detail. Her nails pressed into his skin. Her eyes closed. "Don't," she whispered. "Please, Mike. Don't do this."

Slowly the motion of his hands stilled. "I'm not doing anything you don't want me to do, am I?"

The sensations were riveting. Silk sliding over her nipples beneath his callused palms, heat flowing from his leg to the apex of hers. His breath stirring the hair at her temple. "I don't want…"

She couldn't complete the lie. He was right. He wasn't doing anything she didn't want. She felt vibrantly alive. Each cell in her body quivered with the needs he was stirring up. The truth was she wanted him to do more.

Much more.

Why him? It wasn't the first time she had silently wailed that question. Why did it have to be Mike, a man who had been in prison, who worked for a criminal, who had wrenched her from her home? Why did her bones melt and her will turn to water at his touch?

If he wanted to, he could easily force her. Yet he hadn't. If he pushed, he could probably seduce her. Yet he had stopped. He was waiting, giving her a chance. Letting her make the choice.

Why did life have to be so complicated?

There was no choice. They both knew it. Taking this further was out of the question. The reasons they were here, alone, together, reasserted themselves in an overdue flash of clarity. This wasn't a romantic rendezvous. It never would be.

Forcing her eyes open, she focused on a point in the middle of the opposite wall. She released her grip on his shoulders. Her arms dropped limply to her sides. "It doesn't matter what I want, Mike. I know this is wrong."

He pressed his cheek against the side of her head, slowly sliding his hands from her breasts to her waist. He inhaled deeply several times until his breathing was almost steady. Then he muttered a succinct, pungent curse and withdrew his hands from beneath her sweatshirt, releasing her so suddenly she staggered back against the door.

"I should have known better," he said, turning away from her and pacing across the room. It was a small room. He only took four paces. Pivoting at the bathroom doorway, he turned back.

"We had to stop, Mike."

"I know that, but it doesn't make things any easier." He tugged at the stud on his jeans. "This is definitely not a healthy situation for a man."

Resolutely she kept her gaze above his waist. "Then you shouldn't have started it."

"Don't expect me to apologize."

"I'm not asking you to."

"Good."

"But you know it was wrong."

"Do I?"

She moved in front of the dresser, bracing her hands beside the bag of hamburgers. "I think it might be best if we try to forget what just happened."

"Do you honestly think either one of us can do that?"

No. Not if she lived to be a hundred and one. Her fingers curled around the edge of the wood. "Nothing has changed, Mike. It can't."

He crossed his arms over his chest and stared at her. "You value honesty, don't you, Rebecca?"

"Yes. Yes, of course."

"Well, I'm going to be honest with you right now." His eyes warmed with an echo of the passion that had burned in them minutes ago. "I want you. We both know it's wrong, but I can't help it. I still want you. Whether it's on my bike or against a door or on a king-size bed with satin sheets."

Her stomach clenched and did a flip. "Mike, I already told you I'm not that type of woman. I've never had a casual affair in my life, and I don't intend to start now. Especially…"

"Especially what? With a man like me? Is that what you were going to say?"

Yes, that's what she was going to say, but the excuse was wearing thin.

"I meant what I said at the start, Rebecca. After this is over

I'll be gone. You'll never see me again. I've got no place in my life for a woman like you with her flowered curtains and her porch swing. You can't pack those up on the back of a bike.''

She was stunned by his vehemence. "I know that, Mike. We're just too different.''

"Damn right we are.''

"We want completely different things.''

Deliberately he let his gaze drop to her breasts. "That's not what it felt like to me.''

She slapped her hand against the dresser. "Will you stop doing that? I said I wanted to forget it.''

"What am I doing?'' He spread his hands. "I'm not touching you this time.''

"You're…'' What could she say? That he was looking? "Leave me alone.''

"Tell me something. Is it men in general, or is it just me?''

"What do you mean?''

"Is it only me that you're afraid of?''

"Mike, you know very well the reasons why we can't…I mean we shouldn't…'' She shook her head. "This conversation has gone on long enough.''

"Maybe you should be afraid of me, Rebecca.''

The expression in his eyes was hard to read. Was it defiance? Or pain?

There was nothing she could reply. As the silence lengthened, she dropped her gaze. The shoulders her nails had dug into were still bare. The springy mat of black hair on his broad chest rose and fell slowly with his regular breathing. His jeans rode low on his narrow hips, clinging to his thighs, contouring the knee that had pressed so boldly between hers. Her gaze halted at his feet. They were long, sturdy feet, planted apart with the bravado of a pirate on the deck of his ship…or a boy on the floor of his tree house. Only he'd never had a tree house.

"What are you staring at?''

''Your feet.''

''Why? What's wrong with them?''

''Nothing. They're perfectly...ordinary.'' She raised her gaze. He had revealed his vulnerability to her tonight. The implications of what he had told her about his childhood were only now beginning to register. There was much more to this man than the labels society had placed on him. The more time they spent together and the more she learned about him, the more she was coming to know the real person within.

Something began to niggle at the back of her mind. This didn't fit. His past had no doubt shaped him into the man he was now, yet how could he be a toughened criminal if he was capable of the type of genuine concern and unexpected kindness he had demonstrated from the start?

His mouth moved into one of his devastating naughty-boy grins as he swept his gaze over her body.

She watched him for a moment, unmoving. Then she pointed at his toes. ''The tough guy act doesn't work in bare feet, Mike.''

''What?''

''The act. Like the way you roll a toothpick along your lip. And the way you say 'yeah' all the time.'' She peered at him more closely. ''I bet you never really hated Princess, either.''

He frowned. His hand made a move toward the phantom cigarette pack before he caught himself and hooked his thumb into a belt loop instead. ''That's garbage.''

''Yeah?''

''You should talk. What about that prim and proper school-teacher act of yours.''

She drew back. ''Excuse me?''

''Watching Dirty Harry movies—''

''That's not fair. I told you that in confidence.''

''Cracking a guy's shins with a car door—''

''Good heavens, did I hurt him?''

''And there's your underwear, too.'' Four strides brought him to stand directly in front of her. He pointed at her shoulder, then leaned closer in order to trace his fingertip along her bra strap. "The prim and proper act doesn't work in lace and silk underwear, Rebecca."

She jumped aside, yanking the neckline of the drooping sweatshirt into place.

He reached past her for the motel room key. "I'm going out to check the bike." He slipped on his boots and his jacket and slammed out of the room.

Then again, maybe she was wrong about being wrong about him. Maybe she was trying to justify the way she felt....

Frowning, she grabbed the bag from the dresser and dug out one of the hamburgers. How dare he say that she was putting on an act? She happened to like Dirty Harry, that's all, though after this was over she suspected she wouldn't enjoy those movies quite as much anymore. And there was nothing wrong with silk and lace underwear. She happened to think it was...comfortable.

She bit down hard on the lukewarm hamburger, then glanced at the twin beds. What were the chances of finding a clothesline and some extra blankets at this time of night?

Somehow they managed to make it through to the morning. The tension between them may have been brought temporarily under control, but they both were aware that it hadn't been defused. Their breakfast of doughnuts and coffee passed in silence, and when they climbed onto the bike for the last leg of their trip, neither of them made any comment about Rebecca's decision to shift her body as far back as the seat would allow and to hold on to the metal bar behind her.

They arrived in Independence shortly after noon. Mike wove through the midday traffic with his usual competence. He skirted the downtown area, bringing them to a stop at last in front of a squat, square building on the edge of a litter-strewn vacant lot.

It didn't look too promising to Rebecca. Heat shimmered in the afternoon sunshine. Tufts of grass sprouted here and there through a webbing of cracks in the pavement in front of the building. This must have once been a gas station, but now the old pumps were encased in weathered plastic. Over the open garage door hung a crisply painted black-and-white sign. ''Otto's Autos,'' she read aloud.

''Otto's the name of Sly's brother,'' Mike replied, nosing the bike into the shade of an elm tree that overhung the fence beside the vacant lot.

Rebecca took off her helmet, poking ineffectually at her flattened hair. She straightened her sweatshirt, making sure her straps didn't show. ''Is this where I'll be staying?''

He slid her an exasperated look. ''Give me some credit, Rebecca. Otto and Sly don't live in their garage. They have a house in the suburbs.''

''Oh. Of course.'' She brushed at the front of her jeans. ''Is there somewhere I could clean up a bit before I meet them?''

''They're not going to care what you look like,'' he said, hooking his helmet over a handlebar.

Naturally a man wouldn't understand, she thought as she followed him across the pavement. When a man got rumpled and dusty after wearing the same clothes for three days, he looked rugged. A woman merely looked wrecked.

She took off her glasses, polishing the lenses on the hem of her shirt as she walked. She knew her appearance wasn't her main concern. Ever since Mike had mentioned these friends of his, she had been wondering about what kind of people they were and how she would be able to get along with them for the time she would need to stay here. This run-down garage wasn't doing anything to boost her confidence.

The sharp clunk of a hammer striking metal came through the open door. Mike paused just inside.

The odors of gasoline, oil and cement wafted strongly on the humid air. Rebecca put her glasses back on. An assortment of what she had to assume were car parts were neatly arranged along the side wall. Next to them was a large red-wheeled cabinet with at least a dozen drawers. A canvas tarp draped over what appeared to be a motorcycle. In the center of the floor sat a gleaming yellow car, something from the forties era she would guess. A pair of grease-spattered coveralled legs poked out from underneath the car's passenger side.

"Yo, Sly," Mike called.

With a rattle of wheels on concrete, the rest of the coveralled man appeared.

"Mike?" The man sat up, a grin spreading across his face. He pulled a rag from his pocket and wiped his hands, then pushed himself to his feet.

"I figured we'd find you here."

"Any trouble on the trip out?"

He shook his head. "No problem. Is that the Daimler you were telling me about?"

"Yup. She's a beauty, isn't she? Bought it from a guy who'd been storing it in his barn. I had to rechrome the bumpers, scrounge around for new headlights and do a lot of bodywork, but the engine was still good." He continued to clean his hands as he turned his attention to Rebecca. "Is this your friend from Chicago?"

"This is Rebecca Stanford. Rebecca, meet Sly Boychuk."

It took her half a second to recover from the shock. Extending her hand, she took a step forward, a genuine smile answering Sly's. "How do you do?"

He wasn't what she had expected. Then again, nothing had gone as she had expected since the night she had found that stray dog.

White haired and wiry, with twinkling gray eyes and a Mark Twain mustache, Sly had to be somewhere in his sixties. He was almost as tall as Mike, but his frame had been honed to whipcord leanness by his extra years. His grip was warm as he shook her hand, his face open and welcoming. "Pleased to meet you, Rebecca. I hear our Mikey got you in a jam. That boy just can't seem to keep away from trouble."

Mikey? Anyone who got away with calling a motorcycle riding hood something like that was a man she wanted to know. She felt an instant, instinctive rapport with this kind-eyed stranger. "It's very good of you to agree to let me stay until things get sorted out. The situation is rather complicated."

"I figured that from what the boy told me. He did right to bring you here. You can stay with us as long as you want." He squeezed her hand, then turned to call over his shoulder. "Hey, Otto. We got company."

From out of the glassed-in office on the other side of the garage, another man appeared. He looked to be a few years older than Sly, had a few more wrinkles in his weathered face, but the height and the lean build were the same. As he approached, Rebecca noticed a strong family resemblance in the broad nose and gray eyes.

"Thought we'd seen the last of you, boy," he said, coming forward to give Mike a hearty slap on the back that would have staggered a smaller man. He took Rebecca's hand and shook with the same confident grip as his brother. "Can you cook?" he asked immediately.

"Passably," she answered.

"Good enough. Esther quit last week. Ran off with the bingo caller."

"Who's Esther?" Mike asked.

"The new housekeeper. Made a mean apple pie."

"What happened to Camille?"

"She moved to Dallas."

"You can have her room while you're with us," Sly said to Rebecca. "We haven't gotten around to hiring her replacement."

"Sly's about to poison us both with his cooking," Otto said. He ignored his brother's snort and leaned closer, his gray eyes keen beneath his bushy white eyebrows. "Hope you don't mind cooking a bit while you're here."

"I'd be happy to help any way I could," she said immediately. "I really appreciate your letting me stay."

"Ha! You haven't seen the breakfast dishes."

"Mike, why don't you take Rebecca out to the house and let her get settled," Sly said. "Then you can come back here and give me a hand with the BSA I got under the tarp."

"We haven't finished fixing the Daimler yet, Sly. I want the boy to take a look at that car first."

"He's better at bikes."

Bushy white brows lowered. "Have you read the sign over the door lately, Sly? It's 'Otto's Autos,' not 'Sly's Bikes.' We have to get that Daimler ready for the auction by the thirty-first."

"It may be your sign, but I taught him everything he knows. I say the boy looks at my bike."

"What's an old coot like you need with that bike anyway?"

"Old coot? You're four years older than me, you reject from a scrap yard."

The two brothers argued with the ease of long practice. Rebecca shook her head and glanced at Mike.

He was smiling, the lines of tension easing from his face, making him appear unexpectedly younger. "Come on," he said, taking her elbow and steering her outside. "This could go on for hours."

"They seem like nice people."

"They are. Besides you, they're about the only honest people I know."

They walked back to the Harley. Rebecca paused in the shade of the elm to look back at the garage. "They restore antique cars, don't they? That's the 'car business' they're in."

"Uh-huh. They do pretty well."

She studied the old building for a moment more, then turned to Mike. "I wouldn't want to bring them any trouble. What if Witlock or one of his men finds out where I am?"

"That won't happen. They know nothing at all about Sly or his brother. You'll be perfectly safe staying here. The Boychuks belong to your world, not Witlock's."

"Would you answer a question for me?"

"Sure."

"Who is Sly?"

He hesitated. Picking up his helmet, he fidgeted with the chin strap. "I told you. I knew him before I did my time."

"He said he taught you everything you know."

"Yeah. He did."

The answer came to her slowly, but when it did, she knew for certain that she was right. "Sly Boychuk was that shop teacher you had in high school, wasn't he?"

"Yeah."

More pieces fell into place. "And you worked for his brother when you went straight, didn't you?"

"Yeah."

Before she could stop herself she reached out to take his hand. "I'm glad you had friends like them."

He lifted his helmet to his head, withdrawing from her touch. "We'd better get you out to the house. Then I'll see what I can do with Sly's BSA and Otto's Daimler before I leave."

She had expected the withdrawal, but she didn't let it bother her. The tough guy act probably didn't work with the Boychuk brothers, either. "Whatever you say." She smiled smugly and waited a beat before she added, "Mikey."

He scowled. Without a word he reached up to her shoulder, hooked his forefinger under her loose sweatshirt and gave a brisk snap to the lacy strap of her silky bra.

Chapter 11

Fanning herself with a folded newspaper, Rebecca leaned over the sink to open the window wider. The sound of crickets came in with a breath of warm, damp air. Trees in the yard rustled subtly in a trace of a breeze. If she closed her eyes, she could almost imagine that she was back in her own home.

"I said I wanted to watch the ball game."

"And I already told you I want to watch the movie."

Smiling wryly, she turned away from the window. Sly and Otto were at it again. They were both widowers, both strong personalities and set in their ways. She was beginning to suspect why they couldn't hang on to their housekeepers.

"Kansas City's playing the Jays tonight." Sly's voice could be heard easily over the swishing hum of the dishwasher. "I want to watch the game."

"No way. It's my turn to have the remote. I hate the way you flip around all the time," Otto returned.

"If I didn't change channels now and then you'd fall asleep."

"Oh, go listen to the game on the radio."

"I think I will. Hey, Mikey, get me a beer, would you?" She grinned at the name.

Mike pushed through the swinging door to the kitchen before she could hide her expression. "What are you laughing at?" he demanded.

"Nothing." She tipped her head toward the bickering that was still going on in the living room. "Are they always like this?"

"Usually."

"They really like each other, don't they," she stated.

"Yeah. You won't find two more loyal characters anywhere."

"They're adorable."

"You have a strange definition of adorable." He walked to the fridge and took out a can of beer. Glancing at her, he lifted the can. "Do you want one?"

"Oh, no thanks. I made up a pitcher of lemonade."

He nudged the fridge shut with his hip then moved back to the swinging door. "Do you think you'll be able to manage here? I didn't know Otto was going to expect you to cook."

"I like to feel as if I'm repaying them a little. And I already like your friends."

"I figured you would." He listened a moment, then pushed the door open and held it for her. "Come on, I think they need a referee."

The living room was comfortably homey, like the rest of the two-story house. The furniture was big and plaid, with fat wood knobs on the corners. As Mike and Rebecca sat at opposite ends of the sofa, the argument between the two brothers fizzled out. Otto tuned in a John Wayne western. Beer can in hand, Sly shuffled off to his room upstairs, muttering how anyone who didn't want to watch baseball was un-American. Smiling contentedly, Otto propped his feet on the coffee table, slouched down in his chair and was asleep by the second commercial break.

Mike caught Rebecca's eye as a snore rattled through the

living room. They shared a smile that was oddly intimate. "Sly could have watched the game," Mike said quietly.

"He probably knows that."

"Yeah." He plucked a toothpick from his pocket and clamped it between his teeth, then crossed his arms over his chest. "Sly's okay. For a schoolteacher."

"Yeah," she mimicked.

Otto shifted, his head rolling forward onto his chest with another snore. Across the flickering screen, the Duke advanced on a saloon full of black-hatted bad guys.

"I'll start back for Chicago tomorrow," Mike said as the first villain fell to the floor. "There are a few things I have to get settled here first, but I'll probably be able to leave by noon."

Of course. He wanted to get back to Witlock as quickly as he could, Rebecca thought, trying vainly to fight the disappointment she felt. She wasn't disappointed merely because he wanted to rejoin that criminal. No, the bulk of her disappointment stemmed from the fact that he was leaving her.

"I'll let you know when it's safe for you to go home."

Of course. He wouldn't be coming to get her. Why should he? A quick phone call and she could board a plane or a bus and go home by herself. That way they wouldn't have to see each other again. "I, uh, hope everything goes well for you."

"I'll make sure of it." He clenched his jaw, then stood up. "I'm going to get some fresh air."

The screen door squeaked, then snapped shut behind him. Everything was happening so fast. Less than a day and he'd be gone for good.

She knew it was for the best.

She also knew that there was no way she was going to sit in front of this TV and listen to Otto snore when she could be spending one last evening with Mike. Pointless as it may be, foolish as it may be, she wasn't yet ready to say goodbye. She rose, smoothed the wrinkles from the flowered dress that she'd washed and ironed this afternoon, tucked a stray wisp of hair into her ponytail, pushed her glasses firmly onto her nose and followed Mike out the door.

He hadn't gone far. He was sitting on the front steps, his bad leg stretched out in front of him, the other bent sharply so that his forearm rested on his knee. The soft light from the living room window gilded his shoulders and cast deep shadows over the chiseled planes of his face. In the distance a train whistled, a mournful, lonely sound.

She rubbed her palms over the gooseflesh that had appeared on her arms.

He looked up at her. "Cold?"

"No. That sound always gets to me."

"What sound?"

"The train whistle. It's so lonely."

"Lonely? That's not lonely. It's free, rolling across the countryside, not staying long in any one place."

"I could never live like that."

"I know, Rebecca. You've got roots."

Sinking down beside him, she propped her chin in her hands. "And you want to be on the move like that train."

The toothpick tilted. "What's it like?"

"What's what like?"

"Having roots. Being a teacher. You really enjoy your job, don't you?"

She settled herself more comfortably on the step. "I love it."

"You already know how I got into cars. What made you choose teaching as a profession?"

"I guess it was chosen for me. My father always wanted me to be a teacher like he was." A pair of joggers pounded along the sidewalk in front of the house. They were spotlighted by the lamp on the corner for a moment, then disappeared into the night. "As it turned out, I happen to be suited to it."

"That's because you like kids."

"Yes, I guess I do," she said thoughtfully. "The age I deal

with is ideal. They're old enough to be interesting little individuals."

"But still young enough to do what you say," he put in.

"Still young enough to have all their potential just starting to be uncovered," she corrected.

"Are you one of those people who look at kids as blank slates waiting to be written on?"

"Not at all. I think children already possess the kernel of the adult they will become. I wouldn't be able to change them to any great extent."

"Then why try to teach?"

She was silent for a moment. "When I was in college I read a poem that really touched me. It was about a gardener, but it actually was about raising children. Kids have their own particular strengths. Their environment, like a garden, can determine whether they ever fulfill their potential. The basic message of the poem was that a gardener can't change a willow into an oak, but he can help it grow true."

"True blue," he said quietly.

"What?"

"It's something one of my grade-school teachers used to say. About being everything you were meant to be." The tree in the yard rustled softly. Tipping back his head, he stared at the shifting pattern the streetlight made on the leaves above them.

Rebecca felt an overwhelming urge to stroke her fingers along the sharp ridge of his jaw. She pleated a fold of her skirt instead. "What was she like, this very wise teacher?"

"How do you know it was a female teacher?" he asked, twisting to face her, his naughty-boy grin deepening the folds beside his mouth.

"Woman's intuition."

"Well, you're right. Except she was a battle-ax who regularly sent me to the principal's office. Claimed I needed discipline."

"That's easy to believe."

He stretched an arm behind her and tugged lightly on her ponytail. "I think I was just insulted."

She tipped her head forward until he released her hair. "I wouldn't insult you. You're much bigger than me."

"I'll bet you're a good teacher, despite your size."

"That's nice of you to say, but you've never seen me in action."

"I don't need to. Your whole face lights up when you talk about your kids."

Her laugh was self-conscious, subdued. "I realize I only have the children for one year. Still, I try to do my best."

"I'm sure you do."

"Thanks. I hope so."

His cheek flexed as he shifted the toothpick. "How much does your job depend on people like that cow from the PTA?"

"Do you mean Mrs. Barring?"

"Yeah. Could you lose your job if she didn't like the company you were keeping?"

"I suppose she could put pressure on her husband to pressure the school board," she began.

"Considering the way you jumped on my bike, they all know you left with me."

She frowned. "It really shouldn't matter if they did. I mean, it's a free country, isn't it? People shouldn't be judged by appearances."

"You're an idealist, Rebecca."

"You make it sound as if there's something wrong with that."

"People can't help making judgments. Whether it's from appearance or financial standing or reputation. That's the way it is."

"Maybe." Drawing her heels up onto the step, she tucked her skirt around her ankles and hugged her bent legs. "The Boychuk brothers don't judge you."

"They're different. They've been working around old cars too long."

"Mmm. Maybe I'm different too because of my profession."

"Why?"

"I see kids before they've had a chance to build up the appearance or finances or reputation that they'll have as adults. So I try to look for the child inside of the grown-ups I meet." She rested her chin on her knee and studied Mike's profile. "Take Mrs. Barring as an example."

"Do I have to?"

"I might have called her a cow when I was angry with her for snooping, but deep inside her there's an insecure little girl. She probably started out as a bully because that was the easiest way she could relate to others, so the urge to dominate carried through to her adult relationships."

"You sound as if you've given it some thought."

"I usually do. It's become a habit." She chuckled. "The first night I saw you I was reminded of a little boy who was trying to look like a gangster."

"Was that another insult?"

"Hardly." She hesitated for a moment, then decided to go ahead anyway. "Despite the way you act, I think you're the sensitive, intelligent child who had to build a tough, street-smart shell around himself in order to survive. You keep to yourself and you want to be a loner out of self-defense, so the world won't hurt you anymore."

He grunted, then was silent for a few minutes. "What about you, Rebecca?"

"What do you mean?"

He grasped her ponytail again and gently stroked the ends of her hair across her neck. "Who's the little girl inside of you?"

She smiled wryly. "As far as I can tell I'm the shy little girl with glasses and skinny legs who wanted to please her parents and follow their rules. I equated love to safety and security." She rubbed her cheek against her knee. "I stayed so safe and secure that my husband couldn't stand it anymore and seized the first opportunity he had to escape.''

''You shouldn't keep beating yourself up over that marriage, Rebecca. It was obviously a mistake from the start.''

''You don't know the things Ted said.''

''No, I don't.'' With the edge of his knuckles, he rubbed the bone at the top of her spine. ''But I know you.''

His deep voice and gentle caress were as soothing as the cooling breeze. Somehow her words came naturally. Somehow, sitting here in the cozy darkness, with the sounds of the old movie drifting through the screen door and Mike's solid warmth by her side, she was able to say aloud the thoughts that had never been spoken. ''You're right, about the marriage being a mistake. Ted had been a great favorite of my parents, and they encouraged us to become engaged when I finished high school. My father died when I was in college, but my mother had her heart set on seeing me settled, so somehow the engagement simply carried on. And on. So I started working and a few years later I bought my house with some of the money I inherited from my father. Ted didn't like it. He wanted something more modern.''

''You have a beautiful house.''

''Thanks. Anyhow, Ted kept postponing the wedding, much to both our families' disapproval. I think he realized I wasn't what he wanted after all, but then my mother got very ill. We went through with the wedding, and things weren't too bad for a while, but then my mother died.'' She swallowed, lifting her face. ''Ted didn't understand my need to mourn. He thought I was deliberately rejecting him, so he started badgering me. He called me frigid, and dried up, and ugly—''

Mike made a noise in his throat and moved closer, draping his arm around her back. ''He was a selfish idiot.''

She sniffed. ''It got so that I couldn't even stand him touching me. So he started finding girlfriends. It wasn't enough that he told me about them, he had to flaunt them around town to humiliate me. The last one wasn't even out of her teens, but he told me she was more satisfying than I'd ever be. They ran off to Las Vegas and when I got the divorce papers I signed them and that was that."

"He had it all, and he threw it away," Mike murmured, rubbing his palm in slow circles over her back.

"If he had really loved me, he would have been patient." She was silent a moment. "Or maybe if I had really loved him, I would have let him comfort me."

"How long have you been divorced?"

"Almost four years."

His hand stilled. "That long?"

"I guess Ted's teenager isn't a teenager anymore."

"How do you feel about it now?"

"I feel like it's over." She leaned into his light touch. "And I feel better being able to talk about it. Thanks."

His fingers traced her back through the thin cotton of her dress. "Lucky for me he never realized what a warm, passionate woman you are."

She shook her head. "He said I wasn't woman enough for him."

"It's the other way around. I'd say he wasn't man enough for you." His palm closed over her shoulder, his fingers sliding forward to the slope of her breast. "I know you have a well of passion inside. I've had firsthand experience." He plucked at the front of her dress. "Hand, palm and fingers."

Her breath caught.

Releasing the cotton, he withdrew his hand, resting it safely on the step between them.

"I don't think I want to talk about Ted anymore," she said quickly.

A minute passed. Neither of them moved, yet a tension began to build. A familiar tension. The front steps of the Boychuk's white frame house seemed intimately isolated, enclosed by the darkness and the memory of all that had passed between them. Rebecca looked at his hand, at how the tips of his fingers touched the edge of her skirt. She looked at his legs, at how they were stretched out in front of him with his ankles crossed in a carelessly masculine pose. And for some reason she remembered his bare feet.

He flicked the toothpick onto the lawn and shifted half an inch closer. "I bet he never wanted to make love on a Harley with you."

"Mike!"

"Storms could be interesting, too. Remember that time on the blanket after our picnic?"

Blood rushed to her cheeks. "Mike, stop that."

"Did you know that I wanted you then?" His voice dropped. "I thought about making love in the storm, with the rain slicking your body and the lightning—"

"That's enough!"

"Hey, you're the one who started it this time."

"Started what?"

"Talking about your sex life. Or lack of it."

Jumping off the step, she strode away.

"Rebecca!" Mike called. "Come back."

"Oh, go soak your head."

"I've tried that, but cold showers don't work."

"This is a ridiculous discussion."

"Okay. Let's try body language."

She put her head down and turned onto the sidewalk.

"Hey! Where are you going?"

She heard his boots hit the ground and lengthened her stride.

Despite his uneven gait, he caught up to her before she reached the next streetlight. He materialized out of the darkness, a tall, virile presence by her side.

Refusing to acknowledge him, she walked on in silence.

"If you keep pressing your lips together like that you're going to end up like a battle-ax in thirty years," he remarked.

"Good."

"What are you so mad about anyway?"

"I don't like having my private life laughed at."

"Laughed at? I wasn't laughing at you."

"You were making fun of my lack of a sex life."

"Hell no. I'm volunteering to improve it."

"Don't toy with me about—"

"Rebecca," he said firmly, grasping her arm to halt her in midstride. "I'm not the kind of man who toys with a woman. I've told you I want you. That hasn't changed."

In the dim light, shadows hollowed his cheeks and deepened the lines beside his mouth. His face was all sharp planes and angles, his expression intense. Awareness of him spread from the skin above her elbow where his fingers circled her arm.

"I think we'd better get back to the house," she said shakily.

He didn't move. Another freight whistled weakly from the distance. "Yeah, we should."

"You have a long trip ahead of you tomorrow."

"That's right."

A couple walked past them, heads close together and arms around each other's waists. Rebecca heard their private laughter and saw the way their bodies brushed with their movements. She watched them until they were out of sight, feeling an odd wistfulness and an aching sense of loss.

Mike raised his hand, tipping her chin upward with his index finger. "I'd like to ask you something."

"What?"

"But I don't want you to get mad again."

She sighed. "I won't."

"Has there been anyone else besides Ted?"

"That's none of your business."

"No, it isn't."

"I said I didn't want to talk about him anymore."

With the back of his fingers he stroked her cheek. "There hasn't, has there?"

Why should she hold back on this? She had already told him more than anyone else knew. "No," she whispered.

Before she could move away, he had replaced his fingers

with his lips. Gently he brushed a kiss along her jaw. "I wasn't making fun of you," he said against her skin.

The kiss was tender, sweet, almost…loving. He didn't touch her anywhere else, yet she could feel her body yearn toward the warmth that came from him. The tang of his after-shave, the clean freshness of his skin embraced her on the breeze. The hush of his breath on her cheek meshed naturally with the rhythm of her own.

Gradually he drew back, then silently held out his hand.

She gazed at his outstretched hand. Something had happened here, something that was more than the familiar tug of physical attraction.

Why him?

Lifting her hand slowly, she placed her palm in his. If only things could be different. If only they could wrap their arms around each other's waists and walk off into the darkness, touching their foreheads together, laughing softly. If only…

If only Mike were the man she had first thought him to be.

"Do you have to go back to Witlock?" she asked tentatively.

"We've been through this before. I have no choice."

They walked in silence, their steps slow. Rebecca thought about the way the Boychuks respected and liked him. Despite the fact that he was working for a criminal, and despite the fact that he had been convicted of murder, they welcomed not only him but his friend into their home. She envied them for knowing Mike before he'd been hardened by prison. She would have liked to have known the boy he had once been. He'd had so many tough breaks in his life, especially having to experience the tragedy of his foster sister's death after having turned his own life around. No wonder he had needed to build such a thick wall around his feelings…

Suddenly she stopped, struck by what she had been saying about the child within. She had seen it last night, but she hadn't taken the opportunity to think about it further.

It didn't fit. From the start she had thought that Mike was

a good man, but then she hadn't been able to resolve her initial impression of him with a man who was a criminal and a murderer. She had assumed that she'd been wrong, but there were too many things that didn't fit. The Boychuks, Mike's unselfish determination to keep her safe, the consideration he showed her, his intelligence and wit...

He had gone to prison for murder. He had told her that he'd been found guilty. But he had never said that he *was* guilty.

She hadn't given him the chance.

It seemed so obvious now. Why hadn't she figured it out before? Had she been afraid to see it, afraid to weaken the shield she had erected around her feelings?

She inhaled sharply. She should have had faith in her instincts, no matter how hard Mike had tried to act the part of the hardened criminal. The man who had rescued her and driven her to safety was the same man whose tender kiss had just brought tears to her eyes.

"Rebecca? Is something wrong?"

She whirled to face him, her skirt brushing his legs. "Will you answer a question for me?"

"What?" he said warily.

She looked into his eyes and realized that she no longer needed to ask.

She *knew*.

Some part of her had known it all along. Otherwise she never would have trusted him, never would have come with him, and never would have let him touch her in the first place. "You didn't kill that man, did you," she said.

"What man?"

"The drug pusher, the one who killed Jeannie. You said you were found guilty, but you weren't. You were innocent."

"That's not what the cops said. That's not what the judge said."

Grasping his forearms, she raised onto her toes. "I don't care what they said. You were innocent."

Roughly he pulled away from her and started walking.

"That's why you hate the police, isn't it? That's why you're so adamant about having your freedom. You shouldn't have gone to prison in the first place."

He increased his pace, his boots making uneven thuds on the sidewalk.

Her heart thumped as her certainty grew. Hitching up her skirt, she ran after him. "You deliberately let me think that you were guilty, didn't you? Why, Mike?"

"I told you the truth."

"But only part of it. Why didn't you tell me the rest?"

"You looked like you'd already made up your mind."

"That's not fair. Why didn't you make me listen? Were you afraid of letting me get close to you? Or have you been told you were guilty so often that you started to believe it yourself?"

"You think you've got me all figured out now, school-teacher?" he muttered as she reached his side. "Is this all part of your hobby, the way you analyze people you meet?"

"Stop it." She took his hand. He tried to pull it away but she hung on tighter. "Just stop it. I told you things tonight that I've never said to another living soul. The least you can do is admit the truth."

"Why? What difference will it make?"

"None at all. You'll be driving out of my life for good tomorrow, so what difference will it make if you drop the act long enough to tell me what really happened?"

Mike turned up the walk to the Boychuks', his face an expressionless mask. "Think what you want. Makes no difference to me."

She paused on the sidewalk for only an instant, her resolve wavering. Then she raced for the steps, placing herself directly in front of him to halt his retreat. "You're a fraud, Mike Hogan."

He reeled backward, his eyes widening in surprise. "What did you say?"

"You're a fraud. I don't care what the judge or the police

or people like Mrs. Barring say. You're a good man deep down inside, and you always have been." She softened her voice. "What happened when Jeannie died? Why did you go to prison when you were innocent?"

His breath hissed out between his teeth. He raked both hands through his hair, then brought them down to rub his eyes. "It was a long time ago, Rebecca. It doesn't make any difference anymore."

She wasn't going to back down. This time she wouldn't let him retreat behind that tough-guy facade. She tried to remember the few details he'd told her. "You knew who had caused her death," she persisted. "How did you know?"

"It was her boyfriend," he gritted. "The man she had been living with, the one supplying her habit. I knew it, everyone on the street knew it. Even the cops knew it."

"And they didn't do anything about it."

"No. They didn't have enough proof, they said."

"So you were angry," she said, putting the pieces together in her mind. "You threatened him, and then you went to see him." She looked at Mike, at how he had his hands curled into fists at his side. She thought of how deep his emotions ran. "You never would have used a gun."

"What?"

"You would have used your hands, or your fists, but you never would have shot him." The answers were coming quickly now, with more and more certainty. It was as if a clean wind were blowing the last traces of doubt from her mind. "He must have been already dead when you got there. The gun, the murder weapon, it was still there."

He looked at her closely, his eyes boring into hers. "How did you know all that?"

"I know you," she said simply.

Brushing past her, he yanked open the screen door and went into the house.

She was right on his heels. The living room was dark. Otto must have woken up long enough to shut off the TV and go to bed. She looked around for a moment before she spotted Mike in front of the window. "You picked it up," she continued. "Your fingerprints were on it. And then the police showed up and assumed they had caught the murderer red-handed. That's how it happened, isn't it?"

Slowly he sank down onto the wooden rocking chair beside the window. He extended his leg, rubbing the knee with the palm of his hand. "Did Sly tell you?"

"No one told me. Is it the truth, then? Is that what really happened?"

"I wanted him dead, Rebecca."

"Of course you did. He was an evil man, he had caused the death of your foster sister. But *you didn't kill him.*"

His hand gripped his knee hard. Turning his head, he looked out the window. His chest rose and fell with rapid, shallow breaths. "No," he said at last. "No, he was already dead."

Swallowing down a sob, she crossed the room and knelt at his side. Tentatively she placed her hand over his. "Oh, Mike."

"She had always been so full of life. She was friendly and outgoing and trusted people too easily. I had tried everything I knew to help her. I was on my way to take her to a detox program the night—" He looked at her then, raw pain in his eyes. "I was the one who found her body. I went a little crazy, I think. I made use of what I had learned when I was stealing cars and tracked that bastard through every bar and alley in Chicago. I wanted him to pay for what he'd done to Jeannie, and to so many others like her. I didn't care who knew. When I finally found him in the back room of some seedy liquor store…" Pausing, he stared down at where her hand covered his. "God help me, I was disappointed to find him already dead. Maybe that's why I picked up that gun."

There was no room for relief or satisfaction that she'd been right or any thought of her own feelings. Her heart overflowing, she lifted his hand to her face and pressed her cheek against his knuckles.

His words came faster now, as if a dam had opened somewhere inside him. "I didn't have a chance. The cops had known about my involvement with those car thefts and had been frustrated because they'd never been able to convict me. Sly and Otto were the only character witnesses I had, but their opinions didn't mean spit against being caught with a smoking gun in my hand. It was an open-and-shut case." He swallowed. "They wouldn't even let me out to attend Jeannie's funeral."

The pain in his voice was more than she could bear. Rising from the floor, she leaned over and pressed her lips to his.

His mouth was hard, unmoving.

She pulled back.

"I don't need your pity," he rasped.

"Mike, I don't pity you. I feel your pain and want to help. I…" She paused, uncertain of the word to use. "I care about you."

"Why?"

Why? It wasn't pity—it wasn't purely physical. It wasn't purely friendship. Unwilling to examine her motives too closely, she placed her hands on either side of his face.

"Rebecca," he said, his voice low.

She heard the warning in his tone but chose to ignore it. The urge to feel his lips against hers was too strong to be denied. Holding his head steady, she kissed him again.

This time his lips softened, moving in response under hers. Tentatively she let the tip of her tongue touch his. Her thumbs traced the grooves on either side of his mouth as she drew his lower lip between hers. It was a heady feeling, this sudden sense of freedom to touch him as she wanted. She sucked lightly on his lip, then placed a kiss on his chin and drew back, balancing herself by bracing her arms against the wooden rocking chair.

He hadn't moved. His entire body quivered with tension, yet he hadn't touched her. "What do you want, Rebecca?"

"What do you mean?"

"From me? What do you want from me?" He reached up and grasped her shoulders. "Tell me."

"I don't know."

"You don't kiss a man like that and then say you don't know," he said harshly, his grip tightening.

Did she expect anything in return? No, she had simply wanted to give.

He swore beneath his breath and pulled her against him. His hands slid from her shoulders to her back, stroking possessively over the curve of her spine. "Do you want me to kiss you, Rebecca?" he murmured. "Do you want me to drive you crazy with my tongue and my mouth and my fingers?"

His actions followed his words. Hot and powerful, his kiss seared across her lips. His hands dropped to her waist, then her hips, then grasped intimately at her rounded buttocks, pulling her onto his lap.

The chair creaked and rocked backward. She felt Mike's solid heat beneath her thigh and gasped into his mouth.

He took her with his tongue, sliding it between her lips, probing the hidden folds beside her teeth, mingling his taste with hers until she was breathless with the sensual onslaught. Wrenching her head away, she gasped for air. The gasp became a groan as he moved his mouth to her neck. Arching back, she raised her hands and clutched his shoulders.

A light flicked on over the staircase that led to the second floor. Wood creaked with shuffling footsteps.

Rebecca looked toward the noise in time to see a white-haired man in a paisley dressing gown descend the stairs.

She pushed at Mike's chest, trying to slip from his lap.

He clamped his hands around her wrists. "Don't go."

It was Sly. He was already into the living room before he noticed the couple in the chair by the window. His head jerked back in surprise. "Excuse me, folks. Didn't see you there."

"No problem, Sly," Mike answered.

"Just thought I'd check that the screen door is latched. Otto fell asleep in front of the movie again."

Rebecca tried once more to escape from Mike's lap. He held her fast. "We noticed," he said, as if carrying on a conversation while caught in a clinch with a woman was nothing unusual. "I'll get the door later."

Sly dipped his head, his eyes twinkling. "Well, I guess I'll be turning in, then. I probably won't be down again until the morning," he added.

"Good night, Sly."

The white mustache twitched with a smile. "Good night, Mike. Rebecca."

She cleared her throat. "Good night."

The footsteps retreated. A moment later the light went out. Rebecca's cheeks burned.

"Don't be embarrassed," Mike said, easing his grip on her wrists. "Sly wasn't born yesterday."

"Oh, my goodness." She covered her mouth with her hand. "He must think I'm terrible," she mumbled. "I don't usually…I mean, I'm not the type of…" She sighed. "I've said all that before, haven't I?"

"Every time."

Her eyes had begun to adjust to the darkness once more. "I'd better go. I'm sorry. I didn't mean to tease."

"Then what did you mean to do? Why did you kiss me?"

She had answered so many questions about Mike tonight, her mind was still reeling from the things she had discovered. Yet his softly spoken question was one she wasn't prepared to consider.

Silently she eased from his lap.

Chapter 12

Sleep was elusive that night. Rebecca tried everything, from deep-breathing relaxation exercises to counting sheep, yet nothing helped. Her mind continued to replay each haunting image from the memories Mike had shared.

Now she knew. She kept saying that over and over to herself, trying to put some perspective on the story of Jeannie's death and Mike's imprisonment, but it was no use. How could she possibly distance herself from the tragedies he had endured?

Restlessly she rolled onto her back. No, she wouldn't be getting any sleep tonight. There was nothing wrong with the bed—though it was narrow, it was comfortably soft, made up with smooth sheets that smelled freshly of detergent and sunshine. There was nothing wrong with this spare bedroom, either—it was quietly isolated on the ground floor at the back of the house, a staircase away from the snoring Boychuks, a short hall away from the living room sofa and the sleeping Mike. Was he sleeping? Or was he lying restlessly on his back and staring at the ceiling with his thoughts chasing themselves around in his brain like lost children?

Something had happened tonight. Somewhere between their words and their kisses something had happened. She felt as if she had reached a threshold and was teetering on the brink, poised to cross into some unknown, uncharted territory of the heart.

Yes, the heart. It was no longer any use trying to deny her feelings. The sexual pull she had experienced from the first was only the surface evidence of what had been building deep inside. This was more, much more. It wasn't only his body that drew her, it was his mind, his troubles and his triumphs, his past and his future. His heart, his soul. His love.

She sat up, drawing her knees to her chin and wrapping her arms around her legs. How had it happened? They were from two different worlds. He had said so from the beginning, and what he had revealed tonight only served to confirm it. They were together only until tomorrow. Whatever the reasons behind Mike's plans, she didn't doubt for a moment that he still meant to finish what he had started with Witlock. And afterward she would return to her nice secure job and her cozy little bungalow, and Mike would hit the open road and revel in the freedom that had been so unjustly stolen so many years ago. She would follow the narrow path and he would go wherever his wandering took him. How could she have let herself fall in love?

Let herself? Had she had any choice?

Rubbing her cheek against a fold of her cotton nightgown, she sighed softly. Love wasn't supposed to be like this. Love was security, safety, pleasing people in return for affection. Love was the grandfather clock ticking in the background as her mother stitched up the hem of her new party dress. Love was her father's smile of approval as she presented him with another straight-A report card. Love was the reliable, respectable husband…who ran off with a stripper?

She knew she had loved her parents, but she had never

really loved Ted. She might have thought she did at the time, yet now she was sure she hadn't. She had never before felt like *this*.

When she had kissed Mike tonight, the feeling that had engulfed her was so strong it took her breath away. She had wanted to give him everything, to soothe his pain, to make up for every injustice of fate. She had wanted to tell him that he'd never have to face the world alone anymore. And she had wanted to crawl inside his soul and fill him with the love that overflowed in hers.

Blindly she turned her face toward the window. It was just as well that they had been interrupted. Who could blame Mike if he had misunderstood her impulsive embrace? She knew what he had wanted. She knew he wasn't shy about sex. His frank openness about the subject was one of the many differences between them. Tonight in her own clumsy, inexperienced way she hadn't been offering sex, she had been offering love.

It was just as well they had stopped. What would have happened if they hadn't? No matter what Mike had said before, her marriage had served to prove that she was a failure when it came to sex. And Mike's solitary life might very well have made him unable to respond to love. In less than a day he would leave and they'd never see each other again.

"I can't love him," she breathed.

But she did love him.

"I shouldn't love him."

But she did love him.

"This isn't fair."

Life isn't fair.

She wiped her eyes against her knees and quietly uncurled from the bed. Her bare feet made no noise as she padded to the doorway, tiptoed down the short hall and peered into the living room shadows.

He was stretched out on his back, one arm flung across his forehead, his feet propped on the opposite end of the sofa. A muggy breeze from the open window briefly lifted the edge of the sheet that draped from his waist to his knees, revealing a flash of bare thighs.

Mike was aware of her the instant she stepped into the room. Without moving his head, he could hear her breathing, could imagine the steady beat of her heart. The same breeze that toyed with the edge of his sheet brought a hint of her scent, floral and sweet, feminine and soft. His nostrils flared as he inhaled greedily.

Why was she standing there? Didn't she know how she was tying his body in knots?

He clenched his jaw and suppressed the urge to groan. He had asked for this. He was the one who had involved her with Witlock. He was the one who had taken her away. And despite what he had said before they had left, he was the one who had been unable to keep his hands off her.

Although she moved slowly, her bare feet made small sucking noises as the skin on the soles stuck briefly to the polished floor. Her shadow fell across his eyelids and he knew she had paused in front of the window.

Clenching one hand against the sheet, he forced himself to remain motionless. After several minutes of continued silence he ventured to open his eyes a crack. Immediately he wished he hadn't.

She was silhouetted at the window. Her chestnut hair tumbled in sleep-tossed abandon over her shoulders and down her back. Folds of the nightgown he had bought her skimmed over her rounded bottom, molding her slender legs and brushing lightly against her ankles. Her palms were braced against the windowsill, her shoulders squared as she stared out into the night.

What was she doing here? What was she thinking about? He should never have told her about his past. She was such a decent woman she was probably feeling sorry for him, just like she had felt sorry for a scraggly runaway dog.

He should look away, or try to ignore her, but of course he

didn't. Molded by the breeze and backlit by the streetlight, her nightgown was as insubstantial as a wisp of smoke. Through it he could easily trace the flare of her hips, the delicate indentation of her waist. Unbound and gently lifting with each breath she drew, the curve of a breast brushed the inside of her bare arm.

She trailed her fingers along the back of the rocking chair, her head bowed. Then as quietly as she had come, she turned and moved away. The door to the kitchen squeaked. A moment later a strip of light shone from beneath it.

With a sigh he swung his legs off the sofa arm and sat up, fumbling for his jeans. He walked toward the light, then hesitated for a long minute, his palm flat against the cool metal plate on the edge of the door.

Did he want to go through? Wasn't what had passed between them this evening enough? He wasn't accustomed to sharing his feelings with anyone, and right now he wasn't sure he had a firm grasp on them himself.

This hadn't been part of the plan. He hadn't meant to open up to her like that. Tomorrow he would be gone. By next week he would have his freedom. If he was smart he would turn around and pretend he hadn't seen her, that he hadn't listened while she had unburdened the pain of her marriage, that he hadn't felt a leap of joy when she had looked into his eyes and declared her faith in him.

Yet somehow, as he knew he would all along, he pushed open the door and stepped over the threshold.

She whirled around, clutching a milk carton to her breast. "Oh. I'm sorry. I didn't mean to disturb you."

"You didn't."

"I couldn't sleep."

"Neither could I."

"I thought if I fixed some warm milk it would help."

The dim streetlight hadn't done her justice. Caught in the glare of the overhead light she looked like a nymph, or a wood sprite, poised to flee. Her bare toes peeked out from the hem of the modest cotton nightgown. Rich chestnut hair curled over a row of ruffles that skimmed her bosom. Her moist lips parted in a startled "oh." Thick lashes swept over caramel eyes as she blinked rapidly.

He clenched his hands. She wasn't wearing her glasses. There was no barrier to the warmth he saw in her eyes. Sweet, naive, trusting Rebecca. Did she know how he wanted to wrap his arms around her and take her down to the floor with him and drop his jeans and raise her gown....

Clamping a tight lid on his thoughts, he reminded himself of the trouble he'd already brought into her life. "Warm milk, huh?"

She wished she had put on her glasses. At this range all she could see of him was a flesh-colored blur. On the other hand, maybe it was a good thing that she'd left them off. Squinting, she glanced down at the carton of milk that she held. "Yes. Would you like me to add some for you?"

"Do you think it will do any good?"

"What do you mean?"

"Never mind. I'll get the cups."

In several steps he was close enough to be within the range of her myopic vision. Close enough for her to see the sprinkling of black hair on his forearm as he reached into the cupboard for two mugs, close enough for her to notice the line of pale skin at his waist where the loose jeans slipped an inch. What did he have on underneath? At the motel he had left his jeans on, but there on the sofa she had glimpsed a bare leg. Was he even wearing underwear?

Her hand shook as she poured the milk into the pot.

His hand shook as he placed the mugs on the counter.

They sat on opposite sides of the chrome and linoleum table and sipped their warm milk in silence. A clock ticked somewhere. A freight train whistled in the distance. The atmosphere trembled with clarity as every nuance of the moment was magnified by their mutual, heightened awareness.

Tomorrow he would be gone. She would never see that cocky smile or those crinkles at the corners of his eyes.

Tomorrow he would leave her behind. He would never hold her slender body close to his or hear the tenderness in her voice or see the open warmth of her smile.

This wasn't fair.

Damn, he couldn't let her go.

She was already reaching across the table when he grasped her hand in his. Heart pounding, she watched him lift her fingers to his lips. He kissed each one, his eyes never leaving hers. He pressed a long, slow kiss in the center of her palm, then tugged gently.

"Come here, Rebecca."

She went.

The chair scraped as he pushed it backward, rising to his feet in front of her. Still holding her hand, he pressed her fingers over his heart. "Do you feel it?"

Her palm rubbed over his skin. "It's pounding like mine," she whispered.

"I thought I could make it through to tomorrow. I thought I was strong enough to walk away, but I'm not." He stepped closer, bringing their bodies a breath apart. "I want you."

She tipped back her head to look into his face. What did she see? This was no longer simply the exciting stranger who had given her a ride on his motorcycle or the criminal who had messed up her life. This was…Mike. The man she loved.

There might never be another time. There might never be another place. There was only one thing that she could do, and the decision was the easiest and most natural she'd ever made in her life. Rising up on her toes, she pressed her mouth to his.

"Ah, Rebecca," he murmured against her lips, tasting her gently. His grip on her hand tightened as his heart thudded beneath her fingers.

She lifted herself against him, touching his mouth with the tip of her tongue.

A deep tremor shook his frame. "Are you sure?" he breathed. "Rebecca, please say you're sure."

"Kiss me, Mike." Impatiently she nipped his lower lip. "Really kiss me."

His response was immediate. Intoxicating. As electrifying as the man himself. Before she could ask again, his mouth moved fiercely across hers. There was no coaxing, no gentle wooing. He took complete possession of her lips with a demanding, devouring certainty.

Her fingers curled within his. She brought her other palm to his chest and he caught that hand, too, then pushed them both behind her back, crossing her wrists so that he could circle them with his fingers. The maneuver was sudden, forcing her shoulders back and her breasts into his chest.

Her heart slammed against her ribs, her breath was trapped somewhere between her lungs and her throat. This was like playing with fire. The thrill, the fear. The knowledge that what you've started could rage out of control. The fascination that made you risk it.

He had never touched her like this before. Now she realized that he had been holding himself back, that he hadn't let her feel the full depth of his passion. But now that passion was unleashed. This time he didn't stop. Keeping her wrists trapped with one hand, he gripped the back of her head with the other, turning her face so that their mouths meshed even more closely. His tongue thrust past her lips, insistent, probing while he bent over her, fitting his body to the curves of hers.

He was a powerful man. He had lived his life on the outside of society, with his own set of rules. She was no match for his strength. Yet she felt no fear. She trusted him. She loved him. She knew he would never hurt her.

Closing her eyes, she melted into his rough embrace. A soft whimper escaped her throat as she opened her mouth and met his hunger with her own.

Her surrender left him reeling. The sound she made had been a purr. Her tongue was stroking his in welcome, her lips hot and wet. Through the thin cotton of her nightgown, her nipples puckered emphatically against his chest.

What had he done? After all they had gone through in order to prevent this very thing from happening, what was he doing?

He released her wrists.

She didn't push him away. Instead she brought her palms against his back and held him closer. He shuddered, raising both hands to her sleep-tossed hair, capturing her chestnut curls where they tumbled to her shoulders.

And still the kiss went on. He drew her lower lip between his, tasting it, nibbling gently, tracing its contours from corner to swollen edge to corner. She explored his mouth. She shared his breath. She took his passion and gave him hers.

Somewhere, in the only remaining sane corner of his brain, he knew there were reasons he shouldn't be doing this. Yet right now he couldn't seem to summon up a single one. How could something that felt so right be wrong? How could the fire in his bloodstream be quenched by anyone but Rebecca? How had he existed until now without her? And how could he exist a moment longer unless he made her his?

What had begun here would have to be completed. That was as certain, as inevitable, as the next beat of his heart.

His hands skimmed her shoulders, then grasped her around the waist. Effortlessly he lifted her until her face was level with his.

She broke off the kiss, on a gasp. "M-Mike?"

"We've wasted so much time. I can't wait any longer."

"Here?" she said shakily.

"This first time I want you on a bed, Rebecca."

Her lips, swollen and moist from his kiss, curved in a smile that had nothing of the prim schoolteacher about it.

He nudged aside her hair to nuzzle the side of her neck. "Wrap your legs around my hips."

"What?"

He slid his forearm around the small of her back, anchoring her against him. His other hand slowly skimmed over her hip until he grasped her thigh and lifted her leg forward. "Hang on to me."

"But I've never…"

"It's easy." He inched her leg higher, hiking up her night-gown. "Just think of climbing on the Harley."

She trembled. Seconds later she had locked her ankles behind his back, her thighs squeezing his waist. Her arms coiled behind his neck. "Now what?"

With her body twined around his like that, he almost lost control. He raised his head and took several deep breaths. "I hope to God you know the answer, Rebecca. Because I don't know if I can change my mind."

"Tell me," she whispered.

His hands grasped her bottom, clamping her against him. "Next we go into your bedroom."

"Like this?"

He didn't even notice whether or not his knee hurt as he took the first step. "Yeah. Like this." He shouldered open the swinging door, then carried her down the short hall to the room at the back of the house. He didn't pause when he bumped into the door frame and staggered briefly. His entire consciousness was focused on the woman he clasped in his arms.

She ran one hand through his hair while her lips nibbled a maddening trail of kisses down the side of his neck. "And now?"

"And now, my sweet Rebecca…" He stopped when he reached the edge of the narrow bed. Moonlight streamed in silver patches through the window, casting their joined shadows on the floor. He lifted one foot onto the mattress and settled her weight on his thigh.

"Mike?"

"Now I intend to do what I've wanted since the moment we met," he said, running his hands over her back and into her disheveled hair. "I'm going to make you naked."

Her breath brushed his cheek as she sighed.

He stilled. "You do want this, don't you?"

"Yes." She sounded…amazed. "Yes, I do."

He leaned away to see her face. Her eyes were wide, almost surprised. "We've been fighting this for too long."

"Yes. Yes, we have."

"I like the sound of that word."

"What word?"

With the tip of his finger he traced the shell of her ear, then followed the line of her neck to her collarbone. His knuckles grazed the pulse at the base of her throat. "Yes."

Slowly she untangled her limbs from their grip around his torso and slid down until her feet touched the floor. "I'm not…very good at this."

The laugh that rumbled from his chest was deep, intimate, intensely masculine. "So far you're almost too good."

"I mean, when I was married I didn't—"

"Your husband was a total jerk," he said, moving his hand boldly to her breast. He covered it with his palm, rubbing gently across the soft ruffle of her nightgown, smiling in satisfaction as he felt her taut nipple. Encouraged by her involuntary gasp, he rolled the hard bud between his thumb and forefinger.

"Oh!" She shuddered again and splayed her fingers over his chest. "Oh, that feels…wonderful."

"It gets better." He bent forward, opening his mouth over her breast and sucking right through the layer of fabric. It wasn't enough. He pulled back from the wet area and reached for the hem, skimming it upward and over her head. Before she could draw another breath, she stood completely naked before him and her quivering breasts were filling his waiting hands.

It did feel wonderful. It felt more than wonderful. Rebecca lifted her face to meet Mike's gaze and felt the wonder of what was happening zing down to her curling toes. His eyelids were heavy, half-closed. His lips curved in a smile of promise while his hands awakened her flesh.

How was it possible to love him more? He was stripping away her insecurities about this aspect of love as easily as he had stripped away her gown. She felt vibrantly alive, pulsing with desire. Yearning for something she didn't yet know.

"Touch me." His voice was rough, unsteady. "Rebecca, I want you to touch me."

Touch him? She wanted to absorb him, meld with him, feel him with every nerve ending in her body. Eagerly she explored the smooth skin of his abdomen, tracing his ribs and the rippled contours of his muscles as he inhaled sharply. She brushed the springy hair that curled over his chest, burrowing with her fingertips, dragging her thumb over the tiny male nipples. She found the silky line of hair that arrowed downward and followed it to his navel, dipping her finger inside, reaching for the waistband of his jeans and dipping her finger inside there, too.

"Jeez, woman. You're going to make me pop the buttons on my fly."

She leaned forward, muffling a giggle against his chest. She had never dreamed there could be laughter along with the love. "Then you'd better undo them."

"You read my mind," he growled, wrapping an arm around her back and falling with her onto the bed.

They came together in glorious, uninhibited nakedness. Exploring with fingertips, she traced the contours of his muscled arms and shoulders, thrilling to the power beneath the warm skin. His knee nudged between her legs and his hand stroked her thighs, sending tingles upward. He dipped his head, touching his tongue to her nipple in the same instant his finger rose to touch her pulsing core.

She gasped, trembling with the swiftness of her response.

He made a primitive, purely male sound in his throat and suckled.

Rebecca arched upward, her fingers clutching his head, an answering cry on her lips.

This, this was what love between a man and woman was

supposed to be. It was pure and clean, the natural, ultimate expression of what was held in the heart. It was laughter, and moaning, and crying out. It was joy, wonder, rapture.

It was the mating of two souls, she thought as she stroked his sweat-sheened shoulders.

He rose onto his knees, his gaze burning into hers. No words were spoken. They were beyond language. They were hard and soft, man and woman, two parts that must be joined to form a whole.

She reached between them, taking him into her hand, holding him, marveling at the strength and the awesome vulnerability of the man at that moment.

"Rebecca." It was a plea. And a promise.

She guided him home.

Afterward she must have dozed. She awakened to a gentle but insistent breeze on her face. Her eyes drifted open and she saw Mike leaning over her, his mouth puckered as he blew across her cheek once more.

She smiled. "Hi," she whispered.

He tenderly brushed a stray wisp of hair from her face, then propped his head on his hand. "Hi, yourself."

Her gaze traced the features that were already engraved on her memory. She would never tire of looking at him. Or touching him. Reaching up, she placed her palm on his chest, over his heart. The beat was strong, steady, slower now that their desire had been spent.

A lingering sense of wonder curved her lips into a smile that brimmed with new knowledge. Mike had given her so much more than this shuddering pleasure. He had given her a part of herself that she had never been aware she was missing. With his lips and his hands and his body he had unlocked the depths of her femininity.

She wasn't frigid. The word didn't even have the power to hurt her anymore. Mike had been right about her capacity for passion. And he had proven beyond a doubt that he was man enough to show it to her.

He covered her fingers with his. "You're quite a woman, Rebecca." Bringing their joined hands to his lips, he languidly kissed each of her knuckles in turn. "You could make a man never want to get out of bed."

Her smile softened. Ted had been wrong, so wrong. She did know how to satisfy a man. Deeply. Completely. And it was all because of Mike. And her love for him. "Really?"

With a growl he scraped his teeth across the knuckles he had just kissed. "Give me a minute and I'll demonstrate what I mean."

"A minute?"

"You want it sooner?" A lazy chuckle vibrated through his chest. "I'll do my best."

"You're sounding awfully smug."

"I'm not smug. I'm looking forward to hearing that special little noise you make in the back of your throat."

"Mike!"

He chuckled again. "No, that's not the one."

Rolling away from him, she sat up and fumbled for the sheet. "I didn't think you'd say anything about it."

He was too fast for her. He grabbed the edge of the sheet before she could draw it up. "Don't cover yourself."

"Maybe we'd better get dressed."

"Later." Leaning on an elbow, he nudged the tip of her breast with his nose.

It began again, that pulsing yearning that only Mike could evoke. Her breath catching, she looked down at him.

He grinned, his eyes gleaming. Holding her gaze, he opened his mouth and gently tongued her nipple inside.

Heat, swift and intense, spread instantly to each still-sensitive part of her body. She gasped. "Mike."

"No, that's not the sound, either," he mumbled, his mouth full.

Shakily she grasped his head, falling back against the mattress with a groan.

"Mmm. Getting closer." He skimmed his palm along her thigh, then brought his knee to the other side and straddled her legs. Balancing on his elbows above her, he kissed his way to the side of her neck.

Her fingers slid to his shoulders as she remembered the waves that had shaken her, the throbbing fullness of their joined bodies, the shimmering fulfillment that had swept through her. "I've never felt like this before. I didn't know. I was married for three years, but I'd had no idea…"

He silenced her words with a long, thorough kiss. "I haven't been a monk. But what we just did has never happened to me, either."

"Really?"

"Yeah," he said quietly.

"I felt…I don't have words to describe it."

"The earth moved, huh?"

"It was more than that."

He leaned over her to spread her hair out on the pillow, then looked into her eyes, as if memorizing the picture she made. "You're beautiful, Rebecca."

The way he said it, the way he had held her and kissed her and shown her his honest enjoyment in her made her feel as if she just might be.

He lowered his weight on top of her, pressing her into the bed. "We've still got the rest of the night before I have to leave."

His words sliced through the spell his body had started working. He was going to leave, to return to work for a criminal. These few stolen hours wouldn't change anything. "Don't go back to Chicago, Mike. Please. You don't belong with those people. You're better than that."

His movement stilled. Bracing his arms, he drew back until her face came into focus. "I have to go back."

"You've gotten me safely away. I'll be all right. I won't

be any use to Witlock as long as you stay away. I can go to the police when I go home. I won't mention your name, I won't tell them anything about you, so you can go anywhere." She stroked his jaw, her fingers trembling. "You can have your dream of freedom and the open road. You can go to California or Alaska—"

"Rebecca," he said quietly, "I have to finish the job with Witlock."

She wrapped her arms around him, clinging tightly. She had known this would happen. Reality was poised to crash down on them. This was going too fast. It was like that first motorcycle ride—she didn't want it to end. "Please be careful, Mike. I couldn't bear it if anything happened to you."

He slipped his arm around her waist and rolled to his back, pulling her on top of him. Fingers trailing downward, he stroked his way to the soft skin on the inside of her thighs, pressing his thumb against an exquisitely sensitive spot. "Let's not waste the time we've got left by talking."

The heat that he rekindled was almost enough to make her forget.

Almost.

Maybe it was better this way, to say goodbye to each other with their bodies. This would be the last time.

Dammit, this just wasn't fair! Now that she had finally found a man to love, a man who could bring out all the passion she had never suspected she possessed, she was about to lose him, if not to Witlock then to the open road and the next horizon. Out of all the people in the world, why did she have to fall in love with this one?

"Rebecca?"

Though the moonlight was already fading, she still saw every fascinating detail. The front tooth with the tiny chip in one corner. The overnight growth of beard that folded into the lines bracketing his mouth. The hairline that had begun to recede at the corners of his forehead. What would he look like in ten years? In twenty?

She would never know.

Quickly she slid her fingers into his hair, memorizing the texture. Using her lips, she charted each plane and angle and line of his face. With her body she felt his strength. She had only these precious minutes left to learn him by heart.

She closed her eyes so he would not see her tears.

Chapter 13

At the sudden knocking on the door Rebecca bolted upright, instantly awake. Judging by the slanting sunlight seeping in the window, it was barely dawn. Less than an hour could have passed since they'd both finally fallen asleep.

The knocking stopped. It wasn't the bedroom door, it was the door at the back of the house. Lunging over the side of the mattress, she felt around on the floor until her fingers encountered her glasses.

"Better stay here."

She shoved the wire frames onto the bridge of her nose and looked up. Mike was standing in her doorway. He obviously had been awake no longer than she had. The hastily donned jeans were still unsnapped. A few thin pink sleep lines adorned his cheek and his hair stuck up in rebellious tufts. A smile came automatically to her lips—he looked adorable.

"I'm serious, Rebecca. We don't know who it is."

The smile disappeared as she rolled to her feet. The intimacy of the night before shattered and fell away as she snatched up the sheet and clutched it over her breasts. "You don't think it could be Witlock, do you? Here?"

"I don't think so, but I want you to stay out of sight until I find out."

She reached the bedroom doorway just as a second knock sounded. "Are you going to answer it?"

He caught her arm. With his chin he nodded toward the window. "If there's any trouble, you can get out that way."

"Trouble? What kind of trouble?"

"Believe me, you'll recognize it."

"Mike, I can't leave you. What if you need my help?"

He gave her a swift, hard kiss and steered her back inside the room. "Just stay here, okay? If I need help, you can go out the window and yell for it."

It was probably only one of the Boychuks' friends coming for an early visit. Or maybe Esther had changed her mind about the bingo caller. Or maybe it was some salesman or some canvasser. And even if it was a whole battalion of Witlock's henchmen there was no way Rebecca was going to let Mike face them alone.

The moment he turned around, she pulled on her baggy sweatshirt. Her jeans were still damp from the washing she had given them yesterday but she wriggled into them anyway, hopping from one foot to the other as she followed Mike into the hall.

He snapped shut the stud on his jeans, picked up a crumpled T-shirt and pulled it roughly over his head as he walked toward the back door. He paused to one side of it and called out, "Yeah? Who's there?"

Rebecca pressed herself against the wall and held her breath.

"Prentice. Open up."

"Is that one of Witlock's men?" she whispered.

He twisted around, a scowl on his face. "I thought I told you to stay put."

"I couldn't do that. Do you need help? Do you want me to fetch Sly and Otto? Or call the police?"

The doorknob rattled. A gruff command came from the other side. "Unlock the door, Hogan."

"Aw, hell," he muttered, reaching for the latch.

The man slipped inside and closed the door behind him. He pushed a pair of dark glasses onto the top of his streaked blond hair, then tightened the knot in the sleeves of the sweater he wore draped over his shoulders. In his Bermuda shorts and L.L. Bean deck shoes he looked more like a yuppie on vacation than a criminal.

But then so had Trevor, and he'd had a gun. Rebecca inched backward.

"I want your butt back in Chicago," the man said.

"Have you made the arrangements I asked for?"

He nodded curtly.

"Then I'll leave by noon, like I already said." Mike crossed his arms over his chest. "What's the matter, Prentice? Don't you trust me?"

"We let you get the woman out of town, but it's been three days. Witlock might get impatient."

"I already told him I'd be back by tonight."

"We have a deal, Hogan. Don't forget the consequences, to everyone, if you screw this up."

There was no mistaking the threat in Prentice's tone, or the flash of fear on Mike's face. Soundlessly Rebecca kept backing away. She waited until she was around the corner, then raced for the stairs, taking them two at a time.

She skidded to a stop in the hallway, narrowly avoiding a collision with a yawning Otto.

"Hey, there, Rebecca," he said, smoothing his checkered shirt into his pants. "Is breakfast ready?"

"Otto," she gasped.

"What's wrong?"

"We have to call the police. Mike's in trouble."

His gray eyes bored into hers for a moment. Then he reached out a gnarled fist and pounded once on the door across from them. "Get up, Sly."

There was a muffled grunt. "It's too early."

"Something's happened. The boy's in trouble."

Feet hit the floor. Less than five seconds later Sly appeared in his paisley dressing gown, his white hair flying wildly around his head, a shotgun cradled in the crook of his arm.

Rebecca's eyes widened. "I don't want anyone to get hurt."

Otto took her elbow. "It's only loaded with rock salt. Sly uses it to scare away the varmints that chew up Esther's vegetable garden."

"It works on all kinds of varmints," Sly said, falling into step on her other side. "Now what kind of trouble is Mike in?"

"Did he tell you about Witlock?"

"The guy in Chicago?"

"I guess he did," she said. "Someone came to the door. He knew Mike had brought me here."

Sly moved in front of her, blocking her from going down the stairs. "Otto, call the cops. This time I'm not playing along with him."

Otto reversed direction, heading back to the room he had come from.

Rebecca felt her pulse trip. "Oh, we have to help. What if they don't get here before Prentice hurts him—"

"Who?" Sly demanded. "Who did you say?"

"Uh, he said his name was Prentice."

"Did you hear that, Otto?"

"Yup." He had stopped where he was.

"I didn't see a gun, but I didn't know that last man had one either before he pulled it out—"

"It's a safe bet Prentice has a gun, all right," Sly said, cracking open his shotgun and eyeing the barrels. "But I don't think he's about to use it on anyone here."

Rebecca darted around him. "All right, you two can stand around and discuss it all you want, but I don't intend to let Mike face this on his own. Give me that thing."

Sly stared at her outstretched hand. "I forgot to reload it

after I scared off that gopher last week. Both barrels are empty.''

''Then call the police, dammit!''

Sly's bushy white eyebrows practically met his hairline. ''Calm down, girl. They're already here.''

''What are you talking about? Otto hasn't had a chance to call anyone.''

''That Prentice,'' Otto said, reversing direction once again. ''He's a cop.''

''Then he's after Mike. I've got to give him a chance to get away—''

The brothers each caught one of her arms before she could lunge down the stairs. ''Mike's working for him,'' Sly said. ''I don't know the details, but it's got something to do with what's going on back in Chicago.''

Sounds of raised voices drifted up from the back of the house.

''The boy's not too happy about the situation. He doesn't particularly like the law.''

Rebecca's head swiveled from Sly to Otto. ''Prentice is a policeman?''

''Uh-huh.''

''And Mike's working for him?''

''Yup.''

''Then he's not in danger.''

''Not from Prentice.''

Of course. Given what she now knew about Mike's background she should have figured this out herself, too. Maybe she would have if there'd been enough time. Of course Mike wouldn't have turned back to crime. He had good reasons for not liking the police, but he had even better reasons for hating criminals like Witlock who moved in the same substrata of society as the drug dealer who had caused Jeannie's death.

He really was a good man. He had been all along. She should have trusted her instincts from the start.

In the next instant Mike appeared at the foot of the stairs.

He glanced upward, then froze. "What the hell is going on? Sly, what are you doing with that gun?"

The blond man was right on his heels. He took one look at Rebecca and the Boychuks, then reached behind his back and whipped out a black handgun. Adopting a semicrouch behind a bookshelf, he leveled the pistol at Sly. "Drop your weapon and let the woman go."

In horror Rebecca realized what the policeman must have assumed. "No!" she cried. "Don't shoot!"

Mike had already moved in front of him to block his aim. "Put it away before you make a bigger fool of yourself, Prentice. Sly's on her side."

Immediately the policeman tipped the pistol at the ceiling, straightening from his crouch. "I presume these are your friends?"

Her knees wobbling, Rebecca sank down onto the top step. "Are you really a policeman?"

A small leather rectangle appeared in his hand. He flipped it open with a practiced movement. "Bruce Prentice, Special Task Force on Organized Crime."

She stared, then shook her head as she finally recognized the blond man. "You dug up my street. And you were in that pickup truck at the grocery store." Her gaze moved to Mike. "And you've been working for the police all along. You let me think you were a criminal, but you weren't." Some of the relief she had felt at the discovery was turning to confusion. "Why didn't you tell me the truth in the first place?"

"He was instructed to tell no one." The policeman tucked his pistol into the waistband at the back of his Bermuda shorts and adjusted the dangling sweater to conceal it. "Your involvement was an unfortunate accident, but at least the damage is under control now. Hogan's cowboy tactics turned out to be the best way to maintain his cover as well as get you to safety. We've checked you out, and decided you don't pose a security risk—"

"Checked me out? What does that mean?"

With a flick of his wrist he glanced at his watch. "I'll let Hogan explain. I have to meet with the locals in ten minutes. Hogan," he snapped, turning to Mike, "I want you back in position by tonight. No later. At this critical stage we don't want to have any surprises or raise Witlock's suspicions." He walked to the front door, then paused, bringing his sunglasses back over his eyes and assuming a negligent, relaxed posture. By the time he had stepped outside he appeared once more to be nothing but a yuppie tourist.

As the screen door banged into place all eyes turned back to Mike.

He rubbed his knee. "Prentice is arranging for the local police to have a cruiser in the vicinity and to swing by the house on a regular basis, but he agrees with me that Witlock won't track Rebecca here."

"What did he mean when he said he'd checked me out?"

"He investigated your background and your reputation to make sure you wouldn't jeopardize his investigation."

"That's insulting."

"That's cops."

There were dozens of thoughts beginning to bubble to the surface of her roiling mind, but one dominated the rest. "I really was right about you from the start. About everything. You are and you always have been a basically good person."

"Don't look at me like that. I'm not some kind of hero."

"You deliberately made me think the worst."

"I couldn't say anything—"

"What do you mean, you couldn't say anything?" Two round spots of color burned in her cheeks. "What about last night? Didn't that make any difference?"

Sly cleared his throat and shifted the shotgun to the other arm. "Excuse me, folks. I'll just go put this away." He nudged his brother forward as he retreated. "Why don't you go start the coffee?"

"Not me. I want to hear about last night."

The next nudge wasn't gentle.

Recovering his balance, Otto loped down the stairs.

Mike raked his fingers through his hair, then rubbed the stubble on his cheeks. This wasn't how he'd imagined spending his last morning with Rebecca. "Give me a chance to explain."

Rebecca tightened her arms around her legs, hunching her shoulders. From the kitchen came the sounds of running water and clunking pots.

A moment later Sly reappeared, with his clothes and minus his shotgun. He squeezed Rebecca's shoulder lightly as he passed, then stopped and fixed Mike with a steady look. "You better treat her right, boy. Not many women would be willing to take a shotgun to a cop for you."

"What!"

"That's not exactly what happened," she protested.

"Otto and I'll take our coffee down at the garage," Sly said, heading for the kitchen. "You two have some talking to do."

Mike listened to the sound of the inevitable argument from the kitchen. Five minutes later Otto and Sly had said goodbye, wished him luck when he returned to Chicago, and were on their way downtown.

Rebecca hadn't moved. She was still huddled on the top step, her brow furrowed. If anything, her grip on her legs was even harder.

He patted his shirt and wished for a cigarette. Now that they had privacy and he had Prentice's permission, he didn't know how to start. "Do you want some coffee?"

She shook her head, pressing her chin to her knees.

Tentatively he put his foot on the bottom step. Leaning his forearms on his thigh, he tilted his head to gaze up at her. "I'm sorry, Rebecca."

"You lied to me."

"I never lied. I really am working for Witlock. I've been trying to get into his organization since I got out of prison. I'm there as a plant. The cops need me in order to shut Witlock down for good.'' He told her everything then, the whole complicated mess. He told her about his connection to Guido, about trying to get past the chauffeur's job and the stress of being caught between two sides. While he spoke, he climbed the stairs until he was standing directly in front of her, his face level with hers. ''You're a kind, decent woman,'' he finished. ''I'm sorry for involving you. It was my fault from the start. Once Witlock and his crew are behind bars you'll be free to go back home.''

''And what about you?''

''You already know what I'll do.''

''The empty highway. The next horizon.''

''That's right.''

''Why can't you quit and let Prentice finish things without you? I know you want to bring Witlock and his kind to justice, but you're risking your life.''

''I told you I'm no hero, Rebecca. I'm not risking my life out of some sense of justice. I'm in this for my freedom.''

''But you've served your time. You don't have to—''

''My sentence isn't over. Prentice got me released early and promised me my freedom as long as I delivered Witlock. That's the only reason I'm involved.''

''He can't hold you to that. You were innocent. You shouldn't have been in prison in the first place.''

''And you're an idealist. Prentice and his friends don't care whether I'm guilty or not. To them a deal is a deal. And I mean to hold them to it.''

''But you could launch an appeal, get a new trial.''

''If there wasn't any evidence of my innocence five years ago, there won't be any hope of finding some now. I'd rather take my chances with Witlock than risk even one more minute behind bars.''

''Your freedom means that much to you.''

''It means everything. It's what kept me going for the last five years.''

Slowly she raised her head and met his eyes. "You told Sly and Otto. You could have told me."

"There wasn't a chance—"

"There were any number of chances," she said, her voice hardening. "You've played me for a fool. All this time you knew how I was trying to come to terms with what you were doing. You knew how I felt about it, yet you continued the charade."

"I had my reasons."

"Well, did you have a good laugh? Did you think you'd put one over on the stupid little schoolteacher—"

"It wasn't like that."

"Oh. Right. I had to be 'checked out' first. You had to find out whether I could be trusted."

"Let me explain."

She moved suddenly, springing to her feet and slipping past him.

He caught up to her at the base of the stairs. "I always trusted you. It was myself I didn't trust."

Her eyes were brimming. "What kind of game were you playing with my emotions last night when you told me the truth about your murder conviction? Why couldn't you have told me all of it then?"

"I didn't mean to tell you as much as I did."

"Is that supposed to make me feel better? What about afterward?" She swallowed hard. "After we made love? Why couldn't you tell me then?"

"It didn't make any difference."

"How can you say that?" she cried. "You let me practically beg you not to go back. You could have told me the truth."

"It was for your own good. We're all wrong for each other, Rebecca. I've only brought you trouble. It doesn't matter whether you know I was innocent, or that I was working for the police. In the eyes of everyone else in your world I'll always be just an ex-con drifter."

Blinking hard behind her glasses, she poked her index finger at the center of his chest. "Don't give me that tough-guy, hard-as-nails act anymore, Mike Hogan. It just... doesn't...work," she said, emphasizing each word with another poke at his chest.

He stumbled backward. "Will you think about it for a minute? What would have happened if you had known all of this before?"

"For starters I wouldn't have needed to spend these last few days wondering whether I was going completely insane."

"What else?"

"I wouldn't have needed to agonize about the kind of man you are."

"That's important to you, isn't it? The kind of man I am?"

"Yes, it is."

"Why?"

"That's the type of woman I am, remember? The solid, respectable stick-in-the-mud who can't forget about her ideals of right and wrong."

"The type of woman who would never neck in a park or get hot thinking about making out on a motorcycle. Or have a fling with a killer or a criminal."

"But you're not a killer. And you're not a criminal. Can't you see that it *does* make a difference? It makes a *hell* of a lot of difference."

He grasped her hand in his and moved it behind her back. She placed her other palm on his chest and he grasped that one, too, pulling her against his body as he had last night.

But it wasn't like last night.

"It makes no difference," he gritted, his face hovering over hers. "I'm still going to leave. You're still going back to your cozy little home and I'm going to hit the highway with my Harley."

"But—"

"I never wanted to get involved with you, Rebecca. I knew

that a woman like you wouldn't fit into the plans I have for my life.''

''Yet you kept coming back. You did want me. You brought Princess over so you could see me, didn't you?''

''I brought the dog over because Witlock ordered me to.''

''What?''

''He ordered me to. He was setting me up, but I didn't know it. That's the only reason I came back.''

She wrenched herself from his grasp. ''I thought you wanted—''

''I wanted to stay away from you!'' he thundered. ''Is that so difficult for you to understand?''

Something was breaking inside. She felt it snap and shrivel as she finally listened to what he was saying. The man she loved. She had never told him she loved him. If she told him now, he probably would tell her that it didn't make any difference.

And it didn't, did it?

''I understand,'' she said finally. A numbness was settling over her, a welcome numbness that dulled the pain of her slowly cracking heart.

''Rebecca,'' he began.

''No.'' She held up her palm to stop his words. ''No, you did warn me, Mike.''

''I have to go back.''

They were both breathing hard, staring at each other across a distance of no more than five feet that seemed like five miles. Or five years. This was it. This was what it all had been leading up to. It had been doomed from the start. She watched numbly as Mike slowly began gathering his things. Less than ten minutes later he was ready to go.

For too many years time had passed too slowly. Now Mike wished that it would stand still. He picked up his jacket and walked to the door. ''You'll be all right here, Rebecca.''

She blinked hard, concentrating on a fold of her sweatshirt that she pleated between her fingers. "I'll be fine."

"The police will keep an eye on the house, and the Boychuks are pretty reliable."

"They've been very kind."

"Prentice will let you know when it's safe for you to go home."

"Yes."

"Are you going to phone Mrs. Barring about taking care of your place for you?"

"Oh." She pushed at her glasses. "I'd forgotten about that. Of course. I'll do that today."

He shrugged into his jacket. The leather creaked, then settled around his shoulders. "If the PTA or the school board gives you a rough time over your job, tell Prentice. He'll straighten things out."

"I hadn't thought of that, either."

"We've been kind of busy."

She met his eyes then. "Yes."

It slammed through him without warning, the urge to take her into his arms one last time, to feel her mouth soften under his, to hear that throaty cry she made when the tremors spread through her body.

"Rebecca..."

"No." She shook her head quickly. "Let's not get into all that again. I always knew it would end this way."

"I never wanted to hurt you."

"I know that, too."

He hadn't realized it would be this difficult to leave her, but this was what he had planned, after all. Well, maybe he hadn't planned the bedroom part. That had just happened, like lightning in a storm. Or spontaneous combustion. Quick, intense, inevitable. And over.

"I hope..." She paused to clear her throat. "I hope you get what you want, Mike. You deserve your freedom. You've had so much bad luck in your life it's about time things turned around.''

She was one classy lady. Now that she understood that this was for the best, there were no recriminations, no tears, no clinging. He should have known this was the way she would say goodbye. Then again, he'd never actually thought about how she would say goodbye. He'd never wanted to think about it.

Time wasn't standing still. He could feel the pressure to return to finish his job tearing at him. Part of him wanted to say the hell with it and carry this woman back to bed. But the rest of him knew that would only be delaying what they both knew had to happen.

A car passed by on the street. Mike turned his head to look out the screen and caught sight of a police cruiser, part of Prentice's arrangements to protect Rebecca. "I've got to go."

"Be careful," she said, her smile wobbly.

He nodded, unable to speak. No, he'd never guessed it would be this hard. Pushing open the door, he headed down the steps.

She followed him to the yard. "Mike, I—"

He paused, letting his helmet dangle from his hand. "What?"

"I…" Her gaze dropped to his bike, then moved to the empty street. "I wish you well."

Fitting on his sunglasses, he fixed her image in his mind. She had forgotten to put on her shoes again. Her bare toes curled into the lawn. A muggy breeze flattened her sweatshirt against her slender, delightfully curved figure. Wisps of her chestnut brown hair teased her cheeks and brushed the corners of her mouth.

Then before he could mess his life up any further by prolonging the battle between his reason and the rest of him, he did what he should have done in the first place those many weeks ago.

He got on his bike, gunned the engine and drove away.

Rebecca stood on the lawn until he was out of sight, until she could no longer hear the rumble of the Harley. Then slowly, holding herself stiffly, she went back into the house and locked the door.

"I will not fall apart," she said, lifting up her glasses to wipe the corners of her eyes. "I will not fall apart."

Resolutely she raised her chin. She would simply get through this the best she could. She had gotten through the deaths of her parents and the travesty of her marriage, so she would manage to get through this. No one spent the rest of their lives pining over unrequited love. It was so Victorian. So pathetic. So selfish.

Mike was risking his life for his freedom. He didn't love her. He had never wanted her to get close to him. He would never really let down the wall around his feelings. And she could never burden him with declarations of love. She had known, from the very beginning, from that very first motorcycle ride, that there would be no future for them. They'd had a few intense days together, a few hours of passionate lovemaking, but that was as far as it would go.

This had been like a dream, an adventure in what was otherwise a respectable, stable, ordinary life. Once the police had Witlock and his gang, she would go back to that life. And in the autumn there would be another classroom full of eager young faces, another set of budding personalities to get to know, new challenges to meet. The summer was half-over. She should be already anticipating the new school year. Autumn was usually her favorite season.

So she'd had a fling. She was thirty years old. Maybe it was about time she'd had a fling.

"Who are you kidding," she muttered, feeling a tear spill onto her cheek. This hadn't been some cheap, meaningless affair. This was *love*.

Why did it have to be him? *Why him?* They were opposites. He had lived hard while she was sheltered. He cherished freedom, she security. He was tough and she was soft. He was...

he was six foot three of firm muscle and swagger. He had eyes the true blue of an August sky with laugh lines etched into the corners. He had a smile that was pure charm, lips that could be gentle or possessive or passionate…

He was gone.

All pretense of control cracked and fell away. With a sob that was wrenched from her very soul, she buried her face in her hands and finally let the tears come.

Chapter 14

Beyond the curving driveway, the lush expanse of grass gleamed silver in the moonlight, and the formal flower beds were leached of their carefully plotted colors. Mike's boots thudded on the pavement as he made no attempt to hide his approach to the floodlit house.

From the darkness came the metallic click of a gun being cocked. "Hold it right...hey, Hogan. Is that you?"

Mike stopped where he was and turned his head. A stocky figure in army fatigues loomed toward him. "Hello, Guido. Surprised to see me?"

He slung the strap of his gun onto his shoulder and moved closer. "The boss said you'd be back tonight. Where you been?"

"I had to take care of some private business."

It took a moment for Guido to remember. "Hey, that stuff with your woman wasn't personal, Hogan. Hope there's no hard feelings."

With an effort Mike controlled the sudden surge of anger. "Whose idea was it to go after her, Guido?"

"Trevor's," he said immediately. "Was the boss ever steamed when he found out."

"I wasn't too pleased myself."

"I kinda thought you were gone for good."

"I wouldn't want to miss the action." He resumed his progress toward the front entrance. "Is everything still on for next week?"

"Sure. No sweat. It's just like the boss planned—"

A sudden loud barking cut off his words in midsentence. From the front entrance a little gray fur ball raced down the driveway toward them.

Guido unslung his gun. "The mutt got loose again. I'm going to shoot that thing one of these days."

The dog headed straight for Mike, barking and wagging its tail so hard its back end turned around. Scrambling in a circle, it leapt for Mike's hand, placing a sloppy lick on his fingers.

"Jeez," he muttered, wiping it off on his pants. "Get down, Bootsie. I don't have any beer this time."

"You shouldn't have bothered coming back, Hogan."

At the familiar tone, Mike glanced up. Trevor Dodge was lounging against a pillar on one side of the main entrance. Stepping over the gyrating Bootsie, Mike advanced on him. "Was that why you did it, Trevor? Did you want to provoke me?"

"I don't know what you're talking about."

He grabbed the front of Trevor's alligator-emblazoned polo shirt and twisted until he heard a seam pop. This man had held a gun on Rebecca. The image pushed Mike dangerously close to releasing the rein on his temper.

Trevor's Adam's apple bobbed. "Get your hands off me."

"Hey, come on, Mike. Let him go."

Slowly he eased his grip. "You went too far this time, Trevor. The matter of the woman was between me and Witlock."

He smoothed the front of his shirt. "I don't know why you were so hot to get her out of town. From the looks of her she could have benefited from some attention from a man like me—"

The first blow caught Trevor in the stomach, doubling him over. The second caught him under the chin. Mike shook out his hand, not even feeling the stinging knuckles as he watched Trevor smash backward into a pillar and crumple to the ground.

Guido leapt forward, clamping a restraining hand on Mike's arm.

Bootsie yipped and darted back into the house just as the sound of slow clapping came through the doorway.

Witlock, in all his bulk, was silhouetted in the opening, leisurely applauding. "How noble, Hogan. Now if you're finished, we have some things to discuss." He moved inside. "My office. Now."

Mike shook off Guido's hand and followed.

Witlock settled behind his desk. He tossed a candy to Bootsie, then steepled his fingers and leaned back. Over the rounded cheeks his black eyes probed Mike's blue ones. "What do you suppose I should do with you?"

Crossing his arms over his chest, Mike strove to portray a calmness he didn't feel. His blood was still pumping from the satisfaction of striking Trevor, but he knew the next few moments could be crucial. "I'm a damn good driver," he said finally. "I can fix anything with a motor and make sure it runs better and faster than before. But you already know that I'll do what you ask, since I've been waxing your cars and walking your dog for months."

"You left town."

"Trevor went after my woman. You had guaranteed her safety as long as I measured up. Trust has to go both ways, Mr. Witlock."

Color rose in his face, looking a sickly purple next to the canary-yellow ascot. "I told you that was a mistake."

"That's all the more reason you need someone like me in your organization. I've got brains."

Witlock studied him in silence while Bootsie cracked another humbug between her teeth. Gradually the purple flush faded and the fleshy cheeks relaxed. "You know, Hogan, I didn't really trust you before this. I tend to be suspicious of a man who won't react when he's provoked." He leaned back in order to open the top drawer of his desk. From it he withdrew a large handgun and pointed the muzzle toward Mike.

Sweat trickled down the back of Mike's neck as he forced himself to remain motionless. "If you kill me you can't use me. You're too good a businessman to do something like that."

With a chuckle that vibrated his pendulous chins Witlock reversed the gun in his hand and tossed it at Mike. "You do have brains."

Automatically he caught the weapon in midair. A quick check of the chamber showed it was unloaded. "So am I in or not?"

"You're in, you're in. The plans for next week haven't changed. I want you to be Guido's backup. You'll be right where you'll do the most good."

"That pacing isn't going to do you any good," Otto mumbled as Rebecca made another circuit of the living room.

"Leave the girl alone," Sly said, reaching for the remote control. "You're worried, too."

He slumped back into his favorite chair and tossed another kernel of popcorn into his mouth. "Put on the ball game. Boston's playing the Royals."

"You never watch baseball. And that's the second bowl of popcorn you've gone through tonight."

"She makes good popcorn."

"You're worried, you old goat."

Otto jammed another handful in his mouth and refused to answer.

Sly clicked on the television.

Rebecca paused at the screen door, looking out at the deepening shadows. Distant flashes of silent heat lightning strobed beyond the roofs and treetops, adding a sense of expectancy to a day that was already rife with it. A dark green sedan was parked across the road. It had been there since noon, taking over from the squad cars that had been passing by as regularly as clockwork since Mike had left a week ago. The sky flashed again. Something was going to happen.

It was scheduled for today. She had managed to get that much out of the tight-lipped Prentice before he had disappeared. Sometime today that trap should be sprung. The crooks should be caught. The investigation should be over.

Slapping her hand against the door frame, she pivoted and paced toward the kitchen. This waiting was going to drive her mad.

"You going to make some more popcorn?" Otto called.

She nodded, grateful for something to do, no matter how brief the task.

"I sure would like some of that lemonade you made," Sly added. "I haven't tasted any that good since Betty Lou moved to Houston."

"Betty Lou wasn't the one who made lemonade," Otto said. "That was Rhonda."

"No, Rhonda was the one who starched your coveralls."

"Only because you told her to."

"No, I told her to starch your shorts."

"Ha. So you're the one..."

After a week with the Boychuks, Rebecca was accustomed to the sound of their bickering. Generally it helped to distract her the same way the minor housekeeping tasks distracted her. They didn't really need a housekeeper, though. Both men were surprisingly competent in the kitchen and cleaned up after themselves with no hesitation. They just seemed to need company. It was too bad that neither of them had remarried. But it seemed as if loneliness was a fact of life—

"Oh, God," she moaned. The tears struck once again,

swiftly and unexpectedly. That was the way it had been all week. Ever since Mike had left.

Impatiently she wiped at the corners of her eyes. Was she going to start measuring time by his departure? Would everything in her life now be remembered as before Mike or after Mike?

The Boychuks had been wonderfully understanding, in their unique, crusty manner. Still, at times she caught a glimpse of pity in their faces when they thought she wasn't looking. Sly had even reminded her, gently, of the reasons behind Mike's desire to travel. He had meant well, of course. Who could have failed to make the connection between her reddened eyes and Mike's departure? And he was right to think that a good deal of her tears were selfish ones. Yet today her anxiety had a different focus. She had always known that she would lose him. Today she would find out exactly how.

"Oh, be safe," she whispered, turning her gaze to the window over the sink.

The breeze was freshening, billowing the curtains as a puff of heavy, moist air blew in. The hot spell was poised to break. All day clouds had been building and now the atmosphere was charged with the impending storm.

The first kernel popped, flying out of the electric popper and skittering across the counter. At the sudden noise Rebecca jumped, forgetting for the moment what she had been doing here. Another kernel followed the first before she grabbed a bowl and placed it under the spout to catch the rest. The popping increased, growing in frequency until the rat-a-tat sound was like some kind of machine gun.

Clenching her jaw, she compelled herself to focus on the popcorn. She couldn't help Mike. She couldn't do anything except stand here and wait. Or pace and wait. Or go crazy.

"Rebecca!" Otto called, his voice hoarse. "You better get in here."

She yanked the cord on the popper and ran back to the living room.

Sly had switched the channel from the ball game. He had tuned in the news.

"...in Chicago today. It was the culmination of several months of an ongoing investigation into the activities of a large organization that has been alleged to have participated in numerous criminal ventures."

"Listen to the twenty-dollar words," Sly muttered. "A crook's a crook."

"They don't want to be sued," Otto said.

"You're not an expert—"

"Quiet!" Rebecca ordered, snatching the remote from Sly's hand. She perched on the sofa beside him and turned up the volume.

"...apprehended attempting to hijack an armored truck that was transferring cash and securities to an undisclosed destination. The value of the shipment is estimated to be approximately seventeen and a half million dollars."

"Whooee!"

"Shh!"

"...of the suspects endeavored to flee on foot but were quickly apprehended after a brief gun battle with police."

Neither Sly nor Otto made a comment this time. Like Rebecca, they were leaning forward, waiting for the rest.

"None of the officers involved were injured, however one suspect is dead and two more have been hospitalized with gunshot wounds. Now, in other news, a threat of a trade war is developing over the softwood lumber imports—"

"The boy's all right then," Sly exclaimed. "He was with the police."

"He was undercover," Rebecca said, pressing the mute on the remote. "He was with the other side."

"Now don't go getting yourself all worked up for nothing."

The phone rang. Springing to her feet, Rebecca was the first one to reach it.

"Ms. Stanford?" It was Prentice's voice.

"What's happened? Is Mike all right?"

"The operation was a complete success. You are free to return home whenever it's convenient. I appreciate your co-operation in this matter—"

"Is he all right?"

There was a brief silence from the other end of the line. It only lasted a second, but in that time Rebecca felt her heart stop. Finally the answer came. "Yes."

"Oh, thank God," she breathed.

"He should be out of the hospital by tomorrow."

She fumbled the receiver, her palm suddenly too moist to hold it. "What?"

Otto and Sly rose at the same time, crossing the room to stand on either side of her.

"It was an accident. He was struck when a bullet ricocheted, but his prognosis is good. Overall, our success exceeded our expectations."

"Who shot him?" she demanded.

"As I said, it was an accident. One of our officers—"

"Haven't you done enough to him? Dear Lord, hasn't he endured enough? All he wants is what he should have had anyway, what he deserves."

"Ms. Stanford—"

"You used him. You and your disgusting masquerades, you don't care who gets hurt. All you see is your job, your rigid picture of right and wrong. He's a person, damn you. A human being. You had no right to force him to take those risks. If the police had done their job right five years ago he wouldn't have needed to risk his life like this. He's a good man. He's one of the most decent people I've ever known, but every chance he's ever had has been stolen away from him...."

Sly took the receiver from her and slipped a comforting arm around her shoulders. "Prentice? Sly Boychuk here. I'd be obliged if you told me just what the hell is going on."

The flight back to Chicago was bumpy as the plane fought its way through the turbulence left over from the previous night's storm. Rebecca shook her head at the flight attendant's offer of coffee, clutching her purse more tightly in her lap as the plane hit another air pocket.

Mike had been shot. The bullet had ricocheted from the armored truck and had struck him in the left arm. It had passed through the fleshy part above his elbow. If it had been four inches to the right it would have missed. If it had been four inches to the left it would have gone through his heart.

She drew her lower lip between her teeth, trying to remind herself that he was fine. It was over. Really over.

Mike was all right. He was finally free. Otto had checked with the hospital this morning, but Mike hadn't even stayed the night there before he'd left.

Where was he now? Was he riding in the rain? Was he cold? Wet? Did his knee bother him in the dampness? How far would he get on his first day of freedom? He had talked of seeing the ocean. Which one would he head for first?

"I hope you're happy," she whispered. "You deserve it."

It was over. Witlock would never be a threat to anyone else again. He hadn't been on the scene of the attempted hijacking. He had been in his office on the estate when the police had arrived armed with search warrants and arrest warrants. It had been all so civilized, from what Sly had related after he had spoken with Prentice. Witlock had been advised of his rights, taken into custody and was conferring with his lawyer when the heart attack had occurred.

Witlock had never been convicted of anything, and he never would be. The heart attack had been fatal.

All this misery, she thought, looking out the window at the murky clouds. All this effort and scheming and danger and the man was about to die of a heart attack anyway.

Otto had had a typically acerbic comment about that final ironic twist. "That'll save the taxpayers a trial."

She was going to miss those two old sweethearts. Their goodbyes at the airport had been brief, but their eyes had been suspiciously moist when she had kissed each of them on the cheek and told them to come and visit her if they ever got the chance.

It seemed as if all she did lately was say goodbye.

The seat belt light flashed on as the plane banked for landing. Rebecca straightened her dress and patted her hair into place. It was raining here, too. The gray drops streaked down the window as the plane reentered the clouds and touched down.

She slung her knapsack over her shoulder and walked through the terminal, oblivious to the incongruous picture she presented with her denim jacket and her dainty dress. The windshield wipers of the taxi she took slapped monotonously as it splashed through the streets. She stared straight ahead as she passed the grocery store parking lot with its few scattered shopping carts dripping listlessly. Andrew's plywood skateboard ramp was rain darkened and deserted. Puddles dappled the fresh coat of asphalt that covered the pavement in front of her driveway.

"This is the address you gave me, lady."

She paid her fare and stepped out, not caring about the drops from the willow leaves that were spattering her dress as she watched the taxi pull away. She turned to look at her house. It used to be a secure, cozy refuge from the rest of the world, someplace where she could draw her blinds and indulge her repressed passions in skimpy lingerie and macho movies. She had returned, yet she was no longer the same.

Maybe it would have been better if she had never opened her door that night. If she hadn't invited Mike back, if she hadn't gone for that Sunday picnic she wouldn't have known...

She wouldn't have known love.

It still hurt. It would always hurt, but Mike had given her more than simply the pain. She had finally put her failed marriage behind her, secure in the new confidence she felt as a woman. Her rigid ideas of right and wrong were no longer as rigid. When you loved someone, you learned to accept them for what they were. After all, at the end it had been Mike himself who had forced the barriers between them. He had deceived her deliberately, had carried on his charade for the sole purpose of maintaining his distance. Well, he had his distance now, although as she'd told him once on a morning so long ago, the people you loved stayed with you in your heart.

Slowly she walked to the porch and unlocked the door. Even if she'd had the chance to live the past month over again, she wouldn't change a thing.

It had been a wild, exhilarating ride.

Mike sat on his bike and watched her close the door behind her. The drizzle was beading up on his jacket and making tiny rivulets on the black leather, seeping into his jeans and chilling his skin. His arm throbbed dully beneath the fresh bandage, his eyes burned from too many sleepless nights. Everything he owned was stuffed into the duffel bag that was strapped behind the seat. He had money and road maps and had topped off the gas tank when he'd left Prentice's office in the early hours of the morning.

What was he doing here? It wasn't raining in California.

He'd made it as far as the outskirts of the city before he'd screeched down the nearest ramp and turned around.

"Damn," he muttered, twisting the throttle enough to nose the bike under the weeping willow. He was an idiot. Had he really thought that he would be able to turn his back on what she had come to mean to him?

He shut off the motor and grabbed his duffel bag. He could be halfway to St. Louis by now. He could be wherever he wanted.

He wanted to be here.

Because this was the place she was.

It should have been simple. It would have been simple, if not for the inescapable fact that he would never leave her behind.

He wanted to be here. Or anywhere. As long as she was with him.

Roughly he pulled off his helmet, then ran his fingers distractedly through his flattened hair as he crossed the lawn. After what he had put her through, the best thing she could do would be to slam the door in his face. He had a lot of nerve showing up like this. She wanted to get on with her life. They had already said their goodbyes.

Who was he kidding? If she slammed the door in his face he would probably break the door down.

He strode up the steps and paused on her front porch. The scent of wet petunias drifted up to him. The porch swing moved slightly in the breeze, its chains creaking. What was he doing? This was crazy. Stupid. Hopeless.

"Aw, hell," he growled, closing his hand into a fist.

At the knock on her door, Rebecca sighed. It was probably Mrs. Barring. She had phoned her from the Boychuks to thank her for taking care of her car and her house while she was gone. She should really thank her for having Andrew mow the lawn and water the flowers, too, but she wasn't up to facing her right now.

The knock came again, louder this time.

She took off her glasses, polishing the rain-spattered lenses on her skirt as she walked to the door. She turned the knob, then slipped her glasses back on.

She froze. No. It couldn't be. This was a dream, an illusion conjured out of her shattered heart.

There was a man on her porch. A big man. The top of his head was almost level with the door frame. His midnight-black hair was damp and tousled, his sinfully handsome face, with its lean cheeks and shadowed lines was wet from the rain. Broad, powerful shoulders stretched the glistening leather jacket. A helmet and a duffel bag dangled from his hand.

"No," she whispered.

Eyelashes sparkling with raindrops framed a gaze as true blue as an August sky. "Can I come in?"

She had thought never to hear that voice again. Its deep, rich tones vibrated along nerves that felt scraped raw.

"Rebecca?"

She backed away from him, struggling to keep her conflicting emotions under control. Joy and anger, relief and hopelessness. She had managed to hold herself together during the trip home. She had even thought she would be able to cope with the empty house. She hadn't thought she would see him again. And lose him again.

He tossed his helmet and duffel bag inside and stepped over the threshold. Then he stood there, dripping onto her floor.

"What…" She had to clear her throat, dismayed by the huskiness of her voice. "What happened? Why haven't you left?"

"I did leave. I left at three o'clock this morning, as soon as I could get out of the hospital and finish my report to Prentice." He paused long enough to kick the door shut with his heel. "But I didn't get far."

"Why not?"

The zipper rasped as he undid his jacket.

"Was it the weather?"

He dropped the leather garment carelessly to one side and shook his head. "This rain wouldn't have stopped me."

"Has something gone wrong?"

"Prentice came through with my freedom. Witlock's dead, his organization is rounded up and the last I heard, Trevor's talking his head off in the hopes of getting a lighter sentence, so Prentice doesn't even need me to testify."

Her gaze fell to the bandage that peeked below the sleeve of his shirt. "Is it your arm? Is it too sore to manage the bike?"

He flexed his arm. "It's fine."

"Then why…"

"Why am I here?"

She nodded, unable to string any more words together coherently. Just the sight of him had ripped open the pain of their last parting. She wouldn't be able to survive it again. Next time she really would fall apart.

He smiled. It was one of his endearing, naughty-boy chip-toothed lethal-weapon smiles.

And that's when she knew she was lost.

That's when she knew she would endure anything if only she could touch him one last time.

He read the message in her eyes. Before she could move, he had one arm wrapped around her back. Lifting her off the floor, he covered her mouth with his.

His heat burned through his wet clothes. He braced his legs, clasping her to his body, thigh to thigh, belly to belly. She felt the moisture from his jeans soak the front of her dress, tingling through to her skin. Breathless, she locked her arms behind his neck and sank into the whirlpool of his kiss.

Once more, she thought. One last time. Then she would let him go.

She wriggled downward until her toes touched the floor, then held his face between her palms, putting all the love she felt into the kiss she returned. His skin was damp from the rain, his cheeks slick. He used his lips and his tongue and his teeth, possessing her mouth, driving out all thoughts but those of him.

He backed her across the room. She pulled up his shirt, skimming it over his head and down his arms before she tossed it aside. Her fingers touched the edge of the bandage on his arm and her heart clenched. She had almost lost him. She *would* lose him, but at least it wouldn't be like that. With a sob she spread her fingers over his chest, reaching for the steady beat of his heart.

Her glasses hit the table, her hairpins hit the floor. A button popped, a hook ripped as he opened the back of her dress. His hands eased inside, sliding over skin that screamed for his touch. Nimbly he unhooked the clasp of her bra, then bent down to warm the skin he exposed.

The back of her knees hit the arm of the sofa. She tumbled

backward onto the cushions, her feet in the air. Mike made use of her position to pull off what was left of her clothes.

He gazed down at her, his face glowing with passion, his cheeks flushed, his lips moist. One by one he kicked off his boots. His eyes held hers with a promise she knew he would fulfill as he brought his hands to the front of his jeans and unsnapped the stud.

Her heart would break. She knew it but she didn't care. Recklessly she held out her arms.

Mike took what she offered and gave her more than she asked. As he joined his body with hers he felt the wonder of that first time all over again. This was the knowledge that had come to him as he'd waited in the rain outside her house. This was what had made him turn his bike around and reevaluate all the dreams he'd thought he'd had. This was why it was so different with Rebecca when they were making love.

They were making *love*.

Squeezing his eyes shut, he pressed his face to her neck. The tremors were already starting in her thighs. He moved, taking her higher, shouting to her, without words, the feelings that she had uncovered in his heart.

He had fought it, but it was too late. It might have been too late from the moment he had seen her caramel-warm eyes peering out at him through the crack in her front door all those weeks ago. He might have been a loner then, but not any longer. He had found his mate, the other half of his soul.

They belonged together. Neither would ever be complete without the other.

As the last shudders faded, he felt the tears on her cheeks. He pulled back to look at her face. "Rebecca?"

She shook her head quickly, her lashes sparkling with the tears that continued to fill her eyes. "Damn you!"

"What?"

Her fist struck his chest. "Damn you! Why did you have to come back?"

He enveloped her hand with his. "I couldn't stay away."

She pushed at him until he rolled onto the floor. Dashing the tears from her eyes, she grabbed a crocheted afghan from the back of the sofa and leapt to her feet.

"Rebecca, we have to talk."

Hunching her shoulders, she wrapped the afghan around her nakedness and moved out of reach.

Mike snatched up his jeans and yanked them on, then pushed himself to his feet. "What is it? What's wrong?"

She sniffed, refusing to meet his eyes.

His gaze fell to the rest of their scattered clothing, to the dress with its missing buttons and torn hooks. A sickening fear twisted through his gut. It had happened so fast, so explosively. He hadn't thought… "Oh, God, Rebecca. I'm sorry. I didn't mean to hurt you."

Her laugh was more like a sob. "Didn't mean to hurt me?"

"I hadn't realized I was too rough."

She blinked, then shook her head quickly, clutching the blanket like a shield in front of her. "You mean the sex? Don't worry. That was fine. You've taught me well."

There was no mistaking the pain in her voice. He had done this to her. "Then what is it?"

"Who made you come back this time, Mike?"

"What are you talking about?"

"You never wanted to get involved. The only reason you came back before was because Witlock ordered you to bring the dog over."

"That's how it started. I told you that so you'd see how wrong we were for each other."

"We've been through this already. If that's why you're here again then you can—"

"I said that's how it *started*. But I think that even if Witlock hadn't given me that push, I would have come back on my own. I told you. I couldn't stay away."

"Why? So you can say goodbye all over again?" She rubbed her arms. "What kind of excuse are you going to use this time? How are you planning to push me out of your life again?''

"I was wrong."

"Wrong?" she cried. "You say goodbye, worry me half to death, get yourself shot, ride off into the sunset or the sunrise and then come here and smile that smile and I'm all over you like a bad rash."

"It just sort of happened."

"Do you have any idea what I've gone through? I thought I would manage without you. I thought I would be able to do the right thing, to wish you well with your freedom and watch you ride away again, but do you know something?" She whirled around, her hair flying over her shoulders. "I can't do it."

He took a tentative step closer. "Can't do what?"

"I can't let you go." Her lower lip trembled, but she lifted her chin and firmed her jaw. "I can't let you go, Mike. I know you've said over and over how you don't want a woman like me tying you down—"

"Rebecca," he began.

"No, let me finish. For the first time in my life I'm not going to do the right thing. I'm not going to be noble. I'm not going to be patient. I want it all." She wiped her nose with the back of her hand. "I want it all, Mike. I want a home with you. Whether it's my bungalow or some tiny, furnished apartment or a tent in the forest, it doesn't matter. And I want a family. Your baby, to hold in my arms and rock to sleep while you're in our bed, waiting to hold me in your arms. And I want a future."

His eyes burned. If he'd ever had any doubts about the wisdom of returning, they had just been forever laid to rest.

She strode over to where he had dropped his helmet. Drawing back her foot, she kicked it across the room. "So if you think you're going to get back on that bike and ride out of my life again, you're wrong. Because I'll come after you."

"You'd come after me?"

"Damn right! I'm not going to be left with my nose pressed to my windowpane, renting old movies and wondering why I'm alone."

He ground the heels of his hands against his eyes, feeling wetness on his skin that was no longer from the rain. Slowly he walked toward her. "You're not going to be alone, Rebecca."

"And another thing, I'm not some fragile..." She stopped suddenly and turned to face him. "What did you say?"

"I'm not leaving."

"But you told me—"

"I know what I said. I remembered every word of it while I was lying in the hospital bed last night. I turned it over and over in my mind until I was half-nuts. It wasn't until I was on the road toward everything I had convinced myself that I wanted that I finally saw the truth."

"What truth?"

He swallowed hard. "I'm not good with words. And I'm not good with expressing my feelings." He stepped closer. "This is all new to me, and I'll probably make a lot of mistakes along the way, but..."

She looked at him, just looked at him. Not judging, not condemning, just there for him, as she had been all along even when they were apart.

In his entire life, he had never spoken these words. He had never even heard them. Now he knew he had been saving them for Rebecca. "I love you."

In the silence that followed he could count his heartbeats and each rasping breath that he drew. He watched her face as she began to take in what he was saying. She wavered, raising her hand to press her knuckles to her mouth.

"I thought I wanted freedom, but I've never felt more free than when I was held in your arms. With you I feel as if I can do anything, go anywhere, be anyone. I could ride the open road to the next horizon for the rest of my life and never find what we have with each other. So if that's what people mean by love, then I never want to live without it again.''

Her tears had started anew. Only this time she was smiling. ''Oh, Mike.''

''I know it won't be easy for us. But Sly said he'd help me get a loan if I wanted, and I'm thinking about eventually opening a business like the Boychuks' here in Chicago. I'm good with cars.'' He held her gaze as he finally closed the distance between them. ''As long as you wouldn't mind being married to a man who works with his hands to make a living.''

She hiccuped, then licked at a tear that fell on her mouth. ''Is that a proposal?''

Reaching out, he wiped the moisture from her cheeks with the back of his hand. ''Yes.''

''Yes.''

He paused. ''Yes?''

She rubbed her cheek against his knuckles. ''I like the sound of that word.''

His heart thudded in his chest. ''You'll marry me?''

Grasping the edges of the blanket in each hand, she spread her arms wide and enveloped him in a trembling embrace. ''I love you, Mike Hogan. I'll go with you wherever you want. For the rest of our lives. Because as long as we're together, no matter where we are, we'll be home.''

Epilogue

That night was filled with wonder. There was so much to say, so much to show each other and so much lost time to make up for. There were no more threats or barriers or inhibitions to keep them apart anymore. They greeted the dawn with their mingled sighs, wrapped in each other's arms and in their newfound freedom of love.

Sometime before noon they decided to get dressed and go outside to sit on the porch swing. Robins twittered and darted across the glistening lawn, bees droned peacefully in the garden while wisps of cloud drifted across the fresh-washed sky like the promise of a new beginning.

The swing creaked as Mike pushed it into motion. He curved his arm around Rebecca's back, stroking his hand along the sleeve of her loose sweatshirt. Grinning, he walked his fingers up her arm and nudged the neckline toward her shoulder.

''Mmm,'' she mumbled, sliding her hand onto his thigh.

''Let's get married next week. We can have August for our honeymoon and still be back in time for September.''

"Mmm."

"Pay attention, woman. I'm trying to do the right thing here."

"Yeah?" She squeezed. "Tell me about the honeymoon."

"Oh, I thought we could laze around in some fancy hotel that has a king-size bed and satin sheets and maybe one of those hot tubs or whirlpool things. What do you think?"

She slid her hand higher, then wiggled her fingers. "I was thinking about taking a trip on your Harley."

He chuckled. "What else were you thinking about doing on that Harley?"

Tipping her head back she smiled up at him. "Come back inside and I'll show you."

"What kind of maternity leave do you have in your contract with the school board?"

"Why?"

"The way we're going, I'd say you're going to need it." He grasped her hand and lifted it to his lips, kissing each of the knuckles in turn. "So you want to go back in the house already?"

"Yeah," she whispered.

"Yoo-hoo! Mrs. Stanford?"

Rebecca turned her head, then sat up but didn't pull away from Mike. She smiled as she watched their visitor make her way up the steps and onto the porch. "Hello, Mrs. Barring. It's a beautiful morning, isn't it?"

Mrs. Barring halted in front of the swing, her gaze flicking to Mike then back to Rebecca. "Yes, the rain has finally stopped."

"Thank you so much for all you did while I was out of town. You've been a tremendous help to me."

"As I said before, when Andrew told me what had happened, I simply did what any responsible citizen would do." She looked to the street once, then leaned closer. "I've heard the oddest rumors, Mrs. Stanford."

"And what would those be, Mrs. Barring?" Mike asked.

"That you two were involved in some kind of—" she looked around one more "—police investigation."

"That's true," Rebecca said proudly. "Without Mike's undercover work that robbery attempt on the armored car this week wouldn't have been prevented."

"Well! An undercover operation." She crossed her arms, nodding sagely. "I knew it all along, of course. I wasn't fooled by Mr. Hogan's disguise for a minute."

Mike's shoulders shook. At the delicate jab of Rebecca's elbow in his ribs, he covered his chuckle with a cough.

"My Andrew is very interested in engines," she continued. "Would you mind if he took a look at your motorcycle while you're visiting?"

"Sure. I'll take him for a ride if it's okay with you. But I'm not visiting."

Her gaze sharpened, the practiced busybody sensing news. "Oh?"

"You're the first to know." He smiled. "Rebecca and I are getting married next week."

"Is this true, Mrs. Stanford?"

"Yes," she said simply. And right in front of the neighborhood's worst gossip, she twisted her head and planted a firm kiss on her fiancé's lips.

Smiling delightedly, Mrs. Barring left them just as another visitor crossed the lawn. He nodded to her politely, but she showed no sign of recognition. His blond hair curled boyishly over the tips of his ears, covering the arms of his tortoiseshell glasses. He was wearing a three-piece suit this time, the charcoal-gray fabric tailored perfectly to his solid frame. Rebecca watched him approach with mixed feelings. The last time she had spoken with Prentice she hadn't been particularly polite.

Mike straightened from his slouch as Prentice climbed to the porch. Tension hardened the arm that was still curled around Rebecca's back.

The policeman headed for the door, then stopped and did a

double take as he caught sight of the couple on the swing. "What are you still doing here, Hogan?"

Mike looked him in the eye. "It's a free country, Prentice."

He straightened his tie and approached them. "Hello, Ms. Stanford."

She nodded. "Prentice."

"I'm glad you're here, Hogan. I have some news you might be interested in."

"Go ahead. I'm listening."

For the first time since she'd seen him in his many disguises, Rebecca thought he appeared uncomfortable. She frowned, feeling Mike's tension spread to her.

Prentice reached into his jacket and pulled out a folded paper. "I was at the hospital yesterday afternoon."

"Visiting Guido?"

Rebecca turned to Mike. "Guido? You never told me he was the other one who was injured."

"It slipped my mind. We were kind of busy."

She flushed, then looked back to the policeman. "What happened?"

"Evidently Guido thought he was dying. He wanted to cleanse his soul, so he confessed to his past crimes. It was a long list, including his activities before he joined Witlock."

"He's been around awhile," Mike said.

"Yes. He also confessed to a certain murder in Chicago we had closed the books on five years ago." His gaze steadied on Mike as he handed him the paper. "According to his statement, Guido was simply carrying out orders. He wasn't working for Witlock then. He was an enforcer for an organization that imported heroin. He admits to shooting the man you were convicted of killing."

The paper fell to the floor as Mike leaned forward, a hand over his eyes. Rebecca placed her palm on his shoulder and felt a shudder travel through his strong frame.

"The details are all in there," Prentice continued, retrieving the paper and placing it on the seat beside them. "Of course there are several legal implications. I'm afraid there's nothing we can do about it now, other than arrange for a complete pardon. Naturally you'll be exonerated and your record will be cleared. You also have a right to seek compensation.''

Drawing in a deep breath, Mike rubbed his face. It was a moment before he could speak. Although short, his reply contained a lifetime of meaning. ''Thanks.''

''My office will be in touch. Where can we reach you?''

It was Rebecca who answered. ''He'll be here. We're getting married.''

Prentice's mouth curved in what was probably a seldom-used smile. ''Congratulations.''

''Thank you,'' she said.

He shifted his feet and looked toward the plain brown sedan that was parked at the bottom of her driveway. ''Ms. Stanford, as I said before, I appreciate the cooperation you've given us throughout this operation. Although I have no right to ask you, there's one more thing I would like your help with.''

''What is it?''

''Excuse me for a moment. I need to get something from my car.''

As he left, Rebecca turned worriedly to Mike. ''Are you all right?''

He shook his head. ''It's kind of hard to take in. I've lived with this for so long. I never dared—'' He broke off, his throat working silently. ''I never dared to dream that something like this could happen.''

''It's over, Mike. Really over. Your record will be cleared. You could probably sue someone over this.''

''No. Those years can't be replaced.''

''But they owe you—''

''What? What do they owe me?'' He turned to her, his eyes gleaming with the love that filled his soul. ''What more could I possibly ask for? Or yearn for? I have everything I've ever wanted, right at this moment.''

Yet again the tears welled in her eyes. "I love you, Mike Hogan."

Turning, he pressed his lips to her fingers. "God, I love you, Rebecca. You're the best thing that's ever happened to me in my whole sorry life."

"It starts now."

"What?"

"Your life. Our life. Everything that's gone before no longer matters."

He leaned over, covering her mouth with his in a kiss that was a greeting, a promise and a vow.

Beyond the trailing branches of the weeping willow tree, a car door opened. Shrill barking cut through the calm morning. Moments later a gray fur ball hurtled up the steps and collided with Rebecca's ankles.

Mike broke off the kiss and glared at the four-legged intruder. "I don't believe this."

Rebecca blinked. "Princess?"

The dog yapped and turned around, then leapt up to lick Mike's fingers.

"Jeez," he muttered, wiping his hand on his leg.

"Princess!" Laughing, Rebecca leaned down to scoop the wriggling dog onto her lap. "How did you get here?"

From across the lawn Prentice hurried back to the foot of the steps. "I was on my way to the pound when I remembered that you had taken care of her before. I was wondering whether you'd like to keep her."

"Oh, yes!"

"And I thought I liked the sound of that word," Mike mumbled.

"Thank you," Rebecca said, finally smiling at the blond policeman. "I suspect you might have a heart after all."

"I simply like to tie up loose ends." He brushed dog hair off his gray pants. "If you need any help getting settled, Hogan, let me know. I'll see what I can do." He walked back to his car, leaving them alone on their porch swing once more.

Well, almost alone.

"That mutt hates me," Mike grumbled.

The mutt squirmed ecstatically and licked both their faces.

"No, she doesn't," Rebecca said. "She just needs a good home." She smiled at the handful of fur that already coated her lap. "She also needs a bath."

The dog growled, then leapt to the floor, nails clattering against the boards as she scrambled into the house.

"Good heavens."

"This is where I came in."

Pushing herself to her feet, Rebecca held out her hand to Mike. "And this is where you stay."

*   *   *   *   *

Silhouette Stars

Born this Month

Jerry Hall, Tom Cruise, Tom Stoppard, Nancy Reagan, Ringo Starr, Barbara Cartland, Harrison Ford, Linda Ronstadt.

Star of the Month

Cancer

An excellent year ahead in which progress can be made in all areas of your life. There may be a period of change in the autumn but don't be fearful as the outcome will be better than you could hope and you will see the necessity for change. A lucky break in the second half of the year could have you splashing out.

SILH/HR/0997a

 Leo

You could find yourself pushing too hard to achieve what you want especially in your personal life. So try a little tact and diplomacy and the results could be better than you dreamed.

Virgo

Travel and romance are both well aspected and if linked you could look forward to an extra special month. Late in the month a friend needs a helping hand but be sure of their motives before offering too much.

 Libra

Energy levels are high and there is little you can't achieve. Holidays are well aspected especially those in groups. Career moves at the end of the month get you excited about the future.

Scorpio

Your ability to communicate constructively may help to bring about an improvement in your financial situation. This, in turn, will help you to build towards the future with renewed vigour.

 Sagittarius

Romance is in the air and you will feel in demand both with partners and friends, making this a social, easy going month with very little to trouble you, so enjoy!

Capricorn

A social month in which you may have to make unexpected journeys. Work opportunities will bring an added financial boost and you will realise your talents are being fully appreciated.

 **Aquarius**

Your love life receives a boost and should become more meaningful than of late. As the month ends you may find your energy levels are getting low so take a break and pamper yourself back to full strength.

Pisces

You have a decisive quality to you this month giving you the courage to make the changes you have long desired to make. Be bold and you'll be amazed by what you can achieve.

 Aries

The lack of financial resource has become an area of conflict in your personal life. You need to sit down together and make an effective budget plan. By working in harmony your relationship will improve dramatically.

Taurus

As your confidence returns you will feel more positive and able to tackle life with enthusiasm. A lucky break mid-month gives you cause for a celebration.

  Gemini

Travel is never far from your thoughts especially the more adventurous kind and this month should see you planning another experience. A friend may want to join you but be sure they are as bold as you before you commit.

**Look out for more
Silhouette Stars next month**

SILHOUETTE SENSATION®

AVAILABLE FROM 21ST JULY 2000

EVE'S WEDDING KNIGHT Kathleen Creighton

Heartbreakers & Sisters Waskowitz

FBI agent Jake Redfield had been after Eve Waskowitz's prospective groom for years. But meeting Eve shifted his target. Now he not only wanted to get his man—he wanted his woman, too!

LONE WOLF'S LADY Beverly Barton

Luke McClendon had gone to prison for the murder of Deanna Atchley's father. But Deanna was determined to clear Luke's name, even though Luke just wanted *revenge!*

THE ICE MAN Brittany Young

From the moment undercover investigator Kyra Courtland laid eyes on Jack Allessandro, she was consumed by a fierce desire for the aloof shipping tycoon. But was Jack guilty of treason?

I'LL REMEMBER YOU Barbara Ankrum

Tess Gordon put her life on the line for the brooding stranger who stumbled into her life with no name, no memories, but a bullet lodged in his shoulder. She was betting against the odds trusting her heart to the man called Jack, praying he wouldn't break it…

WIFE ON DEMAND Alexandra Sellers

They'd come together in a whirlwind of passion, but fate had ripped them apart and now he seemed to despise her. She *had* to marry him, but he'd sworn to hate her, even though he still desired her…

ALMOST PERFECT Marilyn Tracy

Almost, Texas

He was an almost perfect protector. He'd rescued her daughters and vowed to protect her family with his life. But who was Pete Jackson? Why had he told her to ask the FBI about him?

Get ready to enter the exclusive,
masculine world of...

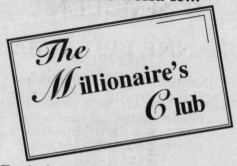

The Millionaire's Club

Desire's powerful new mini-series
features five wealthy bachelors—all
members of a very select, prestigious
club—who set out on a mission to
rescue a princess...and find true love!

August 2000
TEXAS MILLIONAIRE *Dixie Browning*

September 2000
CINDERELLA'S TYCOON *Caroline Cross*

October 2000
BILLIONAIRE BRIDEGROOM *Peggy Moreland*

November 2000
SECRET AGENT DAD *Metsy Hingle*

December 2000
LONE STAR PRINCE *Cindy Gerard*

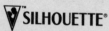

▼™ SILHOUETTE
SENSATION®

SUZANNE BROCKMANN

**continues her popular,
heart-stopping mini-series**

*They're who you call to get you out of
a tight spot—or into one!*

Coming in July 2000
THE ADMIRAL'S BRIDE

Be sure to catch Mitch's story,
IDENTITY: UNKNOWN, in September 2000

And here's Lucky's romance,
GET LUCKY, in November 2000

Then in December be sure to pick up a copy
of Suzanne's powerful instalment in the
Royally Wed mini-series,
UNDERCOVER PRINCESS

2 FREE

books and a surprise gift!

We would like to take this opportunity to thank you for reading this Silhouette® book by offering you the chance to take TWO more specially selected titles from the Sensation™ series absolutely FREE! We're also making this offer to introduce you to the benefits of the Reader Service™—

- ★ FREE home delivery
- ★ FREE gifts and competitions
- ★ FREE monthly Newsletter
- ★ Exclusive Reader Service discounts
- ★ Books available before they're in the shops

Accepting these FREE books and gift places you under no obligation to buy, you may cancel at any time, even after receiving your free shipment. Simply complete your details below and return the entire page to the address below. *You don't even need a stamp!*

YES! Please send me 2 free Sensation books and a surprise gift. I understand that unless you hear from me, I will receive 4 superb new titles every month for just £2.70 each, postage and packing free. I am under no obligation to purchase any books and may cancel my subscription at any time. The free books and gift will be mine to keep in any case.

S0ZEA

Ms/Mrs/Miss/Mr ....Initials................................

BLOCK CAPITALS PLEASE

Surname ....

Address ....

....

....Postcode................................

Send this whole page to:
UK: FREEPOST CN81, Croydon, CR9 3WZ
EIRE: PO Box 4546, Kilcock, County Kildare (stamp required)

Offer valid in UK and Eire only and not available to current Reader Service subscribers to this series. We reserve the right to refuse an application and applicants must be aged 18 years or over. Only one application per household. Terms and prices subject to change without notice. Offer expires 31st January 2001. As a result of this application, you may receive further offers from Harlequin Mills & Boon and other carefully selected companies. If you would prefer not to share in this opportunity please write to The Data Manager at the address above.

Silhouette® is a registered trademark used under license.
Sensation™ is being used as a trademark.